Property of:
Hall Middle School Library
200 Doherty Drive
Larkspur, CA 94939

Jessie's Mountain

Jessie's Mountain

Kerry Madden

Viking

VIKING
Published by Penguin Group
Penguin Young Readers Group, 345 Hudson Street, New York, New York 10014, U.S.A.
Penguin Group (Canada), 90 Eglinton Avenue East, Suite 700, Toronto, Ontario, Canada M4P 2Y3
(a division of Pearson Penguin Canada Inc.)
Penguin Books Ltd, 80 Strand, London WC2R 0RL, England
Penguin Ireland, 25 St Stephen's Green, Dublin 2, Ireland (a division of Penguin Books Ltd)
Penguin Group (Australia), 250 Camberwell Road, Camberwell, Victoria 3124, Australia
(a division of Pearson Australia Group Pty Ltd)
Penguin Books India Pvt Ltd, 11 Community Centre, Panchsheel Park, New Delhi – 110 017, India
Penguin Group (NZ), 67 Apollo Drive, Rosedale, North Shore 0632, New Zealand
(a division of Pearson New Zealand Ltd.)
Penguin Books (South Africa) (Pty) Ltd, 24 Sturdee Avenue, Rosebank,
Johannesburg 2196, South Africa

Penguin Books Ltd, Registered Offices: 80 Strand, London WC2R 0RL, England

First published in 2008 by Viking, a division of Penguin Young Readers Group

1 3 5 7 9 10 8 6 4 2

LIBRARY OF CONGRESS CATALOGING-IN-PUBLICATION DATA IS AVAILABLE
ISBN 978-0-670-06154-9

Printed in U.S.A.
Set in Granjon

"In spite of everything I still believe
that people are really good at heart."
—Anne Frank, 1929–1945

For Shirley Fairchild,
a Maggie Valley girl
who grew up in the shadow of Dirty Britches Mountain

For Crystal Lynn Chesley Iyoha
(1961–2007),
a mother and friend who dwelled in possibility

For my sister, Keely, and my brothers, Duffy and Casey, my first friends,
who joined in the storytelling and making things up

CONTENTS

Jessie's Mountain

CHAPTER ONE

Dear Grasshopper

THE ICICLES CRACK together in the trees like giants' swords, and the freezing rain pounds our tin roof. I hear the old clock chimes stutter midnight. *Gong, wheeze, gong, wheeze, gong.* I count all twelve. I wonder if our cow, Birdy Sweetpea, is asleep in the barn. Wish we could bring her inside and warm her up a bit. It feels like we're living in the last place on earth, with the first winter storm blowing hard into the mountains. Can't sleep a wink with thoughts crowding my brain. Do I go off to Nashville to audition or not? It would mean leaving Maggie Valley without telling a soul. It would also mean going off on the grandest adventure of my life. I'm due one, no doubt.

I get up and my feet hit the icy floor. I light the lantern by the bed and pull on Daddy's old winter coat and heavy socks. All the kids are sound asleep, and nobody wakes up but Uncle Hazard, who hops down out of Cyrus's bed after me. His dog toenails click across the floor as if he's asking, "Where to? Where to?"

"Shhh! Don't wake nobody up, whatever you do!" I warn him, but he only wags his tail. Together, we head down the hallway to the kitchen to scrounge for something to eat. I can always think better after a snack, and Uncle Hazard is not one to miss a chance for food. I cut myself some cornbread left over from supper and break it up into a glass of buttermilk. I toss him a bite, which he gulps down in a single swallow, and he rises up on his haunches to beg for more. When he whimpers at the ice storm raging outside, I pull him onto my lap and whisper into his long wiener-dog ears, "Uncle Hazard, don't be scared. Come morning, our holler will look like a glass city."

He licks my face, and again I wonder what I should do. Wish I had me some kind of sign to help me make up my mind. Would leaving like this constitute running away? Officially? I aim to return directly after I audition for Mr. George Flowers of Music Row and sell some songs in order to buy our house from our cheapo landlady, Madame Cherry Hat. That way we won't have to move to Grandma Horace's house in Enka-Stinka. Feels like we're kin to modern-day sharecroppers living like we do. I saw the last OVERDUE, REMIT PAYMENT NOW letter stuffed inside the "Everything Box" where Mama keeps important papers regarding our lives. I hate Madame Cherry Hat sending mean letters from her office over in Clyde. All the babies from Maggie Valley are born in the hospital in Clyde, but I don't think the name has any poetry at all—not like Balsam or Ivy Hills or Hazelwood or Maggie Valley.

No wonder I can't sleep, worrying over spiteful letters saying PAY UP OR ELSE! Least the cornbread tastes good. I like to be sitting up late while the rest of the world is off dreaming. The lantern light fills the room with a warm radiance, and I pick up my book of Emily Dickinson poems to look for a sign if I should go or not. I come upon one called "I Dwell in Possibility," all about gathering paradise in her narrow hands. It makes me think about "possibility" and what it all means. I got forty dollars saved up from working at the bookmobile all summer. I didn't give it all to Mama like she thought, and I hope to borrow a little more from the Everything Box. Would that be stealing if I aim to replace any borrowed cash immediately? Forty's the most money I've ever had in the world, but somehow fifty sounds better for Nashville. I go back to reading Emily Dickinson, but I don't get more than a few stanzas read when Grandma Horace looms up behind me, casting an impressive shadow on the wall. Hands on her hips, she hisses, "Olivia Hyatt Weems! They Lord!"

My heart beats fast at being sneaked up on, but I try to be sweet. "Can't sleep. Say, let's pretend we're old friends who like to sit up late together and swap stories."

Grandma Horace sputters another "They Lord!" which means "Good God Almighty" in mountain talk, only "They Lord" sounds better.

"Swap stories? What are you getting at?"

"Not a thing. Just don't be mad, please? For once? I'm sorry to say this, Grandma Horace, but don't you ever get tired of getting riled up all the time?"

Something in my tone must sway her because she grunts and sits down in a chair, the legs squeaking under her weight. "I do not get riled up all the time. I just simply do not believe in children prowling around in the dead of night. You'll wake folks up—especially your mama, who needs her sleep. Shocking as this sounds, I have better things to do with my time than get mad."

"You do?"

"Of course I do. What a thing to say!" Insulted, she stands up and puts on the kettle. The wind howls in the trees outside like somebody crying. Grandma Horace fixes her one good eye on me. "Listen to that pitiful wind. I miss my home on nights like this."

I put my book down. "I thought you liked living in the mountains. You said—"

"You want to swap stories? I'll give you one. I can't keep countenance with living out in the sticks forever."

"I think I heard this one before."

"Well, you can hear it again, Lady Jane. Do you know I have the prettiest little brick house in Enka, North Carolina, on a street called Orchard, with snowball bushes in front and fine yellow roses with sweet little finches flying everywhere? Your granddaddy planted them before the cancer got him." Her violet glass eye shines in the lamplight, staring off to her beloved Enka. "Bless his heart."

"I been to that house once."

"And I know you don't think much of it either, but old folks need to go back to the places they know. Winter is the dormant season; plants sucking down in their roots . . . it's a time of resilience. Maybe that's why folks move back *home* in their old age . . . to root themselves and get strong again."

"But Maggie Valley *is* our home."

Instead of debating the subject, she says, "We need to discuss something."

"What?" I don't like it when folks need to "discuss" something with me, because it usually has to do with my faults and ways to improve my sorely lacking character.

"Don't look so woebegone. I found something over at the Enka house for you, and I was going to give it to your mother as a Christmas present, because it's really hers, but when she left all those years ago to run off and marry your daddy—"

"Why did they run off like that?" I know this story, but I never get tired of it.

Grandma Horace says, "You know they were in a big fat hurry to start their lives. Lord, do not marry young!

Get yourself an education. I'm very concerned that your handsome brother is headed down the same path as my brother, which is a meager hand-to-mouth existence, rubbing elbows with the likes of carnival folk from one horse-town to the next. Sad, sad."

"Well, I intend to visit the Egyptian pyramids at Giza, the very last one of the Seven Wonders of the World that still exists," I say. "Mr. Pickle is teaching us about them this whole year. I know there are folks in Haywood County who don't cross the line into Buncombe County, but that won't be me."

"Good, because you don't want a life of regrets."

"Is that what you got?" I don't mention that I sure would if I was her, but Grandma Horace only presses her thin lips together. I suspect I hurt her feelings. The wind blows softer now, icicles tickling each other in the trees, the bells of faraway fairies.

Finally, she says, "Since you can't sleep, you can do something for me. Wash my hair."

"Wash your hair? Me? What for?" I guess I must look scared.

"Well, I won't bite. Is it so odd a request? I like my hair shining clean even if it is iron gray. My arms are achy lately. I get sore picking up grandbabies. Wears me out."

"All right, I'll do it if you want."

She leans over the sink as I pour warm water from

the kettle over her head. I get the bottle of lavender shampoo from the shelf, and she says, "It helps me to breathe easier if I can get my hair washed with lavender. When you're old, smell is about all that's left. Eyes, ears, taste . . . they diminish, but not the sense of smell."

I don't answer. I focus on working the shampoo into Grandma Horace's head real good, and soon, the kitchen is filled with a sweet lavender smell, her head thick with lather. It's not bad, washing old-lady hair. I rinse it and towel-dry it, noticing the thin folds of what looks like crepe-paper skin on her throat. *What's it like to be that old where your skin looks like it could tear in two?* While her long gray hair dries by the woodstove, I try to brush out the tangles, but her hair is full of knots.

"Ow. Quit! You're yanking too hard. I'm tender-headed! Now wait here. I'll get what I was talking about." I hear her snapping open her pocketbook in the other room. While she's gone, the rest of the water finishes boiling, and I pour us cups of sassafras tea, and she comes back into the kitchen. "Here."

It looks like an old notebook. "What is it?"

"Olivia, this is your Mama's diary of when she was just your age. I should give it to her, but a long time ago, she told me she didn't want any of her girlhood things. She wanted to 'leave the past where it was,' I believe is how she put it. When I found her diary, well, the way you love to read and write songs, maybe you'll think of a song about your own mother. Anyhow, it's my early Christmas present to you."

Tears sting my eyes. No one has *ever* given me an early present before. I swear Grandma Horace can be such a grouch, and then she turns around and does something sweet. I kiss her head and say, "Thank you, but will Mama be mad if I take it?" The old notebook is tied with a faded red sash. It feels important, this gift—not just a prayer book meant to improve my mind or save my soul. Grandma Horace's last gift to all us kids was *Prayers for Children, with Suitable Hymns Annexed*. Mama's diary is a real piece of history. My history.

Grandma Horace only says, "Your mother had promise. And dreams."

"Don't you think she still does? She knits the prettiest scarves and sweaters."

"Of course, she does"—one of the babies starts in crying—"but life has a way of . . . oh, never mind." Grandma Horace goes off to check on who's fussing. I pick up the diary and read JESSIE HORACE'S DIARY. NO PEEKING UNLESS ALLOWED. I ignore that and open to the first entry. The first thing I see is a bird drawn beside the words. Some of the entries are real short—just quick thoughts—and in others, it looks like she spills her whole heart out on the page, not holding nothing back. I take the diary back to my bed so I can read in peace—a rare thing in this house of ten kids and three grown-ups.

September 1, 1942
Dear Grasshopper,

You've just arrived. Mother thinks I need to improve my handwriting. But I intend to draw some birds inside your pages, too, and tell you all what they do and where they come from. Maybe I'll be a scientist who studies birds. There is a word for that. Ornithologist. And in honor of your arrival, I've sketched you a cardinal. They bring good luck, those pretty red birds, and they love sunflower seeds. Cardinals also mate for life and raise their babies together. It's also the State Bird of North Carolina, where I was born and raised.

I intend to join the Audubon Society. I hope they let children join. I promise to write in you later and tell you everything. I'm so glad we're going to be friends. Right now, Mother is calling. Bye! Be right back!

Finally! She wants me to frost the coconut cake when it cools, since she has to go out, and I had to promise her ten times I wouldn't forget. Mother thinks I'm flighty and don't face facts enough, but here's a fact: I'm beginning this very first diary entry by calling it JESSIE'S MOUNTAIN. *This book will be a mountain of stories of my life in Enka, North Carolina. We're also living in a time of history, according to*

Mother, since World War II is going on over in Europe. Papa went for a while, but then he came home deaf in one ear. He doesn't talk about the war.

I wish we lived deep in the mountains instead of a stone's throw away from the American Enka Factory, maker of carpets, drapes, and other upholsteries in general, even if American Enka is helping in the war effort. They might start making women's nylons again after the war is over. My papa works in the dye-making part of the factory, so sometimes his fingers are stained blue.

I hope you like your name, Grasshopper. Since I am twelve years old, I have decided to practice my most grown-up-girl voice on these pages, and I will begin by formally introducing myself to you. I am Jessie Rebecca Zilpah Horace. I don't mention the "Zilpah" to folks, but it came from Mother. I am the only daughter of Zilpah and Cal Horace, and in addition to maybe being an ornithologist, if I ever have kids, I intend to have way more than just one. I will have a whole bunch of kids who play together and have themselves a good time. Not only that, they're each going to grow up to be ALL different professions: doctor, lawyer, artist, journalist, juggler, scientist, judge, dancer, and so forth.

I like to draw pictures of the big family that I will have one day. And best of all, I'll have a noisy house. Mother cannot tolerate noise of any kind. I will also teach my children not to be afraid to try things. Mother's always afraid I'm going to hurt myself or get into trouble.

I try to be patient, but as you can imagine, we have VERY, VERY quiet Christmases, birthdays, Easters . . . you name it. Sometimes, the quiet feels screaming loud, but Mother would say to that, "Stop being so dramatic." The other day I dropped a big bowl of apples on purpose just to hear the bowl crash and the apples go rolling every which way. Mother nearly jumped out of her skin. I had to apologize fifty times, at least. And she thinks I'm the one who is "dramatic."

I turn to the next page, but I hear a noise and the door creaks open. Mama peers inside in her long nightgown. "What are you doing still awake? What are you reading?"

"Nothing. Emily Dickinson poems is all." My heart hammers inside my chest.

She yawns and says, "Well, turn off the lantern and go to sleep now."

"Yes ma'am." I turn it off and shut the diary, holding it close to my heart. Uncle Hazard curls up at my feet to warm them. I slide Mama's diary under my pillow. I try to picture her as a little girl drawing her birds, wanting to be an ornithologist. I never even knew that word before. As my eyes grow heavy, I think of the time when Cyrus and Caroline were wanting to dance like a prince and princess in the holler, and Mama started laughing at the two of them tripping over each other in the sally grass. To show them how to do it right, she said, "Watch!" She took me in her arms and taught them how to dance a waltz, demonstrating with me as her partner. *One-two-three, one-two-three* . . . I followed her lead, and we danced together under the branches of the red maple. As I drift off to sleep, breathing in the scent of lavender on my hands, I dream of Music City USA and Mr. George Flowers, the Nashville Music Man who said he liked my songs and my daddy's too. He even sent us both notes of encouragement. I can't wait to audition for him. Show him what he's been missing. Grandma Horace has given me the sign I was seeking, wrapped up in a faded red sash.

CHAPTER TWO

Glass City Holler

AT THE CRACK of dawn the next day, our holler does sparkle like a glass city, tiny rainbows shimmering across the snow through the icicles in the winter trees. Uncle Hazard scampers about, leaping in and out of snowdrifts. Some of the snow banks are so deep that all I see are his brown floppy ears poking out. Me and Gentle are the first ones up. We walk across the blanket of snow, and Gentle holds my hand tight, whispering, "The air feels so white. Let's make angels."

Together, we lie down in the snow and scissor our arms and legs to make snow angels. We've taught Gentle to "see" colors by the way things feel and smell, and being frosty cold is the color of pure white. Lately, Gentle insists her favorite color is green (it used to be purple), and I think she changed it to green because she loves rolling down the grassy hills on a hot summer day, racing the twins to see who will hit the bottom first. I once talked to a blind lady over at Gentle's eye doctor office, and I asked her if she ever missed seeing colors, and she said, "Child, you don't miss what you've never known, but I have heard of other blind folks who do see colors all swirled and mixed together, and they said it was like looking at the world through stained glass."

I close my eyes and think about my midnight talk with Grandma Horace. It was one of the first real talks we've ever had, and I have hopes for more. Maybe my grandmother isn't such a grump after all. I'm tickled to have made up my mind about leaving for Nashville and—*smack!* A snowball hits me right in the face, ice and snow sliding down my neck.

Jitters stands on the porch giggling in her nightshirt and boots. "Sorry! Didn't know I could aim so good. Must be my new glasses!" She grins at me through her new silver cat's-eye glasses from the Red Cross, who came to our school to do eye exams for free. The eye doctor told Jitters she was real nearsighted and ordered her a pair.

"Just you wait! I'll get you good, Jitters!" I stand up to chase her, but she dashes inside the house like the pathetic fraidy-cat that she is. "That's right, you better run, Myrtle Anne Weems, before I knock the holy living tar out of you!"

"You'd better not!" she fires back from the window. "Not with my new glasses. They're breakable! And they make me look smart! Everybody at school says say so."

I wipe the melted snowball off my face; revenge will have to wait.

Louise comes outside. "Boyhowdy, fireworks this early?"

"Jitters hit Livy Two with a snowball! *Smack*. I heard the whole thing," Gentle says. "Hurry, come on, Louise. We're already making snow angels." She lies back in the snow to work on her angel some more.

"I'm coming. I got warm oats I heated up for Birdy Sweetpea. Here, hold them, Livy Two—I want Gentle to touch something."

I take the warm bowl of oats from Louise, who lifts Gentle up to feel the icicles hanging on the porch. Gentle inspects the dagger-shaped icicles with great concentration.

Louise says, "Had enough? Come on, let's go feed Birdy Sweetpea."

Gentle says, "My turn to feed her," so we head into the barn to give our cow breakfast. Louise breaks the ice off the barn door, and it creaks open. In the sunlight, our cow blinks at us in her stall through mournful eyes the color of chocolate. Gentle giggles as Birdy Sweetpea eats the oats off of her hand like a horse. I get the stool and bucket to milk her, trying not to yank hard on her teats. Pretty soon, the warm milk hits the ice-cold bucket. Gentle tries to milk her too, but her little fingers find it hard to grasp the teats. Louise takes over the milking; I lean my head against Birdy Sweetpea for a minute more. She's so warm and strong-smelling. What will happen to Birdy Sweetpea if we move to Enka? Maybe she can stay with Mathew the Mennonite until we work things out to come on back home. A song comes to me as the warm milk fills the pail from our sweet cow.

Glass holler city of daggers and fairy bells
Crystals of ice casting their magic spells, fairy bells
Glass holler city, frozen drops galore
Swirling winter snow makes me want to explore
A glass holler city . . .
A glass holler city . . .

I sing the song as Louise milks Birdy Sweetpea in a barn that stinks to high heaven. I'll have to sweep it out later. Seems like I inherited all Emmett's chores ever since he went off to work at Ghost Town in the Sky. Even in the off-season, he lives up there on Buck Mountain, helping Uncle Buddy, the night watchman, with repairs on all the rides and chairlift and such. Grandma Horace is right—he ought to go back to school—must be right lonely living with Uncle Buddy. I miss my brother, even though he's lived away from home for a long time. Can't be helped. But I don't miss Uncle Buddy. Not a minute.

As we step outside of the barn, Louise says, "Uncle

Hazard's pinecone palace looks like a gingerbread house laced with frost." I breathe in the air that smells of nothing but pure clean cold—like we got a chance to start fresh. I wonder what Grandma Horace meant by a life of regrets. I reckon there are things I regret too . . . like when I made us all hike up Waterrock Knob a few weeks ago, the day President Kennedy was shot, and we lost Daddy for hours. I've only been about half forgiven for that transgression. Sometimes Mama says, "Livy Two. Stop and think what you're doing first." But did she always do that every day of her life? Did she do it when she run off and married Daddy? Did Daddy stop and think first when he brought home Uncle Hazard? Mama didn't want the dog at all at first, but then he saved Gentle from falling in the river, so he was invited to stay and live in a pinecone palace we built him.

Gentle looks like a fairy princess with the sun shining on her yellow hair, sitting high atop Louise's shoulders. I wonder how a kid can be so pretty like that. To my mind, I am what folks call "plain," with braids and an ordinary face with too many freckles. I don't care for mirrors. We only got one in the house, and Becksie hogs it to herself, since she claims the "Queen of the Maggie School" has to look her best.

Gentle sniffs the air and cries, "Can we go sledding?"

Louise says, "All right, but we got to make it quick."

She heads up the hill with Gentle still on her shoulders. I grab the old sled from behind the barn and follow them. It's just an old beat-up sled Daddy found on the side of the road years ago, but every winter, we rub it down with wax to make it slick again. Louise carries Gentle to the top of the hill, and when I catch up with them, she says, "Y'all go first. Gentle, it's right in front of you."

Gentle claps her hands and climbs onto the sled. I get on the back and pull her close to my body. Together, we go flying down, racing like the wind. Uncle Hazard runs along beside us, trying to beat us. Gentle squeals with delight. "Faster, faster!" But pretty soon, we're right back at the bottom.

"Again, again!" Gentle cries just as Louise yells, "Hey, look at that!"

I turn and see the funniest sight—six whistle pigs poking their heads out from under our house. "Gentle," I say, "be real still, there's a whole family of whistle pigs living under our house."

"Take me to them. Show me."

So I take her by the hand and lead her to the rock under the porch where the whistle pig mama and her babies are. Gentle kneels down by the rocks in the snow and says, "Here, whistle pig. Come out."

A window opens and Becksie pokes her head out. "You can't call one of those varmints like a pet dog. It won't to come to you."

"That's right!" Jitters appears next to Becksie. "Not to mention varmints got all kinds of diseases that you could die of in a heartbeat. Whistle pigs, possums—yuck!"

"Diseases? You crazy?" I snap. "Groundhogs aren't varmints at all. They're sweet little critters and prophets of the weather too!"

"Ha!" Becksie says, and old copycat Jitters says, "Yeah, ha!"

Louise calls from the hill. "Uncle Buddy said the only thing a possum is good for is a front tire, but whistle pigs are smart."

"Yeah," Gentle agrees. "They even whistle at each other. I hear them whistling when they're playing, so they can tell where they all are."

"Besides, don't you'uns know that it's *bad luck* to insult a whistle pig?"

"It is not bad luck!" Jitters cries in a panicky voice, as she takes superstitions very seriously. "And besides, I'm wearing my acorn necklace, which is good luck and nothing but. And last spring, I saw three white butterflies, which guarantees good luck for a whole year, thank you very much, Livy Two!"

Me and Gentle can't help but laugh. Right then Grandma Horace shouts from the open window, "Lord have mercy, shut the window! I've never heard such nonsense. Good luck and bad luck. Hogwash! Pure foolish talk. Live a good Christian life, and toss the good and bad luck in the trash where it belongs." The window slams shut.

With the naysayers back inside, two of the whistle pig babies must feel safe, because they poke their heads out from behind the rock to inspect the world again. Gentle tries once more. "Hello, whistle pigs. I hear you. I'm Gentle Weems. I'm five years old." One of them crawls forward, buck-toothed, black nose quivering.

Louise calls from the top of the hill, "You'uns hurry up. Come go sledding with me! They're supposed to be hibernating until the second of February. You must have woke them up." But Gentle is too entranced by the whistle pigs to listen to Louise. The two bravest ones crawl right onto her lap and let her pat them on the head.

Daddy comes outside in his bathrobe and bare feet, holding his banjo. "Good morning, children. Good morning, good morning."

"Daddy, your feet will freeze," I tell him. He forgets things like shoes—even when it's snowing. He needs reminders, since the car wreck stole some of his common sense.

He studies his feet with only mild interest, but then he looks at Gentle and the baby groundhogs on her lap. He smiles. "No finer pet than a whistle pig."

"Did you ever have one, Daddy?" Gentle asks him.

"I did. Once." He listens hard. "Is somebody playing Kitty Wells?"

"That's the radio in your head again. Remember

you get those auditory hallucinations sometimes?" I remind him. At least they're not as loud as they used to be when he first came home from the Rip Van Winkle Rest Home—or as frequent.

"Sure sounds like Kitty Wells to me."

"You had a groundhog for a pet?" Louise asks, to change the subject.

"When you were a little boy?" Gentle wants to know.

He considers this question a moment. "I wish I could tell you, but I believe so."

"What was your whistle pig's name?" I ask.

"Can't recall," Daddy says. "Wait. Andrew Jackson. That was his name."

Gentle pets on all the whistle pigs. "Then this one here is Andrew Jackson the Second. A whole family living right under us. We could make them little clothes."

Mama comes outside with one of her homemade scarves. "Tom, you'll freeze. Put this on." She wraps it around his neck and tucks it into his robe. "Here are your boots."

"Thank you." Daddy steps into his boots. "Look yonder, Jessie—whistle pigs."

"Can I name them, Mama?" Gentle holds up the fattest one. "Please? I want to call this one Sugar Cookie, and here's Andrew Jackson the Second. Please?"

Mama stops. "Name them? Well, all right, but they're not coming inside. They're wild critters. Now, wash your hands for breakfast, girls! Livy Two, bring the pail of milk inside when you come." Her voice scares the whistle pigs, who shuffle back under the house. I try to see the girl in the face of the distracted lady who just went back inside.

I take Gentle back up the hill to give Louise the sled, and together the two of them go racing down the hill through the snow. A red-tailed hawk sails through the air above us, barely flapping his wings. I step behind a tree and reach in my pocket to read more of Mama's diary, stealing a few moments before breakfast. I feel around the tattered edges and flip through yellowed pages of pictures, words, sketches of birds, scribbles, soliloquies from *Romeo and Juliet* and sonnets, and four-leaf clovers. . . .

September 15, 1942
Dear Grasshopper,

What else can I tell you about myself? I'd like to make it a fascinating read, because I am not fascinating in real life. Not even close. Sometimes I just wish I had somebody to talk to. . . . I can talk to Papa, a little. He loves me. It's like we don't need words. Our rhythms match. He showed me how to plant snowball bushes, without hardly talking at all. . . . I can't wait to see them bloom come spring. We take walks down by Enka Lake when he comes home from work. He says it clears his head and lungs after being at the factory. Sometimes Mama comes with us, but she won't leave the house unless it's neat as a pin. She's always scouring something.

I should try to tell you about my life, which you could say is grown-ups, grown-ups, grown-ups, and Methodist church suppers of sweet tea, fried chicken, macaroni and cheese, and green beans cooked with Ritz crackers.

We listen to sermons and we eat and discuss the weather and we eat some more. I may get fat. Mother likes me to put on a clean dress and act like a lady every day, but most especially at church, where we pray for our soldiers at war. I have one dress the color of a bluebird's wings that I got at Schulman's Department Store over in Jackson County in Sylva. We live in Buncombe County, but the tallest mountains are in Haywood County. I want to have a picnic in the mountains, but Mother prefers buffet restaurants in Asheville, where you can eat without waiting and everything's already hot. We went on a picnic once, but Papa left the car engine running. "Just in case."

Yours truly, Jessie Horace

Bye for now . . . P.S. I am calling you "Grasshopper" because the ONE AND ONLY time my Uncle Buddy visited, he taught me how to make a grasshopper spit tobacco juice. It's real fun. You just press your finger real gentle upon the mouth of a grasshopper and it will spit tobacco juice right on your finger. Here's a picture.

In the diary, Mama's sketched a grasshopper. I can't get over how good she used to draw—a little like Louise.

"Breakfast!" Mama calls from the window. "I won't say it again. You'll go without. Where's the milk, Livy Two? Why do I have to repeat myself again and again!"

I wait for Louise and Gentle at the barn, but I put the diary away. She sounds like she was so much fun. How can she be the cranky lady yelling for us to come inside to eat? Is that what happens when you get grown up? It all drains away? I pick up the pail of milk on the front porch.

As we hang up our coats inside, Baby Tom-Bill crawls across the floor toward me, wanting to be picked up. Two-year-old Appelonia races straight into Louise's arms and starts crawling up her like a tree frog. We head to the kitchen to join the rest of the family for a breakfast of corn mush with syrup and biscuits and gravy. I'm glad we'll be getting tangerines for Christmas. I can't wait to taste the sweet citrus on my tongue. Jitters ducks behind Becksie when she sees me. "You still mad at me?" she asks.

Cyrus, who has to know everything, asks, "Why are you mad at Jitters?"

"I'm not mad at all, Cyrus," I tell him, but I whisper to her, "Don't worry. I'll get you back." I scoot in between Gentle and Jitters. "Only you won't know when or where. It'll be my special surprise to you."

"Really?" Her face puckers into a frown.

"No, fakely!" I use Uncle Buddy's favorite line in the world.

Grandma Horace says, "Eat your breakfast and stop this nonsense. And Jessie, we need to find a way to ferret the critters out from under the house."

Gentle yells, "No! They're my whistle pigs. They're a family."

But before there can be any further discussion on the future of the whistle pigs, the man on the radio announces that all schools are closed today because of the ice storm, so everybody cheers, except for Mama and Grandma Horace, who swap secret looks of sorrow. Then he announces that the Haywood County Bookmobile is stuck in the ice down at the Maggie Valley School. Well, no sooner are the words out of the radio and into the air than me and Louise throw back on our coats. The driver of the bookmobile is our beloved Miss Attickson. Even Mama gives us a sack of early Christmas presents to take to her. "You girls hurry!" she says. "Make sure Miss Attickson is all right."

CHAPTER THREE

Ice-Bound Bookmobile

ME AND LOUISE leap through the snowdrifts on our way down the mountain. We're on a mission to save the librarian of the Haywood County Bookmobile. I can see the headline now in the *Smoky Mountain News.* "Weems Girls Brave Ice and Snow to Save Friend and Precious Haywood County Books." Maybe we'll even get a medal from a judge or mayor! It feels great pounding through the snow. Heck, we're used to running through these mountains in all sorts of weather. Truth is, I'd run anywhere for Miss Attickson. Though I can't help but feel a sadness that's she throwing her life away marrying Mr. Pickle. Maybe I ought to sing "Single Girl, Married Girl," an old Carter Family song, to her today to get her to rethink her plans of disaster. That song would make anybody think twice.

"Come on, Livy Two! You're too slow," Louise yells from down the path.

"I'm coming! Pardon me for not having your long legs."

"That's why I'm going out for track in high school."

"I sure hope we're in high school in Waynesville and not Enka!" I run down the mountain to catch up, my thoughts wandering back to Miss Attickson and her impending act of jumping the broom, which is what the old-timers called getting married in the mountains. At least we got her for a few more months before she gets herself hitched. Louise is painting her a wedding picture, though it's still a big secret. Maybe once we get to the bookmobile, I'll be able to tell both Louise and Miss Attickson about another secret. I squeeze Mama's girlhood diary in my pocket. The three of us could make a pact not to say a word ever, and I could read bits of it to them. Miss Attickson is the kind of adult who would carry a secret to her grave, and those adults are few and far between.

When we arrive at the school parking lot, the bookmobile is there. And Rusty Frye, the meanest boy ever to live, is sledding on a metal trash-can lid on the ice. His pack is following close behind with their own lids as sleds, including Billy O'Connor, who helped Daddy the night he got lost on Waterrock Knob, but who is so under Rusty's thumb there is sadly no hope for him. Those mean boys sled toward us, spraying ice and grit in their wake. Rusty yells, "Hey, look, it's the Tater Girls who swap taters and turnips for free lunches."

I stop to try and think of something mean and spiteful to say, but Louise grabs me and says, "Come on. Ignore the possum-breath boys!"

Rusty yells, "Hey, you'uns ever hear the high-pitched scream of a lady in distress up where you live on Fie Top? Usually happens in the middle of the night."

"Beat it, Rusty," I tell him.

"It's a panther, in case you do hear. Watch out or it might eat a Weems child."

Billy O'Connor says, "One time around midnight, I saw a black bear, twelve feet tall, in the clearing. My daddy keeps a shotgun as a general matter of principle."

The boys come sledding and spinning our way with more creatures-of-the-night stories, but we're too quick, and before they know it we slam the door of the bookmobile in their faces. Seconds later snowballs start pelting the side of the truck. Me and Louise stomp the snow off our boots and try to catch our breath. Miss Attickson opens the door and shoos the boys away like they're nothing but winter mosquitoes pestering us.

Then she helps us off with our coats, clearly delighted by our visit. "Well, look who it is! Hello, Weems sisters. Get yourselves warmed up this minute. Can you believe we are stuck here for the time being with all this ice and snow? Good thing the old heater works fine on this bookmobile." She sits in the driver's seat, which swivels right around to make a fine librarian's chair.

It's only then that I notice Mr. Pickle, who looks like

close kin to Ichabod Crane. The man on the radio neglected to mention that Miss Attickson's fiancé was on the scene; otherwise, we might not have bothered to rescue her at all. And for that matter, Miss Attickson don't look the least distressed at her predicament of being stuck in the ice. *Rats!* Why does *he* have to be here too? They're not even married yet. I try to hide the disappointment on my face. Mr. Pickle blows his stuffy sinuses with a tissue and gives a halfhearted wave, as if to say, *It's a snow day, schools are closed, which means we don't have to talk*. He's reading the *Smoky Mountain News* and says, "Look at this article about dumping in the Pigeon River. Folks in East Tennessee are blaming western North Carolina."

Miss Attickson reads the paper over his shoulder and says, "As they should. It's a shame all these factories—Champion, American Enka. Folks have to make a living, I know, but the big shots are responsible for dumping chemicals and waste into the river. I'm sure it is tied into the cancer rates here—I believe it heart and soul."

"There's no proof of a direct correlation, honey."

"Are you joking?" Miss Attickson's eyes widen in disbelief, but I'm stuck on another word. *Honey?* They're already like an old married couple discussing the day's headlines. I head up to the counter with her present from Mama. "Anyhow, didn't mean to interrupt you, but we heard on the radio that you were stuck in the snow. Here is your Christmas present in case you're cold." I hand her a sapphire scarf and some gingerbread from Grandma Horace.

"Oh! This is absolutely beautiful. Your mama's scarves are a thing of beauty." She wraps it around her neck. "Look, Leonard. Feels like a soft blue cloud."

"Very nice," Mr. Pickle agrees, but I'm glad I don't have one for his skinny chicken neck. I stand there with my petty thoughts buzzing like fruit flies in my brain. It's so good to see Miss Attickson, and I almost feel like crying because I realize this will be the last Christmas that she will be Miss Attickson. *It's not too late. Run while you can!*

"Are y'all both just freezing to death?" She puts her warm hands on our cheeks.

"Yeah, we ran the whole way," Louise adds. "Or one of us did, at least."

"It's hard to run on snow and ice." I blow on my fingers to get them warm.

Finally, Mr. Pickle says, "Louisiana. Olivia. Please come sit down."

"Oh, we can't stay long," I explain. "We just wanted to check that you're all right, Miss Attickson. Guess you are since your fiancé is here. Right, Louise?"

Louise nods, but she's already started thumbing through an art book of famous painters. She holds up a painting of a melting clock that I don't understand. She sees my puzzled expression and says, "Salvador Dalí. He likes painting in funny ways."

Miss Attickson says, "Shall I pour two more cups of hot chocolate? Leonard brought some over once he heard the bookmobile was stuck. We've had a fine morning organizing books and drinking cocoa."

I try not to be jealous, but it's my job to organize the books, not Leonard's. "You know I have a real good system organizing books," I remind them in case anyone forgot.

"Yes, I believe it's the very one I taught you," Miss Attickson replies. "Don't worry, I'm not about to give Leonard your job. He was just helping out today. Now sit and tell me some Weems stories. Besides, the roads will be clear soon, and we'll drop you off closer to your house." She pours me and Louise cups of creamy hot chocolate.

Louise sighs with delight at its goodness, and I cradle the hot cup in my hands, feeling a sweetness spread over me—so long as I don't look at Mr. Pickle. How will I ever be able to tell Miss Attickson and Louise about Mama's diary now? Maybe Mr. Pickle will leave? I send him telepathic thoughts to beat it: *You're getting tired of sitting here. You want to leave. Now. Now. Now. Scram!* It's not working. He just sits there, drinking his hot chocolate, grading papers, sucking on ginger drops, blowing his nose. I try to get a peek at whose paper he might be checking, but he's got them covered up good. He gives me a sour look, so I shift in my chair so as to have my back to him.

Louise says, "Guess what, Miss Attickson? We got a family of whistle pigs under the house. Just found them."

"How delightful!" Miss Attickson claps her hands. "How many?"

"Five babies and a mama. Gentle's already claimed them," Louise says. "She—"

But I don't want to talk about the whistle pigs, so I interrupt, "Miss Attickson. How old were you when you first took a trip alone?"

She considers this a moment. "Let me think. I believe I was thirteen, and I rode the Greyhound bus from Memphis, Tennessee, to Yazoo City, Mississippi, to visit my grandparents. I felt very grown-up."

"Were you scared?"

"Scared? What for? Now, it took a long time. I remember it was a hot old August day. Bus seemed to stop everywhere. But that summer Grandmother made homemade peach ice cream, and I got to turn the crank. Grandfather taught me how to drive. I learned to drive all over their farm and fell in love with driving. I love driving, and I love books. My job is the perfect fit."

"I'm almost thirteen too." I let the words linger in the air.

"Going somewhere?" asks Mr. Pickle, but he don't look up from his papers.

"No, not yet anyhow. But I intend to see the Great Pyramid of Giza one day. And anyway, I always like to keep my options open, and I think—" The sound of *honk, honk, honk* blasts outside, only it's more of a bird honk, not a car honk. The door of the bookmobile opens, and it's Randal, the goose boy. I met him last summer over in Dellwood. "Hey, it's you," he says.

"Hey, Randal." I wave back, but then we don't know what else to say.

"What's your name again?" he wants to know.

"Livy Two. Over there is my sister, Louise."

Randal says, "Hey," but Louise is buried back in Salvador Dalí again.

"Randal, what in the world are you and Clancy doing over here in Maggie Valley in this weather?" Miss Atticknson asks.

"Plumb out of books. I surely do need them in all this snow. My daddy brought me in his truck. Snow on Balsam doesn't bother him."

"Where is he?" I ask.

"Truck. He's not partial to reading, but he doesn't mind that I am." Randal limps to the counter in a kind of shuffle/drag walk. He got polio as a baby because his mama forgot about vaccinations, so later on he trained his goose to help him out. He calls his goose Clancy, and he's taught him to carry his books for him on his back. He's got a fondness for E. E. Cummings poems like me. Last summer when I met him, he was reading through the poets alphabetically. Miss Atticknson usually don't allow animals in the truck, but she makes an exception for Clancy.

Randal removes the stack of books from Clancy's

broad feather-downed back. He says, "I like this place better than my own house, but I'd better hurry. My dad's got a load of pulpwood to take over to Champion."

Miss Attickson says, "Here, Randal, you hurry and drink a cup of this hot chocolate before you have to go. Leonard makes the best hot chocolate." She glances in my direction at my shocked face. "Don't look so surprised. He's a man of many talents."

Louise says, "I wish I could drink hot chocolate every day of my life."

I don't compliment Mr. Pickle on his hot chocolate. No sense in him getting a swelled head. I turn to Randal. "You were on the poet E. E. Cummings last time I saw you. Are you up to Emily Dickinson yet? 'Cause you'd like her."

"Passed her already. Now I'm at John Donne. I like his poem 'A Nocturnal upon St. Lucy's Day.'"

"Ain't read it."

"It's about the longest night of the year or the shortest day, right, Clancy?"

Clancy waddles up and down the bookmobile.

"I read him all the poems to practice," Randal explains. "I intend to put lots of poems to memory in case I am ever called upon to recite at social gatherings."

I try not to laugh, but he sounds so dang proper. He looks over at Louise, who is still paging through her art book. "She likes artists?"

Louise laughs and says, "Look at this painting of

skinny flying cows. It's by Salvador Dalí too." She holds up the book, and Randal laughs with her.

Miss Attickson says, "Yes, one of the surrealist painters. Oh, I almost forgot. Your sister's book arrived yesterday."

"What book? Which sister?" me and Louise both ask at the same time.

"Myrtle Anne, of course. Didn't she tell you?"

I shake my head. As far as I can remember, I can't ever recall Jitters ordering a book special unless she was under direct order from Becksie to get a cookbook.

"Yes, it's here somewhere. *8,414 Strange and Fascinating Superstitions.*" She drags out a big thick book and plops it down on the counter. "Your sister seems to take these things very seriously, so I did my best to find her the finest book I could."

Louise says, "I guess we'll have to tote it on home to her."

"We'll drive you in when the roads clear," Miss Attickson says again.

"No thanks," I tell her. "We're all warmed up now and ready for the run home."

Louise says, "We do need to get on home. Just glad you're okay."

I hesitate at the door a minute, tempted to tell her all about me leaving for Nashville, but if I did, she'd try to talk me out of it. And I have to go. I know this as sure as ever I've known anything. I stand there a moment longer, memorizing the bookmobile. I'm just going for a few days, but it feels like it will be a lot longer somehow.

Randal waves good-bye, and so does Miss Attickson, and even Mr. Pickle gives a nod. Clancy honks as the door opens and the cold wind hits him. Louise and me waste no time running fast and furious down the Highway 19 road, taking turns carrying Jitters's silly tome of superstitions. I'm relieved that Rusty and his posse of mean boys are long gone. We race past the Pancake House, the parking lot of Ghost Town in the Sky, where the empty chairs of the chairlift rock back and forth like lonesome ghost chairs. Next to the Maggie Store stands a pitiful building with a cardboard sign that says FOR RENT. Who'd want to rent some old building like that? It's near falling apart with busted-out windows; the FOR RENT sign's been there for as long as I can remember. I can't wait to get out of Maggie Valley and feast my eyes on a beautiful building like the Grand Ole Opry in the middle of downtown Nashville, standing proud and full of music.

As we turn on Fie Top to head up the mountain, I make up my mind to start a list of all the things I'll need in Nashville—it would be awful to forget something and get all the way to Music City USA only to find I've arrived without my guitar or the address of Mr. George Flowers. I need a secret list to help me prepare for the biggest trip of my life.

CHAPTER FOUR

Incidentals of the Traveling Kind

A FEW DAYS later the mountain roads are finally clear, and after school I race to finish packing my schoolbag and guitar case. I check and double-check all the items on my secret list, which is pretty near everything I own in the world anyhow.

1. Guitar
2. Mr. Flowers's address: 1026 Sixteenth Ave. South, Nashville, Tennessee
3. Toothbrush, hairbrush, soap, and hand towel
4. Nashville city map (ordered special from the Nashville Tourism Bureau
5. Money
6. Two clean shirts
7. Two pairs of underwear and socks
8. One sweater
9. Daddy's old winter coat

I make sure my cubby of clothes looks exactly the same by moving some of Louise's and Becksie's things into it. We've each of us got a cubbyhole for our clothes carved into the wall, and I don't want my empty one to lead to any suspicions.

"Livy Two, have you seen the purple-and-gray scarf I knitted?" Mama calls.

"No ma'am!" Whoops. Almost forgot—I pop back open the guitar case and stick in Mama's diary. I shove my schoolbag and guitar case back under the bed out of sight. I offer a quick wish and a prayer to Livy One, my namesake and sister who died at birth, to watch over me real good and not to let Grandma Horace or Mama blow a gasket when they find out I'm gone. I intend to leave a letter under Louise's pillow that will set their minds at ease. After all, this is what musicians do. Daddy left home at fourteen. I'm not leaving home by any stretch. I just intend to start helping my family make a living at this music business. This could possibly be the best Christmas ever when I come home a success from Nashville.

In the front room Daddy's playing with the twins next to a rickety bookshelf with a mostly complete set of Mama's old Childcraft encyclopedias, which have all sorts of volumes, from *Folk and Fairy Tales* to *Life in Many Lands* to *Great Men and Famous Deeds*. Cyrus stands on a chair dressed as Poseidon, yelling, "I'm an earthshaker! Watch me and my water horse rock the waves!" He waves my guitar around to use as his trident, but I grab it back. "Not with my guitar, you don't, buddy."

"But I need a trident! A real one! Where can I get one?" Cyrus pleads. Then Caroline whirls around the room in her fairy wings. "Livy Two, I'm Poseidon's queen Amphitrite. Say howdy to my forty-nine sisters. My only son, Triton, has a fishtail for legs, but he's not sad because he can go swimming all the time."

"Who can I be?" Gentle pleads. "I want to be somebody too."

"You can be Iris," I tell her. "Goddess of the Rainbow and deliverer of secret messages to Zeus. And you were born in the sky just as the sun was coming out."

Gentle says, "Iris! I like that—I'm a rainbow goddess."

"Let's feed the fairies later, Iris," Caroline says. "They love raindrop tea from rainbows."

Miss Attickson sends discarded library books home with me. Lately, I've been reading the little ones *Greek Myths*—something Daddy used to do when we were small. They love the stories of Zeus tossing around his lightning bolts, but Gentle cried over Demeter and her daughter, Persephone, kidnapped by Hades, King of the Underworld. My favorite is Athena—Goddess of Wisdom and a fierce fighter when the times called for it. Not only that, my name "Olivia" means "olive tree," and Athena struck her spear in the ground to plant a sacred olive tree. I have never tasted olives, but I hope to one day.

And I only fight when it's absolutely necessary—just like Athena.

Gentle plays "Jingle Bells" on the piano while Daddy picks out chords on the banjo. He allows Caroline to comb his hair straight up and straight back down again. He plays on the banjo, while she plays on him. He looks up at me and says, "Howdy."

"Say my name, Daddy."

He studies me a moment. "Louisiana."

"Not again!" Cyrus keeps ringing his imaginary bells. "She's Livy Two! When are you going to start remembering, Daddy? How long will it take? How many seconds?"

Daddy smiles and says, "I knew that. Hello, Livy Two."

I sigh and kiss him on the head. Louise paints new flashcards for him all the time. The latest is a series of instruments—Dobro, fiddle, piano, harmonica, mandolin, guitar, banjo, washboard, and even spoons. Becksie's also sharing her *Encyclopedia of Wild Flowers* with him to get him to practice colors and flowers and shapes again.

I whisper into his ear. "Guess what? I've got a surprise, but I can't tell you yet."

He holds the banjo on his lap and plucks a few chords. "That's all right." He gives me one of his old smiles. "Listen to this. . . ." He plays the first verse of an old mountain song called "Jennie Jenkins." It feels so good to hear him playing again. He may not remember our names too well, but the music—the notes, the chords—he's remembering bit by bit. Some folks in the mountains call the banjo "devil's music" and won't put up with it a minute, but I think the sound of Daddy's banjo is pure heaven on earth.

Caroline races to the window and studies the sky. "It's not snowing in the front yet, but maybe it's snowing in the back. I'll go check."

"Livy Two, I need you now!" Mama calls. "I won't call you again."

"I'm here!" I yell as I hit the kitchen, and right off she hands over the washing of the babies to me. A pot of black beans flavored with onions and fatback bubbles on the old woodstove, and cornbread bakes up golden brown in the cast-iron skillet in the oven. Baby Tom-Bill and Appelonia splash in the washtub on the floor by the sink.

"About time you showed up!" Jitters sniffs from behind the taters she's peeling, twirling her good-luck acorn necklace. "Always trying to sneak out of working. Reading, plucking on your guitar. Me, I never try to get out of working. I'm always helping out the very best I can, right, Mama? No matter how tired I get . . . I just keep right on—"

I interrupt her. "You win the grand prize, Jitters."

"For what?" She pushes those cat's-eye glasses up the bridge of her nose.

"World's Greatest Martyr!" I grab the cake of soap and dunk my hands into the babies' bathwater.

"I am not a martyr!" Jitters points a finger at me.

"You are too. Didn't me and Louise drag that *8,414 Strange and Fascinating Superstitions* book all the way up to you in a blizzard, and all you can do is set there and talk about how perfect you are, working your fingers to the bone. Poor you."

"It wasn't a blizzard," Jitters corrects me. "It was an ice storm, and it was over."

Mama cuts in, "Hush now. Livy, you haven't seen my purple-and-gray scarf?"

"No ma'am." I lather up the babies, and Grandma Horace comes into the kitchen to put kindling into the woodstove. She studies the Bradley's Hardware calendar on the wall. "Note the date, Jessie. Monday, December sixteenth. Your papa's birthday was today. He would have been sixty-three."

"Grandpa Cal Horace got the cancer when you were thirteen, right, Mama?" Jitters perks up. "Didn't he work in the textile plant in Enka? Livy Two says the chemicals from the textiles flat-out killed him."

"I never said that." My face turns red. "Not exactly." I don't add that it was Mr. Pickle and Miss Attickson who told us about the pollution dumping into the Pigeon River and cancer rates and the folks in Tennessee getting mad at folks in North Carolina.

"Yes, you did!" Jitters looks pleased with herself. "Heard it with my own ears."

Grandma Horace points an accusing finger at me. "Olivia Hyatt Weems, your Grandpa Cal, God rest his soul, was very proud of his job. The Enka Plant gave us a good life, understand? It most certainly did not give him the cancer. So you will not spread false tales." Her gray glass eye seems tinged with sorrow, staring back into the time of Grandpa Cal Horace. "And you won't find a prettier place than Enka Lake at sunrise or sunset, mark my words."

I could smack Jitters, I really could. Grandma Horace and I are finally getting along all right, and she has to go and spoil it with her flapping jaws.

"Never mind," Mama says. "It was all a long time ago. Now, who wants biscuits with sourwood honey for dessert? I've been saving a jar. Daddy's favorite."

"I'll take some only after everyone has had some first," Jitters says with a sigh.

I ignore the martyr and talk to the babies, scrubbing them clean. "Sourwood honey is the best because it's the first honey of the season.

"Best honey," Appelonia says, but Baby Tom-Bill only splashes in the water.

"That's right. You'uns babies should know this fact. Folks from as far away as California will spend ten dollars on a jar. I've seen them do it, too, at the Maggie Store, where they pull over to cool off their brakes. Some flatlanders, who don't know no better, pump and ride their brakes so hard on mountain roads, it can cause the brakes to catch fire. One spark and that's all she wrote, right, Grandma Horace?" But she gives me the silent treatment for treading on the sacred past of Grandpa Cal Horace and American Enka. I'd almost rather get yelled at than get the silent treatment.

Mama says, "Finish up, Livy Two. Becksie's at the Pancake House, and Jitters has already dropped Appelonia once. The twins and Gentle need to bathe next."

"Ouch!" Appelonia splashes in the water. "She dropped me. Boom!"

"I said sorry!" Jitters's lower lip trembles. "She's too dang slippery. But I've stopped dropping so many things since I got my new glasses. Right, Mama?"

Appelonia plays with bubbles. "I fall down, Livy Two. I fall down."

"You're fine." I pour water over her plump shoulders. "Where's Louise got to?"

"Out hunting the perfect Christmas tree. Then you'uns can go chop it down on Christmas Eve with Emmett like usual." Mama keeps right on knitting.

Grandma Horace rolls out the dough for a stack cake and stares out the window. "Jessie, you ought not to let Louisiana go traipsing off into the woods alone. When we move to Enka, we won't be continuing this tree-chopping tradition. Next year, we'll go to a nice tree lot in Asheville and pick one out like civilized folks."

"Grandma Horace," I tell her, "me and Louise love chopping down the Christmas tree with Emmett. Makes us feel like pioneer kids from the olden days."

"Which none of y'all are!" Grandma Horace fires back. "It's almost 1964, and we're living in the dark ages without even a television set here in the sticks."

"Couldn't get reception anyway." Mama starts another row on the red scarf.

"You're not telling me a thing I don't know." Grandma Horace stirs the simmering apples on the stove to put in between the layers of the stack cake. "Having to listen to poor President Kennedy's death on the radio. I want to get us back to Enka, where we can attend my old church and watch TV and get us a newspaper on a regular basis. It's time to civilize all my heathen grandchildren once and for all. There are good plant jobs for women at American Enka, Jessie." But Mama don't answer.

Gentle touches her way into the kitchen with the new cane that Emmett whittled her. She's getting so tall he had to make her a new one.

Grandma Horace asks, "Did you practice your Braille today, Gentle? I'll be testing you."

"I did, Grandma Horace. Let me help, Livy Two?" A smile plays on her lips. "I was playing with the whistle pigs. They love me and Daddy."

Jitters says, "I wouldn't get near one of them whistle pigs with a ten-foot pole."

At that moment, Louise busts in the back door, her face flushed from the cold wind, with Uncle Hazard, barking and shaking off the snowflakes from his tawny coat. "I found one," she cries. "I found the perfect Christmas tree! Oh, Livy Two, wait until you see it. And look who's behind me." Before anyone can wager a guess, Emmett and Uncle Buddy stomp inside, too, shaking snow off their shoulders.

"Hey, Mama," Emmett says. "Surprise!"

"Emmett!" Mama hugs him hard. "Howdy, Uncle Buddy. Well, y'all wipe your feet now. Come on in and get warm."

Uncle Buddy snarls, "Chimney caved in at Ghost Town. Pile of rubble in the night-watchman cabin. Won't be fixed until after Christmas, so we are here for the duration, Lord help us." He keeps Pearl, the iguana, tucked inside his sweater. Pearl's head sticks out, coal-black eyes blinking at us. A brown bag sticks out of his back pocket. I reckon it's moonshine, though he'd bite my head off if I asked. Probably bought it from Delia Jupiter, the lady who sells moonshine out of her kitchen window to support her kids since her husband hit the road for greener pastures.

Grandma Horace says, "Buddy, why don't you go in there and say hello to Tom?"

"Is that who's picking? Why don't he write something for Johnny Cash?" Uncle Buddy yells, "That music sells. Not that high lonesome banjo crap." He pronounces "banjo" like "banjer." Uncle Buddy is always hitting somebody up for money, even stealing Emmett's paycheck, and I wonder how in the world he knows what would sell and what wouldn't. He's a mean man who don't ever recollect being mean. It's like every day is a new day for him. I once saw a sign that said "A short memory is not a clear conscience." Wish somebody would tell him that, but he'd probably forget it.

Emmett eats a heaping spoonful of beans on the stove. "I'm starving. Hey, any of you'uns want to hear my new plan? I'm thinking of going to Hollywood for real. If I can fall off the roof at Ghost Town for fifty-five dollars a week, I might as well get paid a lot more out there in California. Real life movie stars like Burt Reynolds and Dan Blocker love Ghost Town in the Sky! Heck, they all cut their teeth acting at Ghost Town."

Uncle Buddy says, "Big talker, we got. Wouldn't last two minutes out there."

"Maybe I would if you paid me back the rest of the money you owe me. I could invest in my future out there from all your poker debts. Get me a studio screen test for *Gunsmoke* or *Bonanza* or *Big Valley.*"

"Hey, hold up!" Uncle Buddy shakes a fist in the air. "You don't talk back to your elders. And I paid you back, boy. The rest is my fees in taking you in and giving you advice on life and such. We're square. So Holly-s on you, kid, not me."

Grandma Horace snorts, "Hollywood? You'd do well to go back to school!"

Uncle Buddy repeats, "Wouldn't last two minutes out there."

But Emmett says, "Come on, Grandma Horace, wouldn't you love to turn on your TV set and see your good-looking grandson playing a cowboy? How about you, Livy Two? Wouldn't it be something else to see your brother on the television set performing heroic acts, saving children? Chasing down robbers on horseback?" He fires two fake pistols. "Pow, pow, pow!"

I laugh. "It would be something to see—that is, if we had a television." But Grandma Horace sniffs, "A little humility would suit you, Emmett Weems."

Emmett shrugs. "Humility? What good is that when you don't got money? Hey, by the way, Mama, when did Becksie go and get herself a sweetheart?"

A silence falls across the room. This is news to everyone. *A sweetheart?*

Emmett picks up Gentle, who wraps her arms around him. "They were holding hands in front of the Pancake House. Sure looked like her sweetheart to me."

Gentle whispers, "Sweetheart," and giggles.

Jitters looks downright betrayed. "That's a lie. And besides, she never said a thing to me! I am her confidante. She told me so." Two bright red spots burn on her cheeks.

"Looks like old Becksie is stepping out on you folks." Uncle Buddy picks up Jitters's taters and juggles three or four in the air. "Hey, Jitters, wish you were sneaking out with the boys like big sister? Jealous, Jitters? Get it? Haw, haw."

"Leave her alone, bully!" Emmett orders.

"Who are you calling 'bully'? Can't she take a joke?" Uncle Buddy snarls.

Jitters races out of the room, and Emmett goes after her. Mama says, "I've put up with a lot from you, Uncle Buddy. And only you know the truth about Emmett's money, but tease my children again, and you will leave this house." Her voice is dead serious.

"Heck, it was just a joke. I didn't mean nothing." He glances at me. "So what?" His idea of a conversation opener . . . *so what?* "Sad day when folks got no sense of humor!" He stomps out of the room with Pearl glaring at us. Grandma Horace follows to make sure he won't stir up more trouble.

Gentle asks, "What joke did he tell? I didn't hear one."

Louise says, "'Cause that welcher's jokes ain't funny, Gentle. Come on, let's go find Jitters." She and Gentle leave the kitchen, and then it's just me and Mama and the babies. Mama knits faster than ever, needles flying.

"Aw, Mama, don't worry. She'll be home soon. We all got out of school early on account of teacher meetings, but Becksie wanted to check the Christmas hours at the Pancake House is all," I tell her, but the line only deepens between her eyes, like she wants to keep us from growing up so fast. "Remember, I have to help Miss Attickson tomorrow at the bookmobile before school, so I'll be leaving early. To sort books and get organized for 1964." I don't add that she and Mr. Pickle already got a good start.

"Well, just don't be late for school."

I breathe a sigh of relief. She don't suspect a thing. By the time the school bell rings, I'll already be in Waynesville ready to depart. I dress the little ones in their nightshirts and comb out their wet curls, but I'm thinking about my escape to Music City USA. "I'm leaving, bye-bye," I whisper into their tiny ears, which makes them laugh because it tickles. The babies will keep my secret.

I wonder if the purple-and-gray scarf I stole has made it to Nashville to the office of Mr. George Flowers—a little token to grease the wheels and open the door to my audition. If Miss Attickson thinks so highly of them, surely one of Mama's knit scarves would be the perfect present for Mr. George Flowers too. Once he puts me on WSM radio, I'll be able to explain the whole story, and then I know Mama will understand. With the money I make, I might could even buy her a book on birds for Christmas.

From the front room, Daddy plucks on the banjo for the family. There's a G chord, and then up to C, and it makes me think about the Grand Ole Opry at the Ryman Auditorium, Ernest Tubb Record Shop, Music Row. I get so excited thinking of all I'm about to see and do in Nashville. The forty dollars I got saved up will pay for the round-trip ticket and incidentals on the road. I do like the word "incidentals." Makes me feel like a world-class traveler. Maybe Mr. George Flowers will love my songwriting and singing so much that he'll say, "Use my phone. Call up your family long distance and tell them the good news." I sing low and soft a new song that eases its way into my head.

Incidentals . . . of the traveling kind
Hitting the road . . . I've made up my mind
With my guitar and pack slung over my back
See you later, I've made up my mind!
Oh, I can't wait to see what I'll find!
It's incidentals . . . it's incidentals
Incidentals . . . of the traveling kind!
I've made up my mind, good-bye!
Good-bye!
Good-bye!
Good-bye!
See y'all!

CHAPTER FIVE

A Bedtime Story

A FEW HOURS later, supper over and dishes put up, the front door opens and Becksie comes inside the house, her face soft and smiling like I've never ever seen before. Me and Louise look at each other in shock, but Jitters right off confronts Becksie with kissing noises. "I know where you've been."

The dreamy expression vanishes from her face as Becksie takes off her coat, her voice trembling. "What are you talking about? Get away from me."

"Secret sweethearts. I thought we told each other everything! Ha!"

Mama calls from the kitchen, "Rebecca, I need to speak you. Thank you for calling earlier, but you owe us an explanation, coming home past seven at night."

Caroline twirls up, fairy wings bobbling. "Do you have a secret sweetheart?"

Daddy smiles. "Do you, honey? Well, that's a good thing, right?" But his comment only mortifies Becksie even more. The final straw is Uncle Buddy, who, feet propped up on a stool, asks, "Been off playing smacky-face, kid?" Becksie flies off to the bedroom, slamming the door. Mama follows, and the fireworks begin in an explosion of tears and accusations. Grandma Horace gets in on the action and trails Mama, reminding her, "Your daughter is the same age you were when you took up with that Tom Weems!"

Mama snaps right back, "Don't you think I know that, Mother? Now, this is between me and my daughter."

I vow never to be so stupid as to fall in love. Tomorrow's a good day to go.

That night I try to sleep, but for the life of me I can't do it. Becksie's sobs don't help. I lay there listening to everybody tossing and turning, like they feel a change coming on, too, even though they don't know it yet. I've never left them before—ever—and I feel real scared all of a sudden. What if something awful happens and I don't come back? I sit straight up in my top bunk and come to a decision. Since I can't tell them I'm going, what I'm about to do will be my secret good-bye to my brothers and sisters. I'm not about to leave Maggie Valley without Mama's diary, but Grandma Horace never said I couldn't share it. I climb down the bunk and peek out of the bedroom door to make sure the coast is clear. I don't dare switch on the light even with the electricity back on.

Cyrus sits up. "Hey, where are you going?"

"Noplace—now, hush!" I tell him. "You'll wake up the babies." Appelonia and Baby Tom-Bill are sound asleep in the crib in the corner of the room. Mama dragged their crib in here a few months ago, so our bedroom's more crowded than ever, but she's moved the furniture around to make it look all right. She loves rearranging furniture to give the place a new look. From the crack in the door, I can tell Mama and Daddy and Grandma Horace are sound asleep in their rooms, and Uncle Buddy, the buzz-saw snorer, is in a deep sleep in the front room. I climb back up to my top bunk. "Before you'uns go to sleep," I say in a low voice, "I'm going to read you this very true story, which you can consider as my early Christmas present to you. Only you can't ask me no questions and you got to swear on your life not to say a word. Ever. Swear?"

Cyrus asks, "What you gonna read us?"

"Cyrus! You hush up or I won't read a word of this very true story. Now do you'uns swear to keep this a secret?"

Everybody nods, crossing their hearts, saying, "I swear, I swear."

"But what's it about?" The boy can't help himself.

Emmett says, "Just go on and read it, Livy Two. Cyrus, come climb in bed with me and Uncle Hazard."

So Cyrus climbs into bed with his big bro
dog, and he's happy enough to keep his lips
the moment.

Caroline removes her wings and hangs
side of the bed and says, "The fairies want to hear the story too. They're waiting."

Gentle says, "That's right. They're waiting too."

Becksie cries, "How long is this going to take? I've had a traumatic time being spied on, and I don't like to be read to. Besides, we got school tomorrow."

"That's right. We do have to get up early." Jitters yawns a big fake yawn.

Louise says, "I want to hear the very true story."

And both Gentle and Caroline start chanting real soft, "Read it, read it, read it!"

I look around at all their faces. I'm dying to tell them good-bye, but I can't. So I say, "All right, here goes. But I'm serious—you truly can't ask me a thing until after I'm done reading. All right? Nothing else is required but listening."

Cyrus starts to ask something else, but Emmett covers his mouth, which makes Cyrus get the giggles. Uncle Hazard barks as if to say, *Get going!* and Becksie says, "Lord, where's my popcorn for all this buildup? We ought to at least have a snack."

But before anybody can utter another word, I say,

Ladies and gentlemen, from the 1942 girlhood diary of Jessie Horace, our very own mother, entitled *Jessie's Mountain*, but affectionately called 'Dear Grasshopper,' here goes." I can't help but peek at their shocked faces. I've got their attention, all right. I put on my best storyteller voice, but I keep it down so as not to wake the grown-ups, although with Uncle Buddy drowning out all sound in the front room, I feel safe. I pick up from right where I left off, since I don't want to start over.

October 1, 1942
Dear Grasshopper,

Papa loved his Cherokee medicine book that I bought him on the field trip to the Cherokee Indian Reservation, you'll be happy to know. I made a cake for Mother and Papa. A fine coconut cake—my very first one on my own—and it turned out all right. We even put a candle on it to celebrate, but it was mostly a quiet celebration. I live in a quiet house.

At breakfast today (Cream of Wheat again), Mother announced that I'm to pick a new word, a new hard dictionary word every day, and tell it back to her in a sentence. I found the word "rancid." Should I say, "The Enka plant smells 'rancid' today?"

Sometimes I wonder how all the North Carolina birds can stand the "rancid" odor? Have they all left Canton and Enka in search of the mountains? Folks not from here think that Enka stinks because we have the textile plant, and it does, but not as bad as Canton, yet we get blamed for both and get called ENKA-STINKA. One day, I'd like to walk outside my house and smell tomatoes on the vine, blackberries, and pure honeysuckle.

Yours truly, Jessie Horace

I look around the room. They are all waiting for me to go on. "More?" I ask.

Becksie says, "Where'd you get that?"

"Yeah, did you steal it?" Jitters points an accusing finger at me.

"No questions, I told you."

"Are you making it up?" Emmett asks. "'Cause if you are—"

"I told you no questions, but how could I make this up? And why would I?"

Gentle says, "Read more about Mama. Please, Livy Two."

A respectful silence fills the bedroom even with ten kids in it. Thank the Lord, Appelonia and Baby Tom-Bill stay fast asleep. "I'll read a bit more, but here are the pictures of the birds Mama drew." I kneel down by Gentle and say, "Mama drew pictures of all the birds she writes about, so I'm showing the kids their pictures. No touching, I'm warning you. This is a rare book that don't need no dirty, smudgy fingerprints." The kids crowd around to look, and I keep reading.

October 23, 1942

Dear Grasshopper,

This here is a picture of a catbird. Catbirds build their nests out of grapevine bark and twigs. They love the coast of North Carolina in the winter and have been seen flying around all the way to Florida. The sound of a "gray catbird" is like a tiny "meow," according to the Audubon Society. I bet they have hearts no bigger than a ladybug.

Since Mother is still after me to improve my vocabulary, it seems to me that a "catbird" might be what you call an "oxymoron," which are two opposites meaning one thing, like, say, "jumbo shrimp" or "pretty ugly" or even "Civil War." How in the world is a war supposed to be "civil" or how can a shrimp be "jumbo"? And frankly, I can't think of worse mortal enemies than a cat and a bird. Can you? So in my opinion, a catbird, besides being an actual bird, is also an oxymoron.

I wish I had a real cat. Truly. But Mother is allergic or claims she is. How would she know? We've never had one, and she never had one as a child. I leave bowls of cream for a cat in the neighborhood called Miss Amelia. Mama doesn't know—it's better that way. But I think Papa knows. He likes Miss Amelia too. Sometimes I wish I was a farm girl. I just want one pet to call my own, because much as I love birds, the ones that even get a little bit close in the yard won't let me pet them for all the tea in China.

Yours truly, Jessie Horace

"All the tea in China?" Cyrus asks. "What's she talking about?"

"Never mind," Becksie shushes him. "Keep reading!"

I yawn. "I don't know. We do have school tomorrow."

If whispers can be yelled, that is just what every kid in the room does when they cry in a chorus, *"Read!"*

"Okay, okay," I tell them. "Hold your horses. But this is the last one for tonight, and I'll read more next time. But I mean it, if you'uns ever breathe a word, Mama will find out and surely take it away, and we'll never get to hear her own very true story." Everybody nods in agreement, and I read the next entry.

November 12, 1942
Dear Grasshopper,

I'm trying to draw an American goldfinch, but it's not my best work, that is for sure. All the American goldfinch boys have little black caps on their heads—not the girls. They just have yellow heads.

It's Armistice Day around here now, and pretty soon, it'll be the one-year anniversary to Pearl Harbor, but today we did a play about Christopher Columbus. I painted the scenery, but the boy playing Christopher Columbus got sick during the performance and threw up his lunch on the Santa Maria ship made of cardboard. It was plain awful, but everybody just pretended he got seasick looking for America.

When I got home from school, Mother was coloring the

butter again because of butter rations in the war—I guess they need the extra butter for bomb making or something. Mother has taken to wrapping the margarine in used butter wrappers. She does it to keep Papa's spirits up, though he doesn't know that and she won't let me tell him. It's a big, fat secret. But the wrappers are looking pretty wrinkled. Daddy just thinks the butter company is losing its high standards using bad wrappers.

Yours truly, Jessie Horace

P.S. Grasshopper, here's another secret I would never tell my friends. I'm afraid of the dark. Mother says only silly, foolish girls are afraid of the dark, but I can't help it. Papa says that he was afraid of the dark when he was little too. That's a relief. I keep thinking of ghosts and I have heard that the Cherokee Little People like to play tricks on folks, but I don't think they'd bother coming all the way over here to Enka. Either way, I don't like the dark at all. Does that make me a silly, foolish girl? I'm afraid it might.

When I finish reading, nobody says a word, but I can tell they're not asleep yet. The moonlight shines bright and full into the room, but I quietly close her diary and put it under my pillow. I'll stick it in my guitar case come morning before anyone's awake just before I leave.

Jitters whispers, "Livy Two, this is not a question

about the diary, but why'd you pick tonight to read it to us? That's what I want to know."

"No reason." I yawn and burrow under the covers, almost feeling sleepy.

Jitters whispers, "I don't believe you. Does anybody believe her a minute?"

But nobody answers, mostly because I think we're all too filled with thoughts of Mama and her stories—a bird-loving girl growing up in a too-quiet house in Enka being afraid of the dark. Besides, we're used to Jitters griping and being suspicious in general. Cyrus is already asleep or he'd be asking more questions, and pretty soon the bedroom is filled with soft breathing. I look out the window at the sparkling moon—what Caroline calls a "sparky fairy moon." I wonder if the "sparky fairy moon" looks the same shining down on Nashville, Tennessee. I guess I'll find out. Once I hear the even breathing of my brothers and sisters, I sneak out of bed and swipe ten dollars from the Everything Box. I leave an IOU in place of the ten dollars. I'll be putting it back and much more when I get home from Nashville.

CHAPTER SIX

8,414 Strange and Fascinating Superstitions

EARLY THE NEXT morning in the pitch blackness I put Mama's diary in my guitar case quiet as a mouse, but then I go and bang it against the bed when I stick my good-bye letter under Louise's pillow. Gentle whispers, "That you, Livy Two? Where are you going?" Gentle knows all our individual walks and sounds. She knows Emmett by his whittling and harmonica, and Becksie smacks her lips, dabbing vanilla spice behind her ears as lady's perfume. She knows I drag my feet sometimes, and Jitters drops things, and Louise stirs up jars of paint and pops her knuckles when she gets nervous. Gentle also hears Caroline's fairy wings rustle, and Cyrus never ever walks when he can run. I don't see how she knows each of us so perfectly by sound and smell, but she does—it's like her other senses are razor sharp to make up for not seeing.

I kneel down beside her bed. "I'm going to help Miss Attickson sort out books at the bookmobile. Mama already knows. You be good. Roads are all clear now."

"Why are you bringing your guitar with you?"

"'Cause." I cast around for a lie. "Miss Attickson likes me to play, that's why."

"Read another mama girl story first."

"No! And you can't talk about that ever. I'll read one later. Go back to sleep."

"You'll forget, Livy Two. You don't mean to but—"

"I won't forget, I swear!"

"You might. Hey, guess what me and Daddy named the whistle pig babies? Sugar Cookie, Cinnamon, Sweetie, Andrew Jackson the Second, and Wiggle."

"That's real nice, Gentle." *Am I ever going to get out of here?* Any minute, Mama or Grandma Horace might wake up. Then Caroline sits up in bed and bangs her elbow. "Ouch! Livy Two, how many funny bones are there in your body? And how come when you get lost in your sleep dreams you can't never find your way home?"

"How should I know? Go back to sleep, both of you!" I hug Gentle and Caroline good-bye. Before I leave the room, I glance down at Becksie's tearstained face, probably dreaming of her secret sweetheart. A picture of a new rock band in England called the Beatles is stuck to the wall by her head. I lift up the blanket on the bed where Emmett and Cyrus are sleeping. Uncle Hazard is snuggled between them. He looks at me through the slit of one eye and goes back to sleep. The dog won't never leave a warm bed unless there's hope of food or somebody makes him.

"Bye, Uncle Hazard," I whisper before I leave the room, pulling Daddy's old winter coat tight around me for the trip. Uncle Buddy's still snoring like a buzz saw in the front room, the noise blessedly drowning out my footsteps across the wood floor and out the door to freedom. I pray I don't step on Pearl the iguana in the darkness, but I make it outside clean and clear. I stand real quiet for just a second on the porch, listening for something—I don't know what. When I turn back to look at the house one last time, Daddy is at the window watching me. My stomach dips, but I pretend like I'm heading to milk Birdy Sweetpea at the barn. Funny how I used to be the one waving good-bye to him when he hit the road for his auditions. I smile back at him and then I take off running like hellfire toward Mathew the Mennonite's place. A herd of wild goats watches me fly by them in the silent dawn of morning, but they just keep trekking up yonder in the snow.

Mathew the Mennonite goes into Waynesville like clockwork every Tuesday morning at the crack of dawn for jobs, so I climb into the back of his truck to hide under some lumber for his next carpentry job. A ribbon of black smoke curls out of his chimney. His wife must already be up making breakfast. I see Ruth and Sarah in the window, and Ruth is combing Sarah's hair. Ruth is Louise's best friend and a carpenter herself. She helped us make a pop-up book of an Uncle Hazard fairy tale for Gentle and the twins' birthday. Maybe we can do another one about a rainbow. The family peacock, Samson, squawks, but I lay low until I hear the very last voice in the world that I expect to hear.

"Livy Two!"

I peek out from under the lumber, and who is it but Jitters who has followed me all the way here.

"Go home!" I order.

"Not on your life." She's got her schoolbag slung over her shoulder.

"Please go home. Don't say a word. Please? Jitters? I'll tell you everything later."

"No. I won't stay under the same roof as Uncle Buddy. And I'm so mad at Becksie for getting a secret sweetheart I could spit."

"I'll give you five dollars. Hightail it out of here. Now!"

"Five dollars? You . . . briber! What are you fixing to do anyway? Hiding out in Mathew the Mennonite's truck like a stowaway?" She wears a coat that's too small, Becksie's beat-up boots, a lopsided red cap. The sunlight sparks off her cat's-eye glasses.

"None of your business, now scat! I'm begging you." I feel the tears start to rise. I had planned everything out perfectly. Right then, I hear the front door start to open. Jitters hears it too, and for a moment, I think she's going to take off running back home, but instead she climbs into the flatbed and hides with me under the lumber. I'm about ready to call the whole thing off when I hear Mathew the Mennonite call, "Good-bye, daughters. Help your mother today." I cover Jitters's mouth, and we duck down clean out of sight. Then his wife comes out on the porch with his lunch pail. "Remember, Mathew. Don't forget to stop by the Weems to be paid for your job. It's long overdue."

"They don't have the money. I'll not embarrass them, Alice. They'll pay when they have it." He takes the lunch pail from her.

"Mathew, we have our own family to think of. You rebuilt that smokehouse more than six months ago, and you've barely seen a penny. I think that folks—"

"Mr. Weems is not working yet. This is not a subject for discussion."

"You're not to do any more work for them, and I don't want Ruth going over there either. Those children run wild. They all might have been killed up on Waterrock Knob last month. Ruth was all caught up in it."

Mathew the Mennonite laughs. "They're not wild. They're children, Alice. Good-bye." He starts up his truck, and Jitters whispers into my ear, "You're *a lot* more wild than the rest of us. She was mainly talking about you."

"I'll snatch you bald-headed if you don't quit talking. And when we get to Waynesville, you're going straight back home to Maggie Valley. No fooling, Jitters. I mean it." We bounce up and down under the lumber, holding on tight the five miles to Waynesville. Jitters tries to grab my hand, but I yank it away. I'm ashamed we ain't paid Mathew the Mennonite yet. I don't want him to think we're a bunch of freeloaders.

The very second Mathew the Mennonite parks the truck and goes inside the Waynesville Hardware Store on Main Street, I hop down out of the flatbed. I take five dollars of my Nashville money and leave it in the driver's seat inside his Mennonite prayer book. He'll find it. I still have forty-five dollars and fifty cents. That's plenty for a single bus ticket and incidentals in Nashville. Then I make tracks down Main Street, Jitters at my heels. Mathew the Mennonite never sees a thing, so at least I can yell at her without him catching us and turning us in to Mama. "Beat it! Beat it now or you'll be sorry!"

"No, I'm coming too. You're up to no good."

When we get a few blocks away, I pull her off behind a tree. "You have no idea what I'm up to, and I ain't about to tell you, nosy thing. But it's not my fault Becksie found a sweetheart and Uncle Buddy's got a screw loose. Go home and ignore them. Why did you follow me for in the first place?"

"I don't have to answer bribers. You tried to bribe me. Your own beloved sister." Jitters folds her arms together, lips sealed. She's the spitting combination of a miniature Grandma Horace and Becksie.

"Look here. I got plans that don't involve you, so you might as well go on back to Maggie Valley and get to school. Uncle Buddy won't stay. He never does. Now scram."

"Think you can get rid of me that easy? Ha."

"Please, Jitters. I have something that needs doing and you're *not invited*."

"Maybe you shouldn't be so noisy when you leave the house at the crack of dawn and make up fake stories to Gentle. Taking your guitar to the bookmobile to play songs for Miss Attickson? Lies, lies!"

"For the love of God, please go home."

"No way. I'm not going back there. Uncle Buddy's a skunk, and Becksie's a traitor. Either I'm coming with you wherever you're going, or I'm telling on you for reading us Mama's diary."

Her threat horrifies me because I know she'd do it, but I say, "Who cares anymore? Go on and tell the world. That's what you do best anyway, you little brat."

"Don't think I won't either!" she calls after me, but I storm away from the tiny tyrant. How are we even related? Beloved sister? Ha. I'm sorry she got her feelings so deeply wounded, but I am going to Nashville. She can find her own way back to Maggie Valley. I keep walking in the direction of the Trailways, hoping and praying she goes on back home. I send her telepathic messages: *Go home, Jitters. Go home.* But it's not working. Every time I look behind me, I'm being followed. She ducks behind trees—her lurking self shadows my every step.

I got to just plain ignore her, and I try my best with Christmastime in the air. At a filling station, a Salvation Army Santa Claus rings a bell next to a donation bucket. "Merry Christmas!" The movie *It's a Mad, Mad, Mad, Mad World* plays at the Strand Theatre. Brand-new toys crowd the shops—honey-haired dolls that blink their eyes, shiny racer sleds, fishing rods, baseball mitts, toy dump trucks, and Tinker Toys. Next to the toy store is a music shop where rows of sparkling banjos, guitars, mandolins, and Dobros seem to whisper, *Buy me!* Down the street a ways is a pawnshop with a bunch of used everything in the window, including guitars. Law, I would never buy a used guitar. In fact, I don't intend to ever give up or swap my Sears & Roebuck guitar from Daddy for a new or used one. My guitar is as much a part of me as my arm or leg. I sure would like to come home from Nashville with presents spilling out of my arms, though, wrapped up with ribbons and bows.

But I got no time to think of that now. Why can't a person go off and have an adventure in peace? I cross the street toward the Trailways, heading straight inside to the ticket window. I'll buy a ticket first, and then I'll go look for her and make her go home.

"Where to, miss?" The clerk's face is shaped like a crook-neck squash, and he's got himself a mustache that twirls into stiff circles on each end. Fancy. He calls to mind that painter Louise showed me, who painted that melting-clock picture.

"Nashville, Tennessee. Thank you." My voice cracks the tiniest bit. I stand up straight, hoping to seem older than almost thirteen. I want to be a regular person taking a regular trip on the Trailways. I lean my guitar case against the counter. My cheeks feel hot, and I shove my trembling hands in my pockets.

"Nashville, Tennessee. Nashville, Tennessee." He shuffles through papers.

"Yep, Music City USA. That's my daddy's nickname for it. He says—"

The clerk interrupts with, "You don't say? Traveling on your own to Nashville?"

Just as I'm about to say, "Yes sir," the little stalker pops up beside me. "No sir, she's not. We're traveling together to Nashville, Tennessee. Two tickets, please," she says with a smile. Butter wouldn't melt in that girl's mouth. "Thank you very much."

I try to keep my breath from flaring like a fire-breathing dragon's. "That's right," I tell him, my heart sinking fast and low.

"Is there a problem? You don't sound so sure?" The clerk aims his question at me.

"I'm sure." I try to keep my voice from shaking. What choice do I have? If I get into a fight with her at the Trailways, the man will get suspicious. He might call the school or the truant officer or worse. Home.

"Departing when?"

"As soon as possible," Jitters says. "We're traveling together because it's safer, especially to a big huge city like Nashville. Right, Livy Two?"

Mr. Fancy Mustache Clerk drums his fingers on the countertop. The beat of his nails distracts me; they sound like the tiny galloping hooves of a miniature horse. "One-way or round-trip?"

"Round-trip, please," I tell him, but my voice sounds far away.

Jitters says, "That's right. Round-trip. This is our first trip together as sisters."

I elbow her to hush up, but the clerk is too busy punching tickets to notice. Why, oh why, wasn't I on the watch-out for lowdown dirty spies? Now I'll have no money left for incidentals. Oh, why did I have to be so sweet and read Mama's dang diary?

"Let's see," he says, "that will be two round-trip tickets from Waynesville, North Carolina, to Nashville, Tennessee. Thirty dollars and fifty cents."

I dig it out of my pocket in change and crumpled

bills, mostly ones. It will leave only fifteen dollars and fifty cents for Nashville. *And Jitters.* Will it be enough for the two of us? Mr. Fancy Mustache Clerk counts my pile of wadded-up bills. I smile, but it comes out fake 'cause my face feels froze up.

"Two round-trip tickets to Nashville." But y'all missed the morning bus. Next one don't leave until late afternoon near suppertime. Five ten on the nose to be exact."

Jitters smiles at him. "We'll wait."

I'm so mad I could spit. If that fool kid hadn't followed me, I'd have caught that early bus right on schedule. Now we'll be stuck waiting around all day.

"You two can sit over there then." He points to the room behind us. "Gets in at four in the morning, Central time. Mighty late or early, depending on how you look at it."

Jitters says, "Well, then it's a good thing we're traveling together and that we'll have our long-lost kin waiting for us, right, Livy Two?"

A lady in behind us lets loose a sharp suffering sigh. "*Woe is me*, have mercy! We're in a big hurry. Could we move it along, *please*, children?" Her husband buries his face in the *Smoky Mountain News*. I grab my guitar and schoolbag and head straight to the waiting room with the other fellow travelers who are getting ready to go to all sorts of towns and cities across the country. I hand Jitters her ticket without a word, and then I find a seat in the waiting room. She sits next to me, but I flat-out ignore her.

A pretty young woman puts on lipstick without using a mirror, which is amazing to me—not a smudge. A little boy eats Sugar Babies from a box by pouring them all into his mouth at once. His mom swats him with a rolled-up newspaper, but he keeps eating. I had expected the smell of the station to be the aroma of travel and excitement—a dash of lady's perfume, exhaust fumes, hot coffee. And it is all those smells, but there's another one too—one I can't figure out, but it hangs in the air, lonesome. I try to think of what songs I should play for Mr. George Flowers. I swear, sometimes I try to play my old songs, and more than one sounds like a bawling baby wrote them. I look around the crowded waiting room. I feel like everyone's staring at me, knowing my secrets. Jitters sits on the chair, swinging her legs, looking like she won the prize. She takes out *8,414 Strange and Fascinating Superstitions* by Claudia DeLys, compliments of the Haywood County Bookmobile. I can't believe I drug it home in the snow for her. I'd like to whack her over her mule head with it.

"How did you know to even pack?" I hiss at her.

"I didn't. I brought my schoolbag is all. I happen to carry this book everywhere. You wouldn't believe all the valuable information they got inside it."

"You're right, I wouldn't. Why don't you give me back your ticket so I can cash it in and you can go on back home where you belong?" I stand up to walk away, carrying my guitar and schoolbag with me.

"No, thanks. Hey, where are you going?"

"Away from you." I step outside the depot. Why couldn't Louise have followed me, or even Emmett? We could have had a good time. But Jitters? She's nothing but a ten-year-old pill that I'll have to babysit all three hundred miles and back again. I work on keeping my temper by looking at the mountains. Sometimes I think they're alive with personalities. Buck Mountain is the strict father, Setzer Mountain is the loving mama, and Dirty Britches is the wild brother, and Waterrock Knob is the dancing fairy sister. The mountains stand proud around Maggie Valley, bathed in pearly smoke after a rain.

My belly aches. How can I do this audition with Jitters tagging along? I should just go home and . . . then the doughy face of our landlady, Madame Cherry Hat, looms up in my mind, carping, "Where's the rent? We all got troubles. Life is hard. Where's the rent?" Madame Cherry Hat has had nine operations, and she likes to tell you about each and every one. She also clunks around in high heels that sink in the mud. She brought us candy once, but it was old orange-jelly candy, stuck together in a bag, like she had dug it out from a corner of her house. Mama wouldn't let us touch it.

"Livy Two?" A familiar voice makes me jump about a foot in the air.

I whip around to face Evie Pepper, the girl who never did forgive Becksie for beating her in the Maggie Queen contest last year. *What's she doing here?* Evie eyes my schoolbag and guitar, smoothing out her new lavender dress. She catches me looking at her dress and says, "Like it? I got it over at Schulman's Department Store in Sylva. They have high-quality dresses and sales, including '*imperfect*' dresses, marked down, so maybe even your family could afford to buy one."

"How the heck do you know about what we can or can't afford?" Though I suddenly recall Mama writing in her diary about her dress from Schulman's too.

Her face flames pink. "Good gosh, I happen to know your family has had a hard time is all. We go to the same church, you know. And we *pray* for you. You'd know that if y'all bothered to *show* up once in a while."

"You can keep your old prayers."

"Fine. I will. You taking a trip—on your own? Is that why you're not in school?"

"Can't pull nothing over on you, Nancy Drew."

"Where to? Does your mama know?"

"Course she does, Nosy! Who do you think is sending me over to Knoxville to pick up one of Daddy's old banjos that he left on the set of the *Cas Walker Show*?" The lie comes out easy as pie, but my heart is thudding hard against my chest. Still, the phrase "Easy-Pie Lie" strikes me as an idea for a song.

"Why do you got your guitar and schoolbag?" Evie puts her hands on her hips.

"'Cause—you never know when the idea for a song might strike, that's why! I happen to be a professional musician myself."

"Well, touch you!"

"Evie, there you are. Come on!" A woman with a gray ponytail yanks Evie by the arm. "The prison bus to Brushy Mountain won't wait. Your big brother will be so disappointed if we miss it again."

Evie looks at the ground. "Don't tell." Tears crowd her eyes, and I almost feel bad for her. Then she and her mama get on a bus that says WARTBURG, TENN. They lock up the worst of the worst over at Brushy Mountain, and don't turn them loose for nothing. Wonder what Evie Pepper's brother did? Murder? Robbery? Arson? Only prisoners I ever heard about are the ones that put out fires on Sheepback Mountain.

Jitters slinks up behind me and whispers, "Well, that was close. But you can come up with better lies than that. Daddy'd never in his life leave a banjo behind."

"Jitters, couldn't you have thought of another punishment besides following me?"

She plays with the strings on her cap, considering my question. "Nope. This one will do. I'm going to Nashville." She reaches down to scratch her foot. "My right foot's been itching something awful lately. Now I know why. Finally. It all makes sense. Itchy right foot means a trip. It says so in my book. I'm ready. I hope you're ready. You can borrow *8,414 Strange and Fascinating Superstitions* anytime."

"No, thanks."

"Suit yourself. Say, why did we go to all the trouble of catching the Trailways bus in Waynesville when we could have caught it at the Maggie Store just down the road?"

"Because we can be *a whole lot* more anonymous in a big town like Waynesville. It would spread like wildfire if we left in Maggie on the Trailways."

As the long, slow hours tick by, we wait in the far corner of the bus station, keeping low and quiet so as not to draw attention to ourselves.

A policeman with a big belly walks in the depot at one point, causing Jitters to make a strangled whimper in her throat. I elbow her in the ribs, and she hushes up quick. He glances around the depot like he's looking for something, but then he leaves.

Miraculously, the announcer calls, "Nashville, Tennessee, now boarding," just as it's growing dark outside.

Home free!

We run toward the bus in a swirl of dead leaves that dance through in the December wind, my younger sister following along behind me. But before we get on the bus,

Jitters says, "Wait!" She stops and spits over her left shoulder and takes three steps right and three steps left and jumps three times and spits over her left shoulder again. "Now the evil eye won't follow us to Tennessee. You're lucky to have me along. You just don't know it yet."

I pretend that we're not related as we get on the bus, and I write down the words to a new song, inspired by my chance meeting with Evie Pepper.

Tell a lie easy as pie
How are you? Happy as a lark . . . Easy-pie lie.
How's your daddy? Right as rain . . .
How's your mama? Sweet as sugar . . .
How's Grandma? Pretty as a picture . . .
Where you going? Over to Knoxville . . .
Easy-pie lie . . . Tell a lie easy as pie.
Tell some easy-pie lies . . . Tell them what they want to hear . . .
Easy-pie lie, easy-pie lie, easy-pie lie . . .

CHAPTER SEVEN

Spearfinger

JITTERS AND I do not sit in the same seats. I won't stand for it, the sneaky sneak. She sits six rows in front of me next to three tiny wrestling boys and their tired mama, who keeps saying "Quit," only she says it like "Queeeeiiit." Her heart ain't in it, and the boys keep at it. Jitters won't stop looking back at me with sad eyes, but I will not bend or weaken. I beam telepathic thoughts her way: *Stay where you are, stay where you are.* And for once, she listens. I want to escape into the pages of Mama's diary. When will they first miss us? Probably right away, since Jitters wasn't supposed to come with me to the bookmobile. Maybe they'll think she just left early for school? Probably, so that means we got almost a day to get away, but what if they send the police to fetch us? And what will Mr. George Flowers say to Jitters coming along? I think of the letter I sent him along with Mama's scarf.

Dear Mr. George Flowers,

Merry Christmas and Happy New Year! Here's my latest song to say thanks for writing me and asking after my daddy's health, which is improving by the minute. See you real soon when I visit Nashville.

Sincerely, Olivia Hyatt Weems

P.S. I am sending you a scarf my mama knit. Folks love mama's knitting and buy it up like hotcakes around here. Hope it keeps you warm.

The woe-is-me lady and her newspaper-reading husband from the ticket counter are back from sightseeing and sit directly across the aisle from me. Her husband is now reading the sports page. The lady says aloud to all in earshot, "Oh, I can't wait to see our baby grandson. He's the sweetest thing on God's green earth, and let me tell you, I intend to spoil him rotten with Meemaw love. Anything he wants, he can have it. By the time I'm through loving on him, he won't be worth killing."

The husband says, "That Brian Piccolo had a great season rushing at Wake Forest. Boy is some kind of athlete, telling you what now."

The woe-is-me lady says, "Don't say? I surely hope this trip won't take forever. My poor old back can't take it. I suffer, but I can't wait to hug on my grandbaby in Jackson, Mississippi. If this old bus ever gets there." She glances toward me, clearly in hopes of conversation, but I look away. I have enough babies in my life, and I don't need to gush over pictures of unknown ones. Jitters leans over her seat six rows up, waves, and mouths, "*Please! I need to talk to you! Please!*"

The woe-is-me lady points. "That child seems to want your attention."

"She's just some crazy child, following me. She must have me mistaken for someone else." The nosy lady looks suspicious, but I turn away to look out the window as the Trailways bus barrels west along Highway 19, winter trees rushing by outside. In December, our North Carolina trees are jagged limbs that claw the milky sky, but in the summer they're so thick with leaves, the sky only peeks through in indigo triangles. Abandoned bird nests sit high in the bare branches, and I spy another red-tailed hawk. Caroline hates hawks because a big one ate the school chicken that the first-graders were feeding as part of an animal project. It was a tragedy, but the teacher let Caroline take the dead chicken home to bury it, so we had to have a chicken funeral in the backyard with Uncle Hazard as one of the mourners, because of how good he can howl.

I peek up to see what Jitters is doing, and she gives me another hopeful smile, but I pay no mind. My breath makes soft ghost clouds against the pane when I breathe. I make fingerprints in the shape of flowers on the window. As we head over the mountain into Cherokee, I swipe away traitorous tears. I will not, by God, be afraid. I won't be what Uncle Buddy calls a "big-old-bawling-mama's-sweet-baby." I do not care for Uncle Buddy, even if he is blood, so I don't blame Jitters for running off in that respect, but it's made the whole plan so much more complicated. I'll call the minute I get to Nashville to tell them we're fine, because if I call along the way, Mama or Grandma Horace might try to catch up with the Trailways bus, or worse, send Uncle Buddy to fetch us home in the Ghost Town truck. Then we won't never hear the end of it.

The bus brakes groan and gripe all the way down the mountain to Cherokee. I hope the bus driver has the sense to put the bus in low gear and not pump the brakes. Sure would hate to go up in flames before we reach Music City USA.

When the bus pulls into Cherokee, Jitters marches back to my seat and plops down beside me. "I won't bother you, Livy Two, I swear. I can't take those wild boys anymore."

"Do I know you?" I ask. "You should go back to your own seat, little girl."

"Very funny. Ha, ha. Those wild boys' mama just sits there doing nothing, letting them get away with acting the fool! I've been hit three times and kicked four and not a one of them has even said 'sorry' yet." Jitters wiggles beside me. "Scoot."

"Good. Serves you right." I move over, but I notice the woe-is-me lady grows big ears all the sudden, pretending not to listen to our business.

Jitters gazes out the window at Cherokee. "Look at all the teepees. Wish I had one. Don't you? Wouldn't it be fun to live in a teepee like the Cherokee Indians?"

"Everybody who knows anything about the Cherokee knows they *did not live in teepees.* They just stuck them up around town to attract tourists who don't know any better."

"Well, I still want a teepee. Don't you?"

"I thought you said you weren't going to bother me."

"Sorry. I'll quit." But instead, she does just the opposite and turns and starts talking directly to the woe-is-me lady across the aisle. "Have you ever been to Ghost Town in the Sky? My favorite place there is the Cherokee Indian Village and also the Silver Dollar Saloon. They have the best chocolate milk shakes at the Silver Dollar Saloon. You ever been there?"

"I have not, sugarpie, but I will make a note of it. I never did travel much in my youth or dotage. Couldn't afford it. Money doesn't grow on trees."

"Sure doesn't. But you ought to go to Ghost Town.

Ride the chairlift to the top. Go to the Cherokee Indian Village or the Tilt House or ride the Wild Mouse. And there's also Moonshine Manor Arcades, with hoops, milk cans, roller balls, a dunking machine."

The lady smiles at Jitters. "Maybe we will. Maybe we'll take our grandbaby. Fatten him up on cotton candy and snow cones and funnel cakes. But our daughter-in-law doesn't believe in sugar. Have you ever heard of such a foolish notion?"

Jitters says, "Well, if you go to Ghost Town, lady, be sure to look for our brother. He's a gunslinger-in-training up there."

The woe-is-me lady says to me, "So you two are sisters. I thought so. Wasn't sure, the way you denied her just like the Apostle Peter did our Lord Jesus Christ over in Jerusalem." She's clearly wanting an explanation—too bad for her.

Jitters says, "Yep, we're sisters all right. This is Livy Two, and I'm Jitters, but her real name is Olivia Hyatt Weems, and I'm Myrtle Anne Weems. She is a professional musician like our daddy, and we're going to Nashville. . . . *Hey! Hey!* Now I know why we're going, Livy Two." She jumps up and down and gets all excited. "I just figured it out. You're going to audition, right? I knew it. Everybody who plays the guitar goes to Nashville to audition and make it in the big-time. It's all our daddy ever talked about before the car wreck. I can't believe I didn't think of it before now."

I interrupt, "Please excuse this child. She runs at the mouth."

"I do not!" Jitters cries. "In fact, I could help you. I could be your music manager. Maybe Daddy never sold a banjo hit because he didn't have a manager? Do you think?"

"Jitters, not everybody in the world needs to know our business," I whisper.

"Heavens, don't stop on my account. I am enjoying this immensely," the woe-is-me lady says. "I think good conversation between travelers helps to pass the time of day when you're stuck on a Trailways bus for hours and hours of your ever-shortening life."

"Thank you!" Jitters gives her a triumphant smile and says to me, "See."

The woe-is-me lady must be inspired, too, because then she says, "And I think that since y'all are going to Nashville to find fame and fortune, y'all should visit the Parthenon too. I hear they got some wonderful Greek god statues there. Unfortunately, I have never seen it myself as I have lived a very frugal life." She directs the last comment at her husband, but he's snoring, mouth agape.

"The Parthenon? That's in Greece," I tell her.

"That's correct, child, but Nashville has got itself an exact replica. I hope to take my grandbaby there someday too. If the good Lord is willing and sees fit to—"

Jitters says, "Well, our daddy used to all the time tell us about the Greek gods. He could do the voices of all them, from Cronus to Athena. Right, Livy Two? Our little brother likes to pretend he's Poseidon."

The woe-is-me lady asks, "And what does your daddy think of y'all heading off to Nashville on your own in the bleakness of winter? Two little girls like yourselves."

"Well, he—" Jitters begins, but I kick her under the seat, and she seals her lips quick.

"He couldn't be prouder," I tell her, and to get off the subject in a hurry, I say, "Jitters, I have a good Cherokee Indian legend. You want to hear it?"

"Of course I do." Jitters gets excited, waiting for the story.

I make my voice low and scary. "Ever hear of Spearfinger?" I pick the scariest story I can think of to shut her up, before the woe-is-me lady decides that we're runaways and turns us in to the authorities. It's a story Emmett used to tell me when we went fishing and he wanted to scare the holy living daylights out of me.

Her eyes get wide and fearful. "Will I like this story?"

"How should I know? But let me tell you, you don't ever want to meet Spearfinger, a Cherokee woman spirit who lives in the mountains. Know why? She'll sneak up behind and dig out your liver with her bony-knife finger. Folks don't even know she done it until it's too late. She's fast, never leaves a scar, and the life just drains right out of you then and there . . . and folks stick you in the cold grave for all eternity."

Jitters's face pales, and I know I'm low-down evil for tormenting her, but I want her quiet. The lady gives me a frosty look and says, "Woe is me, have mercy, if I had a sweet sister like you got, I'd be kinder. Sisters don't grow on trees, you know. Especially sweet ones like this one here."

"They sure don't!" Jitters says in a squeaky voice, but I don't answer either of them. I'm merely relieved when the next sign says, WELCOME TO THE THREE GREAT STATES OF TENNESSEE! Only two hundred more miles to go. . . .

CHAPTER EIGHT

Outer Space

January 10, 1943
Dear Grasshopper,

This here is a sketch of an indigo bunting . . . the female picks her mate by which male bird can sing the best of all her suitors. Isn't that funny? After she chooses the best musician husband bird, she builds their nest. I think indigo is about the prettiest color in the whole world. Our class just went on a field trip to see the Cherokee Indian Reservation. We went right over the mountain through a little town called Maggie Valley. I love the name Maggie Valley. I learned that the Cherokee Indians don't have a word for good-bye. The only word they have for it means "Until we meet again, my friend."

I almost forgot, Miss Amelia, the red calico cat, keeps coming over for saucers of cream. Meow, meow! I have to feed her early before Mother wakes up. I set my alarm for the crack of dawn. American Enka smells funny in the morn-

ing—sharp, acrid. I wonder what it smells like over in Europe in the morning? What does war smell like? It's so quiet here in the dawn, but is it loud and scary over there? Are kids my age afraid? American Enka makes materials for the war. . . . Does that mean the war smells a little like Enka? My questions irritate Mother no end.

Papa hasn't been feeling well, so I haven't had time to write to you. In fact, I am writing in the backseat of our car while Papa drives us over to Asheville. A doctor in Asheville is supposed to tell us what's the matter. Papa says we're making a fuss over nothing and that he needed to lose a few pounds anyway. We have to cross the French Broad River, which I learned is 210 miles long, which makes it the longest river in North Carolina.

Yours truly, Jessie Horace

P.S. Good news! The doctor told us that Papa is a-okay, and then Papa said to Mother, "Told you so!" It made her smile. He's one of the few folks with that talent. But then she said, "I still wouldn't mind a second opinion," and Papa said, "Didn't think you would." Mother always has to have the last word on EVERYTHING.

I put down Mama's diary as we head into Knoxville. I'm relieved to read that Grandpa Cal Horace is all right. I wonder whatever happened to Miss Amelia, the cat?

Jitters tries to read the diary over my shoulder, but I shift it away from her, blocking her view. *No mama stories for the stowaway!* The traffic is heavy as we cross over the Gay Street Bridge into the heart of Knoxville, the wide Tennessee River swirling below us with riverboats sailing by big as life. I crack open the window to breathe in the muddy river smell of fish, gasoline, and the air right before it snows. I like it. A lot. Maybe I'll travel by river one day. *ALONE, thank you very much.* Giant glowing snowflake ornaments hang on each downtown streetlamp as dusk gathers, and more Christmas trees shine from storefront windows. But by the time the bus pulls into the Trailways station, the brakes gasp and shudder. The bus driver parks and says, "Thirty minutes, folks. Possibly longer. We'll keep you posted."

I get off the bus, and the wind steals my breath away, it's so bitter cold after being on the stuffy bus. Jitters sticks close, looking forlorn in her little red cap, and I almost feel bad for her. My stomach growls with hunger, so I know she must be hungry too. We go wash up in the bathroom before eating supper. Jitters says, "I'm scared to pee here."

"What are you scared of?"

"Diseases. It smells funny."

"Put some toilet paper down and quit whining."

"Don't leave me."

"I won't. Though I ought to. About what you deserve."

"Please?"

Her voice sounds so scared I feel low-down mean. "I won't! Just hurry." When we both finish washing up, we go out into the lobby of the Trailways. I unpack some cornbread with sourwood honey, apples, and raisins for supper. We sit on hard chairs in the lobby. It feels lonely at dusk on a winter night in Knoxville, the sun gone. I spot the red glow of the Coca-Cola machine. I stick a nickel in the machine and a bottle rolls out. Jitters watches without saying a word. I put in another nickel and buy a second bottle. I hand it to her along with a slice of cornbread and raisins.

"Thank you." Jitters pops it open and takes a big long drink.

"You're welcome."

"Livy Two?"

"What?"

"You think next time, you could get me an orange sody-pop instead?"

"Next time, buy it yourself." I watch some folks go into the café, where I smell meat loaf and potatoes cooking.

"I'm just saying." She takes a few bites of her cornbread before she points to a pay telephone. "You think maybe we should call home? So they don't think we been kidnapped by bad guys or sold into child slavery?"

"They're not going to think that."

"What if they think Spearfinger got us? Why'd you have to tell me that terrible story anyhow? We should call home and tell them we're safe and sound."

"We'll call from Nashville."

"But we don't get there until the middle of the night. Central time middle of the night! Whatever that is."

"We're in the Eastern time zone. It means we're an hour ahead."

"An hour ahead of what?"

"It's ten o'clock here in East Tennessee, but it's only nine o'clock in Nashville. There's Eastern and Central time. And Western too, but that's all the way in California."

"Why? What for? What do we have all those time zones for?"

"'Cause the sun gets to us faster in the East. Now no more questions. I have to think." Miraculously, she gets quiet eating her cornbread and sipping on her Coca-Cola. I try to figure out what to do next. Long distance is expensive, and we don't have much money as it is. I am getting more and more uneasy about this whole trip, so I repeat "Mr. George Flowers, Mr. George Flowers" in my head to keep focused on what I set out to do. The Coca-Cola tastes fizzy and sweet and feels good going down my dry throat.

An old man with a yellow dog comes up to the Coca-

Cola machine. He's lanky and wears a suit, but his back is bent with age, and he leans on a cane near the machine. He fumbles with the change in his pocket like he can't get his fingers to work right. He looks at us watching him and asks, "Would one of you kids fetch me a Dr Pepper? Here is a nickel. I'm fond of Dr Pepper. I got the arthritis of the fingers. Be grateful for your youth." As he talks, I hear the sound of soft whistling, but I can't figure out from where.

Jitters takes his nickel and drops it in the machine. "I'll get it for you, mister."

We both watch the way his Adam's apple bobs up and down when he swallows. We sit there in silence. Even though he's old and feeble-looking, I'm wary of scurrilous crooks like what Mr. Fagan was in *Oliver Twist*, recruiting pickpockets. Jitters needs to watch out too, but she's already petting his dog. "What's its name, mister?"

"Laika. Named after the first dog in space." The whistling is louder now. "Sent into space by the Russians. I climb water towers and such myself. To conquer my fears."

"You work on water towers?" Jitters asks.

"No, just climb 'em."

I don't know what to say to that, so I hug my guitar and schoolbag closer. Jitters is too busy petting on Laika to pay him any mind. "Do you get to take your dog on the bus?" she asks him.

"Yeah, I got a medical condition. I got permission from the authorities."

I don't want to know what his medical condition is, so I nudge at Jitters to come on, but she asks, "Why did them Russians send a dog into outer space anyhow?"

"To see how a living creature would survive." His tired voice sounds like he's got wet pebbles in his throat. "She did not. Survive. On a spaceship called *Sputnik Two*."

"Oh, that's so sad." Jitters looks like she might bust out crying.

"I did a current-event report on the first woman in space," I tell Jitters. "Remember? A Russian cosmonaut, Valentina Tereshkova."

"Funny thing," the old man remarks, "sending a female to outer space."

"Why is it funny?" I say it louder than I mean to. "Valentina Tereshkova was called 'the seagull.' She was so talented at driving her spaceship around the world, she orbited it forty-eight times without a hitch."

"Just a peculiar thing—a female astronaut—but that's the Russian Communists for you." His lower lip practically touches his nose. "But I'm a curmudgeon—old-fashioned in my thinking. Mean no harm. It's nice to see two kids traveling together. Reminds me of me and my brother. How do, I'm Fletcher Partridge."

"Nice to meet you, Mr. Partridge." Jitters beams.

At that second, I realize the whistling I've been hearing is coming from the old man's nose. One of his nostrils whistles like a flute.

"Y'all kids have far to go?" he asks.

"Not far," I say, but then Jitters pipes up, "Nashville! Where are you headed?"

"Me and Laika here are going on to Memphis. But Nashville! That's some kind of town. Y'all watch yourselves in the big city. Integrity is in short supply these days."

"We'd better go now," I say. "Nice talking to you." I pull Jitters away with me, and she calls, "Have fun in Memphis! Bye, Laika, I'm glad you're not in outer space like the other poor Laika, headed to your doom in the outer galaxies."

"You don't have to tell strangers our business," I say after we're out of earshot.

"I was just being nice. And he's not a stranger anymore. He's Mr. Partridge."

"He is so a stranger with a whistling nose who don't believe in girl astronauts."

"But I thought you liked meeting new folks."

"I do—I just—I thought it'd be different is all." I can't explain it, but where are my fellow travelers who are kindred spirits off on adventures like me? I guess I just ain't met them yet. I smell bread baking from somewhere far away. The sound of a train wails in the distance along with the peal of church bells. It must be almost supper-time, and I feel a lump in my throat, thinking of Daddy staring at the window this morning, smiling at me. What's Mama doing now? Is Jitters right? Should we call home?

A few hours later in Cookeville, we get delayed due to "mechanical difficulty." To pass the time, Jitters reads tidbits from her superstitions book until I want to cry for mercy. She warns me about how it's bad luck to leave a hat on a bed or shoes on a table and how it's important to spit into a new baseball mitt to make it lucky for the player or how you should never fly on a plane where the flight numbers add up to thirteen.

"Since when are you catching a plane?" I ask.

"This is also for future reference."

Then she says, "If a frog hops into your house, it's good luck! And if a bee flies inside, it means company is coming, but if you kill the bee, it will be bad company. This book could map out your whole, entire life for you. It's the best."

"Don't read me any more."

"Why not?"

But the bus driver gets on the speaker and says, "Sorry for the delay, folks. Our brakes have been suffering since

Knoxville, so to keep y'all folks on schedule to Nashville, our good colleagues from the Cookeville Greyhound depot have agreed to help out. There is a bus from the Greyhound station, ready to carry you the rest of the way to Nashville. You won't be too much later arriving, but bundle up. We may break the temperature record this December, according to the weather reports."

I start to feel a little desperate at the dire forecast. Can we sleep in the bus station in Nashville? Jitters and I start to walk toward the Greyhound bus that pulls into the parking lot, along with the rest of the folks.

Jitters grabs my arm and says, "Livy Two, wait. Is it bad luck not to call home?"

"How should I know? I'm sick of hearing about good luck and bad luck!"

"You don't have to bite my head off."

"Well, all I know is that I was supposed to be off on an adventure by now, and then you showed up and used up half my money for your ticket, and you go around telling everybody our business. And instead of meeting kindred spirits, the only folks I've met so far are a woe-is-me lady and an old man with a whistling nostril. And you keep telling me about superstitions! This wasn't the plan. I haven't had a moment to even think about my audition for Mr. George Flowers."

Jitters's lower lip starts trembling.

The bus driver calls, "Step it up. Y'all girls coming? Shake a leg!"

"Just a minute, sir." I turn to her. "Jitters, don't you dare cry. Come on."

But it's too late. She really starts blubbering. "I'm going home. I'll stay here in Cookeville and take the next bus back to Maggie. You hate me! It's plain as day."

"I don't hate you . . . but don't you play the martyr now, or I'll knock you into next week." I grab her arm, but she wriggles free.

"I'm not playing nothing, for your information. Go on to Nashville. I'll tell Mama you're safe—that you're off chasing your dream like Daddy." She looks miserable as she wipes away a tear with the sleeve of her coat.

"Quit it, Jitters. I'm sorry. Come on, please?" I can't believe I'm begging her.

The bus driver toots a warning honk. "Get the lead out, kids!"

"Leave me alone! I'm going back to the Eastern time zone where I belong."

My face gets hot. All the folks on the bus are staring at us. "Jitters, I am truly sorry. Don't do this. Please? We've made it this far. I'll quit being so mean."

Tears stream down Jitters's face, but she says, "You mean it?"

"Course I do. I just said it."

"And no more Spearfinger stories either!"

"No more, I swear." The bus driver honks the horn, a final warning, and Jitters relents and follows me on the bus. We sit together this time, and as the bus heads toward Nashville, the woe-is-me lady leans over to us. "Thought y'all girls weren't going to make it. Been a sad thing to get stuck in Cookeville on a bitter night as tonight."

"Awful." Jitters nods. "Why is it called the 'Three Great States of Tennessee'?"

The woe-is-me lady says, "Here's a tissue, honey. I have no idea why they call it that," but her husband leans around her and says, "I know. 'Cause East Tennessee is mountains, Middle Tennessee is rolling hills, and West Tennessee is flat as a pancake."

She pokes her husband. "Well, send you to the head of the class! See, isn't he just chock-full of facts? But you'd never know it. Got to pry the information and the pennies out of him."

Teary-eyed, Jitters says, "That makes sense." Then she turns to me and says, "Can I please be your music manager? All musicians have them. Please?"

"What do you want to be my manager for?"

"'Cause we're going to Nashville, and I want a job to do."

"All right, I'll think about it. Just go to sleep." Jitters curls up next to me, and I don't shove her off. I aim for patience and love toward my annoying sister, though I don't feel a whiff of none of it. The night is blue-black and full of stars as we leave Cookeville behind. The full moon hangs creamy and white in the sky. Why shouldn't a girl fly into outer space if she wants to? I bet Emily Dickinson, always dwelling in possibility, would have liked to see a girl astronaut fly to the moon and back again.

CHAPTER NINE

Music City, USA

January 28, 1943
Dear Grasshopper,

I got up early to see the sunrise on Enka Lake. Miss Amelia followed me the whole way. It was so pretty, Grasshopper. So icy cold in darkness, but then the sun came up spilling gold rays across the lake. The plant doesn't smell so bad in the winter. Papa works real hard there, mixing up all sorts of dyes, and it's what puts food on the table. But it's winter now, so on weekends, he's stuck inside studying the seed catalog for the spring. He's going to plant some garlic, as it "purifies the blood." He learned this in the Cherokee Medicine Book. Mother loves onions and because spring onions, known as ramps, grow so big and wild around here, they have Ramp Queen and Ramp Princess contests to celebrate the wild onions over in Canton. Mother wants me to try to be the "Ramp Princess" at the Ramp Festival someday, but I don't much want to be an onion princess.

Yours truly, Jessie Horace

Jitters's head rests heavy on my shoulder as the bus rolls west in the darkness. I close Mama's diary and slide it back into my guitar case, where I know it will be safe. My eyes grow heavy, and all the rest of the way to Nashville, I dream of Mama with her snowball bushes, wearing a crown of onions, waving at me, "Livy Two! Livy Two!" But as my dream of Mama ends, I am inside another—visiting some of the Seven Wonders of the World. I start at the Great Pyramid of Giza in Egypt, then on to the Hanging Gardens of Babylon on the Euphrates River. Then I'm zoomed to the Temple of Artemis at Ephesus in Turkey and the Lighthouse of Alexandria off the coast of Egypt. I must be on a super time machine, but the thing is, at the tail end of the dream, I still land smack back on the shores of Enka Lake, located in the shadow of American Enka. Grandma Horace and Jitters are both shouting, "Olivia! Over here! Come see the 'Eighth Wonder of the World'! You're gonna love it! Athena just dropped by for a visit too."

I try to run away, but I feel somebody shaking me awake. "Livy Two! We're here. The driver said, 'Welcome to Nashville, Tennessee!' Look at that big old dog there."

I sit up to see the giant statue of a greyhound dog standing perched on the roof of the Greyhound bus station. A sign says, WELCOME TO YOUR HOME OF COUNTRY MUSIC!

Jitters stretches and yawns. "I'm hungry. You got any scrap of food left?"

"No, you ate it, so you'll have to wait. Come on and watch out for pickpockets."

"I will. I ain't seen any yet. Hey, it's getting light outside, Livy Two. Look!"

Sure enough, the gray dawn of this winter morning shines on the old face of the woe-is-me lady and her husband. They never even wake up, as they're going on to Jackson, Mississippi, to love on their grandbaby. They sleep curled up together like they're best friends, and maybe in sleep they are. I look outside the window of the bus just in time to see Fletcher Partridge and his dog, Laika, turning the corner away from the Greyhound depot. I thought they were headed to Memphis.

The split second we get off the bus, the wind blows hard against us. Trees are bending, almost bowing sideways, but it don't matter. We're in Nashville. We did it. It's a good thing I got my city map that I ordered special from the tourist bureau. We slide and slip across the patches of ice in the parking lot into the station. The bus must be late because of all the bad winter weather, but who cares? We made it. Signs say: WELCOME TO THE ATHENS OF THE SOUTH, WEARY TRAVELERS! and FORT NASHBOROUGH TOURS DAILY! LISTEN TO THE TALE OF "THE BATTLE OF THE BLUFF, 1781"!

Once inside the toasty bus station, Jitters asks, "Now what?"

"Let's get cleaned up so we can look professional. And listen to me, I know you think you're my manager now, but while we're there at Mr. George Flowers's office, don't go running at the mouth the way you do the minute we meet him, all right? You can say hello, but that's all. He and I are the ones been corresponding. Not you."

"What if he asks me if I'm a musician too?"

"You'll say no."

"But I clog."

"This is not your audition. If you clog for him, Jitters Weems, I'll make you regret it the rest of your born days."

"All right, I won't clog. But can I at least tell him I'm your manager?"

"Fine, now come on!" I prod her toward the ladies' room, where I give myself a birdbath with funny-smelling soap. I make Jitters give herself one too. I feel real grubby from traveling so long. I brush my teeth at the sink and clean it out. Usually, I'm sharing a sink with a bunch of other kids, so it's easy to get cleaned up in this public bathroom, but it smells wrong, full of industrial cleansers and disinfectant. I brush my hair and braid it back up again. I go inside a stall to put on a clean shirt and jeans. When I come back out, Jitters says, "You almost look like a professional."

"What's that supposed to mean?"

"It means that as your manager I think you almost look like a professional."

I ignore her and go out to the lobby to a newspaper stand. I read a headline that says, "Reading Near Record Here: Cold to Stay," and a caption that says, "What's a Duck to Do?" It shows a picture of a crowd of ducks outside the Parthenon, waddling out onto the frozen Centennial Lake in the eleven-degree temperatures.

Jitters whistles. "That lady was right. There is a Parthenon here. Whoops! No whistling inside. It's bad luck. Means you won't make any money. But oh, those poor, poor ducks! I bet they're scared. Let's go see them after your audition."

I read another headline. "'Chimp-Man Kidney Transplant Success.' Dockworker is doing fine after receiving a chimpanzee's kidneys in a 'historic operation.'"

Jitters gasps, "How in the world did those doctors do such a thing?"

"Beats me."

"All I know is I sure wouldn't want some chimpanzee heart beating away inside me," Jitters says with a nervous expression on her face.

It's easy to get lost in all the folks that are coming and going in the Nashville Greyhound bus station. Some detour for breakfast, and me and Jitters linger in the café doorway to smell the bacon and eggs sizzling on the griddle, stacks of pancakes and sausage and jugs of sweet maple syrup. Men in cowboy hats carry around steaming cups of hot coffee to wake themselves up. I'm tempted to buy a cup myself even though I only like the smell, not the taste. My stomach growls with hunger too, except we got to be strong and save our money for emergencies. I hold tight to my guitar, trying to figure out what to do next.

Outside, trucks and cars whiz by on Sixth Avenue as more buses start pulling in and out of the Greyhound. Jitters asks, "How much money we got left?

"Less than fifteen dollars. And it's got to last us."

"But a doughnut ain't nothing but a nickel. Come on, let's get a doughnut? Please?"

"Fine, get me one too." I give her a quarter. I study the city map. I pretty much know the streets to Music Row, having studied the map before I left. It's not far—about a mile at the most up to Sixteenth Avenue. We'll have to go to Broadway to catch the bus, but I want to stay on Sixth Avenue awhile and then cut down on Fifth Avenue, so we can see the Ryman.

Jitters comes back with two warm glazed doughnuts. Both of us try not to swallow them whole, but they taste so good, and the sweetness spreads in our bellies. "Guess what?" Jitters informs me. "We're on Central time now."

"I told you we would be."

"It's funny to think how they're an hour older than

us back at home just because we got on a bus and headed west."

An announcer calls out schedules: "Cleveland, boarding. New York City, delayed. Memphis, arriving. Birmingham, Alabama, final call." After we finish our doughnuts, I find myself hoping that my singing voice don't crack today. I hope Mr. George Flowers gives me an audition and a chance at WSM Radio, home of the Grand Ole Opry.

We head out of the bus station, walking fast. Nashville seems to go on forever with stoplights, sirens, taxis, cafés, and tall brick buildings with faded lettering on them with words like "Mercantile" and "Hermitage Hotel." I try to take it all in, and even Jitters stands there gape-mouthed at everything there is to see. Stone churches with spires seem to scrape the sky, and I hear the sound of a distant train. Nashville sits right on the Cumberland River. People dash from one building to the next to get out of the cold, in cowboy hats and boots with rhinestone jackets, carrying guitar and fiddle cases. We're near a place called Printers Alley, packed with all sorts of tall buildings and business offices. I see a sign VISIT THE LIFE & CASUALTY TOWER: TALLEST BUILDING IN THE SOUTHEAST! SIGHTSEEING AT OBSERVATION DECK—PLEASE DO NOT DISTURB OTHER BUSINESSES. Another sign says,

VISIT OLD HICKORY . . . PRESIDENT ANDREW JACKSON'S HOME, and it makes me think of Gentle's whistle pig, Andrew Jackson the Second, with a lump in my throat. *I will not be scared. I will not be scared.*

The women wear a lot of makeup with high hair in this city. I never seen such high hair in one place. How do they get it to do that? We crouch in doorways to warm up, and I see places called the Rainbow Room and the Brass Stables. I reckon we must look like a real pair of backwoods girls in frayed winter coats, but it ain't my style to get gussied up. We pass by an old green 1949 Ford truck with a sign in the window:

OLD CARS ARE LIKE PRETY WOMEN.
LOOK AND ENJOY.
BUT DON'T TUCH UNLES THEY ARE YOURS.
THANK YOU. HAVE A NICE DAY.

I think someone ought to learn to spell, and then I see it—right on Fifth Avenue—the Ryman Auditorium, where all the country-music stars got their starts to fame and fortune. It's in near spitting distance from the bus station. I can't hardly believe it. "Jitters, this is it. We're standing in front of the Ryman Auditorium. Home of the Grand Ole Opry."

"Just looks like some old church to me."

"Some old church? That just shows how much you know. That just—"

"Look, Livy Two." Jitters points to something else in front of the Grand Ole Opry. "There's that Fletcher Partridge man we met back in Knoxville. I thought he was going on to Memphis. What's he doing? Is he acting like a—?"

I try to figure out what I'm seeing, but it's like my brain is playing tricks. The old man with the yellow dog, Laika, is standing near us on the steps of the Grand Ole Opry with a tin cup. He has on dark glasses, carries a white cane, and he's got a lead on the dog like she's a guide dog for the blind. He's faking it, being blind, and making the dog fake it too. Is that his "medical condition"? Lying? He calls out, "Repent and be saved!"

Before I can stop her, Jitters snaps her fingers and says, "Howdy, Laika. What are you doing here, Mr. Partridge? I thought you'uns were going to Memphis." The dog wags her tail at Jitters. *Thump, thump, thump.*

I pull her away. "What are you doing, Jitters? Don't even talk to him. The faker."

The old man yells, "Who's there? Who's there? Can't see a thing."

And I can't help myself. I yell, "You see us plain as day, Mr. Partridge, or did you go blind overnight, which would about serve you right."

But he sputters, "Mistook. You kids got me mistook for somebody else. Mistook."

"Doubt it. We talked about outer space. You don't believe in girl astronauts. You named your dog Laika. Your eyes were working fine in Knoxville. Faker."

"Mistook, I say. Almost Christmas. Help an old blind man—save your soul."

Jitters says, "You said 'integrity was in short supply.' Why are you faking it?"

"So is money, sister. Spare a quarter?"

"No, sorry, my sister has the money."

"Jitters!" I snap at her. "Shut up right now! Come on."

"But he's one of the poor, Livy Two," she argues. "Even if he is a faker."

"Your sister is right, Livy Two. I'm poor as they come." The old faker blind man lurches toward us, going for Jitters's schoolbag, which seems to knock some sense into her. We light off south toward Broadway, but Laika howls and barks in misery, *Don't leave me!* The man yanks hard on Laika's leash, and the poor dog cries out in pain.

Jitters stops. "He's mean to her. Listen. Should we go back?"

"No, Jitters, we can't. Now come on."

She looks like she might argue, but it's so cold in the freezing wind at Broadway and Second Avenue, she clings onto my arm to wait to catch the bus to Mr. George

Flowers' address on Sixteenth Avenue. I want to forget what we just seen. It makes my head pound to think on it. I look toward the Nashville skyline, which is buck-naked, not a mountain in sight. Where are the mountains to hold the city together the way they hug Maggie Valley? The homesickness gathers in my chest like a knot. There's a pay phone next to us, and I know in my heart that we should call home this very minute. They got to be real scared, but I just can't. I need to do this audition first and get our family on the path to success, or at least out from under the thumb of Madame Cherry Hat.

We wait for the bus on Broadway on a corner up from the Ernest Tubb Record Shop, where "Waltz across Texas" plays outside on some speakers. Across the street and down a ways on the right, I see Tootsies Orchid Lounge, and I know that's where Opry singers wait in between sets and sip Coca-Colas (and other drinks, I expect). I bet Loretta and Patsy and Kitty have all sat at the bar in Tootsies waiting to cross the alley to the Ryman. I have read all about how it used to be called Mom's until a lady named Tootsie Bess bought it.

Finally the bus comes, and we climb aboard. I get settled expecting a long ride, but the bus delivers us to Sixteenth Avenue in a matter of minutes. It's all happening so fast now. I feel sick at my stomach, like I might throw up. We get off the bus and start following the numbers to Mr. George Flowers. Will he be a kindred spirit?

"I swear I hate folks that are mean to dogs. Remember when Uncle Hazard got stung by the hornets? Grandma Horace was sweet to him and got him feeling better."

"I remember—now, come on, I'm freezing." We walk down Sixteenth Avenue looking for Mr. George Flowers's address, but instead of a building, we come to a house, a brick house with a wide front porch and a yard covered in snow. "This is it," I tell her.

Jitters inspects the fiddle-shaped mailbox. "I think that's a good sign. It's homey. But you'd better do some singing warm-ups. Is your guitar tuned?"

"Can't tune it until we're inside." I knock on the front door. No answer. We sit down on the porch swing to wait in the bitter cold. We huddle up together, and for the first time, I secretly admit to myself that I'm glad she's along.

"Isn't it work time for folks yet, Livy Two?"

"I reckon it's early yet for Nashville. Now remember I'll do all the talking."

"You told me a hundred times already."

"Well, he and I have been writing lots of letters, so I'm more prepared than you." I blow on my fingers in the raw cold. Church bells chime ten o'clock in the morning.

Jitters says, "I'm hungry. Maybe being a manager makes a person extra hungry."

Instead of answering, I turn to the sound of clicking high heels on the sidewalk, followed by a jangle of keys. A woman in a red coat is headed straight toward us with a sensible walk and a no-nonsense air about her. She don't look too happy to see us waiting on her porch swing, but it's a free country. I got a right to come to Nashville to audition—even with a younger sister tagging along. Jitters whispers, "You scared?"

"Yeah, I'm scared. What do you think? Try to show a lick of sense, all right?"

"I was just thinking that you ought to be scared is all. I'm sure glad it's not my audition." Jitters steps along the side of the front porch like she's walking on a tightrope.

CHAPTER TEN

"Nothing Personal, Little Lady!"

THE WOMAN HAS black hair swooped up high, and it resembles a warrior helmet. Even though it's real windy, her hair don't move an inch. She stares at us, taking note of my schoolbag and guitar. "No school today, girls?"

Before I can utter a word, Jitters says, "Howdy. My sister here would like to see Mr. George Flowers. I am accompanying her. I'm her music manager."

I see the woman try to hide a smile. I swear I could smack Jitters. "Hey. How are you?" I cut in, trying to sound professional in spite of the kid beside me. "I'm Olivia Hyatt Weems from North Carolina. It's a—a holiday over there." I try to force out an easy-pie lie, but I can hear my voice trembling. "Do you know Mr. George Flowers?"

"I am his secretary. What holiday is happening over in North Carolina?"

This catches me off guard, but Jitters says, "It's the—

the—the Snowball Holiday, to welcome the wintertime. Kids get off school. Even grown-ups get off work."

"Is that so?" She looks wary. "Well, I'm sorry, but George Flowers is a busy man. If y'all girls didn't make an appointment, you can't see him. Have a nice day. Bye."

"Wait!" I try to stay calm. "Me and him—we been writing letters back and forth since the summer, so that's why I'm here. Please?"

"What did you say your name was again?"

"It's Olivia Hyatt Weems."

"I know that name. You're the child from Maggie Valley, North Carolina, aren't you? You've been writing to George at a pretty regular clip, I'd say."

"Yes ma'am."

"All right, step inside a minute."

Immediately, Jitters's glasses fog up, but she don't care. "Thank the Lord! We were like to freeze to death out there." She smiles at the lady. "You hear about the ducks at the Parthenon? Their lake froze, and they don't know what to do, right, Livy Two?"

"Mr. Flowers wrote me back too." I try to stay on the subject.

"Once," the secretary corrects me. "I sent it." She turns on the lights and heat.

"Just once?" Jitters asks me. "I thought you said you two were near pen pals—"

"Hush!" I whisper. But I'm at a loss for words. In my

mind, me and Mr. Flowers had a much more lively exchange. "Anyhow, here I am. Would you please let him know that I want to see him for an audition? My sister will be happy to wait outside in the hallway, so as not to crowd up your office, right, Jitters?"

"So now it's an audition, is it?" The lady sounds miffed. "Look, did somebody drive you over here? Where are your parents?"

"Back in Maggie," I tell her.

"Taking care of the little ones," Jitters continues. "Well, Daddy's probably not. He's probably playing the banjo, trying to remember the details of his life. As for Mama, I bet she's—" Jitters gets revved up to spill the whole epic story, but the split second the secretary has her back turned to make coffee, I yank her braid to make her quit. "Ouch!" She rubs her head.

"Something the matter?" the secretary asks.

"Nothing!" we both say at the same time, but Jitters edges away from me toward a wall of country singer pictures. It's filled with the likes of Hank Williams, Patsy Cline, Loretta Lynn, Little Jimmy Dickens, and so many others. I ask, "Did Mr. Flowers get my present? It was a scarf my mama made."

Jitters gasps, and then I realize I'd forgotten to explain to her about the scarf. She points an accusing finger and mouths, *"Thief! Thief!"*

The secretary sits at her desk. "Girls, Mr. Flowers

receives a lot of mail from hopefuls and wannabes." This phrase sticks in my mind. *Hopefuls and wannabes?* Is that all I am to him? I sit down on one side of the couch, Jitters on the other. I try to remember the words to a Christmas song I wrote about Maggie Valley.

After a silence, Jitters says, "Not only am I her manager, I can clog."

"You don't say?" The secretary lights a cigarette.

Finally, around lunchtime, a man busts into the room in a cowboy hat and string tie and the whitest, shiniest pair of cowboy boots I've ever seen. Even Jitters is staring at his white boots. "Cold as a well-digger's instep out there!" the man shouts, shaking the snow off of him. "Holy Moses, where's my coffee, Mildred! Better be hot!"

The secretary says, "George, you have someone here to see you." And then, finally, after all these months, Mr. George Flowers is staring straight at me, looking more confused than happy. Yet, as I stand up to shake hands with him the way Daddy taught me, firm and strong, not like a dead fish, he turns away. "Mildred, I don't got any appointments this morning. I got that lunch date at Merchant's. Then I got to meet with some pickers at the Ryman." He pours himself a gigantic cup of coffee and spoons in three whopping spoonfuls of sugar. Boy, wouldn't Grandma Horace take note of that?

Mildred says, "Well, this kid and her 'manager' showed

up all the way from the Tar Heel State where, apparently, they're having some kind of special holiday today."

"Manager?"

"That's me," Jitters says from her perch on the couch. "I'm Myrtle Anne Weems, and this is Olivia Hyatt Weems. How do you do, Mr. George Flowers?"

"Is this a joke? Come on, now. What can I do you for, kids?" He drinks down his coffee, black and sugary. I look over at the secretary, but she's now typing.

"Mr. Flowers," I say, "I wrote you letters. You liked my daddy's songs," I say, but my voice sounds flat and scared. What's wrong with me? Where's my gumption?

"You know how many letters and songs I get? Whooo-dog, tell her, Mildred!"

"But you wrote me back, and you wrote my daddy back too. Tom Weems."

Mildred stops typing. "George, it's the child from Maggie Valley."

"The mountain kid? Was it your daddy who had the car wreck? We felt real bad about that, didn't we, Mildred? Well, nice to meet you. How do y'all like Nashville?"

"Cold," Jitters replies, but I want to quit with the small talk, and I interrupt, "We like Nashville just fine. Before the accident happened, Daddy sent you a song that you liked, and you told him to 'keep it up.' I found your note in my mama's Everything Box, where we keep our important files and such. And that's how I came to write to you, and you liked my music too, especially 'Louisiana's Song' and 'Strike It Rich'—I think that was the other one you liked."

Jitters shakes her head and says under her breath. "You went peeking in the Everything Box too? Lord, Lord."

"George, the child has come to audition for you!" Mildred spells it out for him, never missing a beat in her typing.

Mr. George Flowers says, "Audition? Holy—I don't have time. I apologize, but I don't have time. And I don't rep kids. Nothing personal, little lady."

Little lady? Who's he calling "little lady"? But Jitters stands up. "Mr. Flowers, Livy Two is a professional musician with a lot of experience playing all sorts of venues."

"Lily Two? What kind of name is that?"

"Livy! Livy Two," Jitters corrects. "And she has sung at Settlers' Days, the Mountain Dance and Folk Music Festival over in Asheville, and plenty of other places."

My heart beats fast. None of this is going according to plan, but I got no choice but to plow forth. "Mr. Flowers, I been playing since I was nine. I played at Ghost Town in the Sky too." He motions us to follow him inside his office, attached to Mildred's. It's crowded with boxes and albums.

He sits down at his desk. "Girls, I apologize. Not only am I a busy man, I am a distracted man." His phone is already ringing. I look at the stack of mail on his desk, and

I recognize my present I sent to him with Mama's scarf. The big envelope sits unopened. My heart feels scalded, but I've come too far to quit.

Jitters asks, "What song would you like to hear first, Mr. Flowers?"

Mr. Flowers says, "See here. My advice to y'all kids is to come back when you're eighteen years old, if you still want to pursue this music thing. Go on back home to the mountains now and be kids awhile longer. Heck, it's almost Christmas. Santy Claus is sure to be coming, right? Besides, a whole lot of heartbreak here—you know how many songs and songwriters I get in here a week? Thousands from every backwoods holler and Podunk across the country."

And just like he ain't said single a word, Jitters asks again, "What song would you like my sister to sing first for you, Mr. Flowers?"

I look out the window, waves of hurt breaking over me one at a time. I bite my lip hard so he won't see it quiver. I will not cry, by God, I will not cry in front of this big shot who thinks he knows everything. I look around his office at records and more pictures hanging on the wall. I see Dolly Parton, the Skillet Lickers, Reno & Smiley. I could name them all. "You represent all these folks, Mr. Flowers?" I ask him.

"That's confidential. Now I have to get to work."

Jitters nods at my guitar case. I get it out, but in my

mind's eye, I see Daddy sitting on the porch, picking the banjo, trying to remember the chords. I see Caroline, Gentle, and Cyrus running around Uncle Hazard's pinecone palace in the smoky mist, trying to catch fairies and Cherokee Little People or pretending to be Greek gods.

Jitters asks for a third time, "Mr. Flowers, what song would you like first?"

"Look here, what's working for us are love songs, cheating songs. Got any?"

"Love songs?" My voice squeaks. "Cheating songs?"

"I didn't think so, but come on back when you do and not a minute before."

Jitters turns to me and says, "I reckon you'd better just play something."

I strum my newest song, "Stack Cakes and Christmas." I tell him, "Mr. Flowers, I wrote this for my brothers and sisters." My voice quivers, but I start singing louder, and it comes back to me strong, steady, and sweet.

"Stack Cakes and Christmas"

Snowflakes and stack cakes, a Maggie Valley Christmas
Wool socks and fairy rocks, a sweet mountain Christmas
May the holler fill with snow— let the December winds blow
And bring us . . .
Snowflakes and stack cakes, a Maggie Valley Christmas
Wool socks and fairy rocks, a sweet mountain Christmas

Leave a tangerine in each stocking
When Santa Claus comes a-knocking
And bring us . . .
Snowflakes and stack cakes, a Maggie Valley Christmas
Wool socks and fairy rocks, a sweet mountain
Christmas . . .
in our North Carolina home!

My guitar feels so right in my hands. I know what to make it do. This instrument is part of me, no matter what he thinks. He sits at his desk watching and listening, tapping his busy-man fingers on his desk. Then before he can tell us to beat it again, Jitters says, "Sing the rest, Livy Two." So I launch into all the songs I can think of: "Mama's Biscuits," "Daddy's Roasted Peanuts," "Grandma's Glass Eye," "Strike It Rich," "Colors," "Buttermilk Moon." He listens, but I can't tell a thing from the stone expression on his face. Finally, when I'm done, I say, "More? I got more."

Mr. George Flowers tries to find his words. "Little girl, you sing all right. You really do. I'm impressed. Okay. So what I'm about to say is nothing personal, you understand? I ain't a babysitter. I don't represent kids. In fact, I don't much like kids."

"What about my daddy's song 'Mountain Mint'? Can't I just sell you some of his songs? Does Loretta need songs? Does Dottie West? Bashful Brother Oswald?"

"You done your homework."

"Yes sir. I study songwriters and songwriting. I even looked up the writer of 'Mountain Dew,' since near everybody sings that song. His name was Bascom Lamar Lunsford. The songcatcher. He went up to the hollers to record folks singing the old songs. Wish I could write me a song like 'Mountain Dew,' only better."

"Better keep practicing then."

"Yes sir, she intends to," Jitters says. "As her manager, I'll make sure of it."

"You know, Mr. Lunsford sold 'Mountain Dew' for a twenty-five-dollar bus ticket to get home? He had to get home to his family, so he wrote it real quick and sold it to buy the bus ticket home. And then it became a huge hit. Can you believe that?"

"Yes, I can believe it. Now—"

The secretary sticks her head in the door. "New recording session this afternoon."

For a split second, I think he will invite us to tag along. But he says, "Thank you for taking the time to come see me. Good meeting you little old gals from Maggie Valley, North Carolina. Have a nice trip home. Now, if you two will excuse me."

He walks out of the office, and I look back at the package on his desk one more time. Jitters sees it, too, and recognizes my handwriting. She whispers, "Mama could sell that scarf for ten dollars at least at the Christmas Fair. And you know it."

I hesitate for maybe two seconds before I swipe it. Jitters is right. He don't deserve the scarf that I stole in the first place. I shove it into my guitar case next to Mama's diary, and set my guitar on top of it real careful. We walk out of his office back to where Mildred is still typing like gangbusters. We stand there a moment, but they don't even look up, like we're long forgotten. Then Mildred says, "There will be more chances, Miss Weems. Just not today. Now, it may be a holiday over there in North Carolina, but we folks in Nashville got work to do."

CHAPTER ELEVEN

Don't Kick the Devil Dog

THE WHOLE WORLD feels like one huge betrayal as we step back into savage wind on Sixteenth Avenue. What just happened? One minute we were talking and I was singing, and the next we're back out here again? All that for this? I try to not to feel sick. I hoist my guitar and schoolbag on my back and look down the street. What are we supposed to do? Should I ask somebody where the Trailways is, so me and Jitters can get on home? Should I go hunting another music man? Why didn't I have two or three lined up, just in case? Why'd I put all my apples in the devil-dog man's cart? That's what he is to me—the devil-dog man. A car rides by, the Beatles singing "A Hard Day's Night" on the radio.

Jitters whispers, "Now can we call home?"

"All right." My feet already feel like blocks of ice back out in the cold. "Come on, Jitters. Let's find a telephone. Hope I got enough nickels. I ain't about to call collect.

Rub salt in the wound." But when I think of hearing their voices, I am ashamed. I was supposed to be a success today, with good news. Now I'm just another kid who caused her parents grief for nothing. I glance back at George Flowers's fiddle-shaped mailbox, and I don't know what comes over me. I lean over and pick up some snow and start packing together a hard snowball. When I'm done, I throw it. *Bam!* Jitters picks up some snow and packs it real good too. *Smack!* I pack another. *Pow! Little lady, little lady!*

Jitters yells at the house, "All I got to say is, you'uns missed out. So don't come crying when my sister gets on the Grand Ole Opry without a sniff of help from the likes of you. And talk about *bad luck.* Boy, y'all just inherited a lifetime of bad luck. Being mean to kids? That'll earn you the *very worst luck of all!*"

Pretty soon, we're making snowball after snowball, aiming them everywhere. At the mailbox, the porch swing, the door, the window! *Bam, smack, splat!* Take that. *Bam, smack, splat.* I never felt so good in my life. Take that, and that, and that!

Suddenly, the devil-dog man himself opens the door to see what is happening, and Jitters beams him with a snowball in the face. He starts hollering, giving chase, and we bust out laughing, running like hellfire down Sixteenth Avenue. Try and catch us! We run with our schoolbags and my guitar case banging and bouncing hard between us, but who cares? Finally, we come to a stop near a filling station, gasping for breath. We can't stop laughing, thinking of all those flying snowballs. I look at Jitters, and then, without warning, I bust out crying like some dumb girl who got her feelings hurt.

Jitters says, "Oh, don't cry, Livy Two."

"I'm not—I wouldn't cry over that devil-dog man. Wind just hurts my eyes. I wouldn't shed a tear over that man back there. Remember how Daddy used to tell us that story? About how you had to watch out for the devil dog on a dark night, and never kick it if it came up close to you growling, because if you did kick the devil dog, it would split in two, and both sides would run up the street in opposite directions."

Jitters shivers. "I never liked that story so much."

"Well, as far as I'm concerned, Mr. George Flowers is the devil-dog man made of two parts: a nice man in letters, but not in person." I try to hold back more stupid tears.

Jitters squints at me through her cat's-eye glasses. "Livy Two? After we call home, can we eat? I'm starving and freezing. I can't believe how cold it is in Tennessee."

"Wait a second, Jitters." I reach in my guitar case and open the package to Mr. George Flowers. I take out Mama's beautiful purple-and-gray scarf, and I wrap it around Jitters's neck. "This will keep you warm." As we retrace our steps and head back to the Ernest Tubb Record Shop, the only landmark I know how to get to by city bus, a new song plays in my mind, and I can hear the words plain as day.

Don't kick the devil dog
'less you want to see it split in two
Come a-growling at you on a coal-black night
But don't stop for nothing till you're clean out of sight . . .
Here comes the devil dog
Watch out for the devil dog
Come a-growling at you on a coal-black night
But don't stop for nothing till you're clean out of sight . . .
Don't kick the devil dog
Watch out! Whoops! Too late . . .
He's done gone split in two . . .

We take the bus back to lower Broadway and find a pay phone near the flashing sign of the Ernest Tubb Record Shop. My fingers are so cold I can't keep hold of the coins. I miss the slot and drop a few onto the ground, and they go rolling, but I grab them up. Lots of folks crowd inside the record shop. Dottie West's song "Let Me Off at the Corner" starts playing right after a Loretta song finishes. What's it like to walk in a record shop and buy armfuls of records? Across the street people are already crowding inside Tootsies Orchid Lounge, and it's only just after lunchtime.

Jitters says, "Well, what are you waiting on? Dial already!"

"I'm doing it. Hold your horses." I slide my nickels into the slot. *Clink. Clink.* I smell stinky aftershave on the receiver, which makes feel so sad for no reason at all. The operator says I have three minutes for ten nickels. On the fourth or fifth ring, Grandma Horace picks it up and says, "Hello, who's calling?" Her voice sounds old and far away.

"Grandma Horace?" I say. "It's me. Livy Two."

I hear a wheeze of breath. "Livy Two, honey, is that really you?" Grandma Horace sounds like she's crying, and she *never ever* cries, or calls me "Livy Two." "Answer me, child? You got us worried sick—have you got Myrtle Anne with you?"

"Yes, she followed me. She's all right. She's fine. Didn't you get my letter?"

"What letter, honey? Where in the world are you?"

Becksie gets on the phone. "Is it you? Were y'all kidnapped by gangsters?"

What letter? Why didn't Louise give it to them? But the next thing I hear is, "Give me that phone!" There's a scuffle, and Uncle Buddy gets on the line. "Well, if it ain't the little prodigals. You got your folks and Grandma and your brothers and sisters worried to death, bless their hearts. Even the dog's been crying, and your daddy won't leave the window, watching for you'uns. It's pitiful. Say, where you'uns are, now!"

"Put Mama on, please?" I feel sick. *How could they not have got my letter?*

"Be prepared for a box and five nails when I get my hands on you'uns!" Uncle Buddy yells into the phone. "Be prepared. Your day of reckoning has come."

My stomach turns over at the thought of him spanking us hard enough to leave a red palm print with five crimson fingers on our legs.

"Answer! Where are you anyhow?" he snarls again.

"Nashville," I say in a small voice.

"Asheville?"

Jitters grabs the receiver. "*Nashville*, Music City USA."

Uncle Buddy shouts, "*Nashville?* Forget it, Zilpah. I ain't driving the Ghost Town truck all the way to Nashville. Yes, Nashville! Two rotten kids got themselves to Nashville. They ought to be hog-tied and horsewhipped!"

Grandma Horace gets back on the line. "Give me that phone, Buddy! Livy Two? You scared your brother Emmett so bad he took off in my Rambler to Knoxville to look for you. He's not back, and we have no way of reaching him. That Evie Pepper called when she heard you were missing and said that she saw you at the Trailways, and you told her that you were going to Knoxville to get your daddy's banjo at the *Cas Walker Show.* Lies upon lies. Explain yourself, child!"

But then Mama grabs the phone, "Livy Two, Nashville? Are you safe? Hurt?"

"Mama, we're fine. I left a letter under Louise's pillow explaining the whole thing, but then Jitters followed me even though I tried to make her go home."

"Let me explain!" Jitters tries to grab the telephone, but I push her off.

"There was *no letter*!" Mama cries. "We thought— Miss Attickson is beside herself with worry. The last thing you said was you were going to help her organize books. How could you run off without a word and take poor Jitters with you?"

"I didn't! I wrote it *all down*. But then Jitters followed me, and there was no time to turn around. Mama, I'm sorry. I wanted to make it a special Christmas. Louise was supposed to give the letter to you."

Louise gets on the line. "I only found it now—it fell back behind the bed. Why didn't you just tell me, so I could know? How's a person supposed to know?"

"I'm sorry, Louise. I thought you'd see it first thing when you woke up."

"It's been awful here. Awful. What were you thinking? Wait, Daddy wants—"

Then there is a scuffle and I hear breathing, and finally, "Livy Two? This is your daddy. Talk to me, right now. Where are you and your sister? I been looking and looking for you. Where in tarnation are you? Been wracking my brains. My head hurts, and my heart hurts. Where are you?"

"I'm fine, Daddy. We're fine. I just had to come see Mr. George Flowers."

"Who is that?"

"Mr. George Flowers. He's the music man that you wrote to a long time back before your accident, and Mr. Flowers liked our songs, so I went to audition for him, but it didn't go like I thought. It was bad. He don't represent kids. Jitters came with me."

"What kind of crazy idea put it in your head to go to Nashville? What kind of crazy idea? Tell me. Tell me now."

I hesitate for a second. . . . "Because you can't, Daddy. So I had to. I thought I could sell a song and we wouldn't have to move to Grandma Horace's place in Enka. I wanted to buy our place from Madame Cherry Hat so she'd quit sending mean letters. I was only trying to be a professional musician like you were at my age. You left home at fourteen, Daddy, and I'm almost thirteen. I mean—"

"Please, come home." It sounds like Daddy is crying. "I been thinking and looking, and I can't find you or the other little one. My head and heart hurt." His words are so plain now—Daddy says whatever he's feeling, it just pops out.

"We're coming," I tell him. Then there is silence, and the phone makes a clicking sound and the operator says to add another nickel. "Daddy, we'll take the Trailways bus back to Maggie Valley." The phone makes more clicking sounds. "I don't got any nickels left. I'm sorry I worried you for nothing. I'll explain the rest when I get home."

Mama gets back on the line. "Livy Two and Jitters, you get on the bus. We'll be waiting for you'uns. Every one of us—you hear? You got the rest of your life to be a big-shot singer in Nashville. Daddy needs you. I need you. Everybody does. We were so scared. Can Jitters hear me too?"

Jitters says, "Yes, Mama. I hear you."

But the line clicks dead. I stare at the receiver as if all the voices from North Carolina are still clamoring inside the wires. But Daddy was listening to me. I could hear it in his voice. It was a real conversation, the first one in such a long time.

Jitters says, "Well, we're gonna catch it good."

"Yeah, I reckon we will."

"But you'll get it worse, though—since the whole thing was your idea."

I can't believe what I'm hearing, so I grab her by the collar. "You listen to me, you little brat. It was both our ideas, got it? Who followed who, remember? Nobody asked you to come. I begged you to go home. You're in it just as much as me now, like it or not." I step inside the Ernest Tubb Record Shop to get warmed up. Jitters follows along after me, stomping her feet to get them warm.

"Wait, Livy Two. I didn't mean—I ain't sorry I come. No matter what, I ain't sorry." Then she notices all the bins of records stretching all the way to the back near the stage. "*Wow!* Look at this place," Jitters whispers. "This is great!"

Folks thumb through stacks of shiny records, studying album covers. Posters and headshots of country singers and concert announcements cover the walls. The voice of Mr. Tubb sings "Walking the Floor Over You" on the jukebox. I wonder how many musicians have sung here. Loretta Lynn did, in a special tribute to Patsy Cline back when Patsy was in a car accident. Plenty of other folks have got their start there. Somehow, it's the smell of home, these vinyl records in their fancy jackets. I remember Mama and Daddy dancing in the living room when the Grand Ole Opry came on the radio, and all the Martha White Flour commercials cutting in between sets.

I lean against the brick wall to watch Christmas shoppers, and then Patsy Cline starts singing "I Fall to Pieces." And her voice is so clear and beautiful, it's like she didn't die in the plane wreck but is alive and singing in Nashville. It's pure relief and comfort running through my blood. What if I could one day give that to people myself? That's why I got to be a singer and a songwriter, no matter what the devil-dog man said.

Jitters comes up to me. "Don't forget that I'm still hungry, and I want to go see the ducks at the Parthenon to tell them it will be all right. I asked the cashier and that froze-up lake is only one mile away. The city bus stops right out front."

"Jitters, you heard Mama and Daddy. We scared them real bad. We'll eat but then we have to get on home. We don't got time to fool with ducks."

"Look here, I'm going to see the ducks with or without you. I bet they're just setting there by this big old frozen lake not sure what to do. If you were a duck and a lake froze over, you'd be scared, so I'm going to see the ducks."

"What do you care about some old ducks for? They'll figure it out."

"I went to your audition and was your strength and support. Don't deny it. You can come with me to say howdy to the ducks over by that Greek place."

"We are going home, Myrtle Anne Weems. We're in enough trouble as it is!"

"Who said we weren't going home? Of course we're going home. We're just going to see the ducks first."

CHAPTER TWELVE

Moses from Memphis

ON OUR WAY to the Parthenon with its froze-up lake, we spy a restaurant called Moses from Memphis. A sign in the window says: TRY OUR DRY-RUB BARBECUE! NO REGRETS. $1.79!

I'm so hungry I can't see straight. "We'll eat first, and then see the ducks."

Jitters sniffs the air outside the café. "All right. Barbecue, ducks, home."

The sweet smells of barbecue sauce, brown sugar, hush puppies, cornbread, and baked beans overtake us the second we step into Moses from Memphis. It's the aroma of covered-dish suppers at the Methodist church in Maggie with folks and kids talking and laughing, only better. The place is mostly empty because it's already the middle of the afternoon, and the man who is boss of the place wears a name tag that says MOSES. His skin is the color of coffee, and his teeth are white and strong. I hardly ever seen a black man before—not in Maggie Valley, anyhow.

Jitters says, "Earth to Livy Two!" She snaps her fingers in front of my face. "He's asked our order three times now."

"Sorry. We want two specials of barbecue beef sandwiches and a plate of onion rings to share." I count our money just to make sure we'll be all right. It dawns on me that we shouldn't even eat since I can't pay back the ten dollars to the Everything Box like I thought. I'll have to work extra shifts at the bookmobile to pay Mama back. We have just under eight dollars left, and this is the biggest splurge of all, eating at a café like city folks. Are we supposed to leave him a tip? I remember Mama left a fifty-cent tip at the Pancake House when Daddy wandered off last summer and ordered mountain blackberry pancakes, so I want to be like her—not cheap. I'll leave fifty cents too. Jitters waves her hand in the air like she's in school and asks, "Could I have an orange soda pop, please?"

"Coming right up," Moses from Memphis says. "And how about you?"

"Water." I look at Jitters. "Put your hand down. You're not in school."

Jitters puts her hand in her lap. In the background, Red Rector plays "Tennessee Blues" on the mandolin. We sit on stools and watch the snowflakes drifting outside the window like some winter painting. I can't think of a quieter, sweeter thing than softly falling snow. On the wall is a picture of President John F. Kennedy and Dr. Martin Luther King, and it makes me sad to see it, only because I know the Kennedy kids will be missing their daddy something awful this first Christmas after he was killed in Dallas.

Jitters says, "Read me more of Mama's diary? I think I'm homesick."

I get the diary out of my guitar case and find the next entry. I look at Jitters. "Now listen to me. You can't tell Mama about this diary. You're the worst tattletale of all, Jitters, and I don't say that to be mean—it's the truth. So you can't tell."

"I won't. I promise. This trip has changed me. I mean it."

And so I read the next entry to Jitters while we wait for Moses from Memphis to bring our barbecue plate specials.

February 10, 1943
Dear Grasshopper,

These birds are vultures . . . they are bad news. I don't like them at all. . . . I've seen them circle a dead cow in a creek over in Madison County once when Papa took us out for a long Sunday drive. They're big old mean-looking birds. They have bald heads, big wings, and talons like thorns. Vul-

tures make me afraid of things I can't see or explain.

We took a trip to Georgia to see Papa's people last weekend, and while we were there we attended a shape-note singing day. I never heard such music before and I love it. You got to sing it loud and strong. Mother thinks shape-note singing is too old-fashioned, and strictly for the primitive Baptist churches, but me and Papa love the "sacred harp"—even if we are Methodists. Some of Daddy's people are Baptists, and shape-note singers, which is how we got invited. The shape notes on the scale are FA SO LA MI . . . just four notes . . . but I could sing those old songs all day. I left the church feeling like I was floating in the air, especially afterward when we ate fried chicken, coleslaw, and sweet potato pie. There are no instruments with shape-note singing—just the voice—the human voice is the "sacred harp." How can music do that to a body? It's funny to think I have a "sacred harp" inside me.

Yours truly, Jessie Horace

P.S. Papa let us stop in Cherokee on the way home from Georgia, and I spent my allowance on a dreamcatcher to hang above my bed. Mother said I'd do better to send my allowance to help the war effort, but I prefer a dreamcatcher. I help out the scrap iron collection at school. I've been collecting metal—bottle caps and flattened cans. I collect newspapers too.

Just as I finish reading the diary entry to Jitters, Moses from Memphis puts the plates of dry-rub barbecue sandwich in front of us, but it looks so perfect that I hate to touch it. I put the diary back in my guitar case and click it shut.

"Thank you," I tell him, but I don't eat. Not yet.

Jitters says, "What are you waiting on, Livy Two?" She starts wolfing her sandwich down like some starving mountain child. "I love Mama's stories, don't you?" She talks with her mouth full.

"Jitters, mind your manners! Close your mouth!" I snap at her.

"Sorry!" She takes another bite and drinks a big gulp of her orange soda pop.

"Sandwiches are hot off the barbecue. Where y'all kids from?" Moses from Memphis smiles as he wipes up the counter.

"Maggie Valley, North Carolina." Jitters smiles back at him before chomping into an onion ring drizzled in ketchup. "We're going to go see the ducks up yonder, because we heard your lake got froze up. I'm worried about them. My sister ain't worried, though. She thinks they'll be just fine." She jabs a thumb in my direction.

"That's right," he says. "I saw the picture in the *Nashville Banner* myself of Centennial Lake. Well, welcome to town. Now eat up. Before it gets cold."

Jitters asks, "Are you Moses from Memphis, like the sign?"

"The one and only."

I smile at him, but I'm all talked out. He goes off to take another order, and I tell Jitters, "You don't have to broadcast our business."

"Why not?" Jitter polishes off her drink. "I'm getting used to it. This orange sody pop is some kind of good! Whoops. Look, an eyelash." She takes an eyelash off her cheek, puts it on the back of her hand, and throws it over her shoulder." She inspects her hand. "Goody. Gone. That means my wish will come true. But I can't tell you what it is. . . . Surest way to kill a wish is to blab about it."

"Did I ask you? I didn't even ask about your wish, Jitters."

"I'm just saying."

Moses from Memphis refills a ketchup bottle, listening to our conversation. Finally, he asks, "What brings y'all to Nashville at Christmastime? Got kin here?"

Jitters points at me. "Audition. She didn't get it. She's pretty mad and sad, which is why she's so dang grouchy. Usually she'd talk your ear off. She's the biggest talker in our whole family. Shoot, usually you can't get a word in, but—"

"I am fine, Jitters." But I want to smack her. I feel like a boring lump just sitting there, tongue-tied and dull as mud. The devil dog's words echo in my head: *Nothing personal, little lady . . .*

Moses from Memphis says, "Oh, anybody can see plain as day that you're fine."

"Well, I am fine. That's all there is to it," I insist, taking a bite of my sandwich.

He glances toward my guitar case like he's heard that whole story before. "Let me tell you that you're not the first musician to come in with a guitar wearing that face. Nashville's a hard town. No getting around it. But don't you know you've done the hardest thing of all? You got yourself here and you tried. Lot of folks never make it that far. You understand what I'm saying? Because—"

"I do!" Jitters interrupts. "I been trying to tell her the very same thing myself."

"Be quiet, Jitters, for once in your life," I hiss.

Moses says, "All I'm saying is plenty of grown-up folks sit around on their front porches or on their lunch shifts talking about coming to Nashville. Boo-hooing about lots of things . . . 'If I had enough money . . .' or 'I could sing as good as Elvis or Muddy himself if only somebody would listen.' But they won't get off the front porch or leave their jobs even for a minute to make somebody listen. You did."

"Didn't do no good, though."

"How are you supposed to know that yet? How in

the world are you supposed to know such a thing yet?" Moses erases the chalkboard of specials.

"Mr. George Flowers said no, didn't he? I come all this way and he said no."

"And one no is all it takes to make you quit?" Moses looks disgusted. "That's sad. That's a downright shame. How many times you think I heard no in my life?"

I shrug. "I don't know. I don't even know you."

"That's right, we don't know you," Jitters repeats.

"Well, let me tell y'all, I heard no my whole life. 'Boy, you won't amount to a hill of beans.' 'Boy, you think you can open up an eating establishment in Nashville? Who do you think you are?' But did I quit? You think I'd give those turkeys the satisfaction?"

"No sir. I guess not." I like this Moses, and Jitters is right—usually, I would talk up a storm to him, but like Daddy, my head and heart hurt. I feel like quitting. I want to go home to my porch and set there and look at Setzer Mountain and never leave again.

"I'll tell you two something else," Moses from Memphis says, but he's looking at me. "Today, you're feeling blue, so you sit there as long as it takes, but I want you to eat every bite, all right? I make the best dry-rub barbecue in the state of Tennessee, and I promise you, you're going to feel better. Sometimes all you need is some food and some sleep to give you some fresh perspective on the world. Okay? How old are you anyway?"

"She's almost thirteen," Jitters answers for me. "I'm ten and a half."

He whistles. "Ten and near thirteen. That's some kind of young. That's plenty of time. How about y'all write a song together and call it 'Moses from Memphis'?"

Jitters says, "Sure, we can do that. We'll mail it to you. We could be pen pals."

Moses says, "That sounds all right to me."

I look at my barbecue sandwich, which comes with relish and pickles and potato salad too. Suddenly, I am so hungry I eat every bite. I've never tasted nothing as good as dry-rub barbecue. I could eat it every day for the rest of my life. When I finish the last bite, Moses puts two slices of hot apple pie by our plates. "I don't think we have enough money for dessert," I tell him, "but thank you."

"Apple pie is on the house for musicians. Don't forget to write that song now."

"We won't," Jitters assures him. "Not on your life."

After we swallow the last bite of pie that fills us with hope and hot apples and plain goodness, I leave a fifty-cent tip on the counter. Sure hope it's enough.

We say good-bye to Moses from Memphis and walk across the lawn of Centennial Park to go check on the ducks. The lake is froze up just like the newspaper said, and it's true, the ducks don't exactly know what to do with themselves. They quack and waddle up and down and across the frozen pond, trying to figure out what's different. Jitters takes out several rolls of bread crammed in her pocket. "I took this from the café. For the ducks." She breaks up little pieces and starts to feed them, and they all come squawking toward her. "It's okay, ducks. Don't be scared. Spring will come, and the ice will melt, and you'uns can go swimming again. I just come to tell you that. You listening, ducks?"

I gaze at the wintry sky and the gray-brown Parthenon beneath it. In between each column is the shape of an urn, just like Daddy showed us in the pictures. He said it was an optical illusion. There's a stone sculpture at the tiptop of the Parthenon stretching across the whole building. It's got horses, kids with water jugs, musicians, and other folks, having a big time up there. I remember Miss Atickson called it an "Athenian frieze." On the giant bronze doors to the Parthenon, the doorknobs are growling lion heads—almost looks like it could bite your hand off when you open the door. Jitters chases after the ducks, talking to them, tossing them more bits of bread crumbs.

The Parthenon stands proud and ancient in Music City USA in the late afternoon sky of lavender. It's already getting dark. I wish I could see a statue of Athena—but instead I almost see something else. One by one, I imagine all the heroes in my life rising up before me like ghosts on the steps of the Parthenon. Patsy Cline, Helen Keller, Miss Attickson, Mama, Daddy . . . even Moses from Memphis, who fed us and tried to make me feel better. They're dressed like Greek gods, smiling and talking. I bet Patsy Cline didn't think she was a hero, but I do.

Jitters says, "Well, I reckon the ducks are happy now. They ate up all the bread anyway. How soon will it take for the lake to melt, so they can go swimming again?"

"Month or two, maybe?"

"Oh. You still sorry I followed you?" She pushes her glasses up her nose and blinks her eyes at me like a scrawny owl, waiting for an answer.

"I reckon not. Not anymore, Jitters."

"I feel different on the road than I do at home. And don't call me that. Jitters—what kind of name is that? I'm Myrtle Anne. I want to go by my real and true name."

"All right, Myrtle Anne."

"That's better." She skips ahead. "Let's go home, but be careful not to step on a crack or you'll break your mother's back." She jumps over cracks I can't even see on the snowy sidewalk as we head back to catch a city bus that will deliver us to the Trailways.

We wind up taking the same bus back toward the Ernest Tubb Record Shop. Then we get on a different bus to the Trailways bus depot, which lets us off about a block away. I'm so relieved to be going home, and Jitters, her teeth chattering, can't wait either. From the corner, I can already see a bus that says ASHEVILLE lit up like a beacon that whispers HOME. The bus driver is loading suitcases on it. That's our bus, by God, but just as we're about to cross the street into the Trailways, who should come barreling up to us from nowhere, but Laika, the gold-yellow dog. Shivering, she dives behind us, whimpering for dear life. I look around for that thieving panhandler.

Jitters yells, "Laika! What are you doing here? Look, Livy Two!"

Out of the darkness behind us, I hear a faint but familiar whistling. Then a hoarse voice shouts, "You get back here, crazy dog!" The old man, Fletcher Partridge, is chasing after the dog, his tin cup and dark glasses gone. He can run pretty fast for a faker blind man. Then he sees us plain as day and hollers, "Hey there, that's my dog! Not you two again! I'll have you runaways sent to kid prison where they lock you up and throw away the key. Now give me back my dog. No fooling. Now. Or there will be trouble."

Sometimes, there's only a split second to make a decision before the chance is gone. I nod for Jitters to grab Laika's leash, and we take off running across the street and through the Trailways parking lot toward the entrance, but near the door I slip on some ice, cracking my knees hard. Pain shoots through my legs, and I drop my guitar case, which goes skittering across the sidewalk. I jump to my feet to get it, but the old man grabs it up first and holds it above his head. "Well. Looks like we got a trade to make, kid. Dog or guitar? Give her back now."

"No!" I shout.

"Looks like I'm keeping this here guitar then. Always did fancy myself a musician. Guess I'll find out, or you could just go on and be a nice girl and hand over my moneymaking dog, and we'll call it even."

I glance at Jitters's pinched face as she clings tighter to Laika's leash. Daddy ordered my guitar from the Sears & Roebuck catalog for me, and if I lose it, who knows when I'll ever get another? But another far more horrible thought occurs to me. Mama's diary is in my guitar case.

"Listen, Mr. Patridge, you can take my guitar. Go on, take it. But I got to get something out of the case first."

"And what would that be?"

I take a deep breath. I'm gonna have to fool him. If he knows how bad I want that diary, he'll never turn it over. So I say, "I got a present in there for Mama and money. I'll leave you the money and the guitar, but I just need the present. It's an old book tied with a sash. The money is in the lining of the guitar case. I brought extra.

A lot extra. You can have every penny, but I just need that book."

He debates for a moment. "I get the guitar and money?"

"That's right."

"And no funny business."

"No sir."

"I was getting sick of that dog anyway, always needing to eat." He pops open the guitar case to where Mama's diary sits up on top. "What? This old thing?" He lifts it up and inspects it.

"Yeah, that old thing." I hate his dirty fingers on Mama's diary.

He inspects my guitar. "Hold up. This here is a kid guitar. No thanks. Why don't y'all just give me back my dog? Probably lying about the money anyhow."

Without any warning, Jitters starts screaming her head off, and I got no choice now but to join in, pointing at the old faker blind man. "Thief! Thief!"

The Trailways bus driver and some travelers look up to check out the commotion. "He's trying to steal my guitar," I shout, and Jitters yells, "And our dog too!"

Somebody yells, "Hey, I seen you before. I gave you money earlier today. I thought you were a blind man. You bothering these girls?" The small crowd of folks gathers, making angry noises. Fletcher Partridge fumbles with the latch on the guitar case and takes off running. Only before he gets very far, Mama's diary falls out into the ice and snow, pages scattering into the wind. Me and Jitters pick up the flying pages, but the old faker blind man has escaped into the darkness with my guitar.

And our address is pasted inside the guitar case. What if he comes to Maggie Valley hunting his dog and revenge?

CHAPTER THIRTEEN

"My Name Is Myrtle Anne"

AFTER ALL THE excitement dies down and Mama's diary is all put back together in one piece, Laika nudges her head under Jitters's hand to be petted, and Jitters pets her like she's rubbing that golden head for good luck. She slips her acorn necklace on Laika's collar, and we head over to the bus driver to convince him to allow the dog to go with us on the Trailways. The bus driver scratches his head, debating, and Jitters squeezes my hand tight while we wait for the verdict. Jitters says, "Please don't say no, mister, to our Smoky Mountain rescue dog. My sister's guitar was just stolen, and she's like to bust out crying for days. Please don't say no."

Whether it's the good-luck acorn necklace around Laika's collar, or he believes our story of Laika being a rescue dog, or it's just plain Christmas spirit, he agrees to let her on board. Thank goodness the bus is near empty, with nobody wanting to travel on such a cold night. Laika settles down on the floor between us for the ride, and

Jitters whispers, "I told you I had a lot of good luck stored up. Lucky for us and for Laika."

"Yeah? Why didn't you get George Flowers to say yes to me then?"

"It don't work that way."

"What way does it work? Explain it. And what about my guitar? Where was all your stored-up good luck then?"

"Look, I already told you—"

"Never mind!" There's no reasoning with Jitters, and I try not to cry as the bus pulls out of Nashville. I can't believe I don't got my guitar. I'm relieved to have Mama's diary, but it's like somebody cut off my hand or arm. That's silly, I know, but not only am I a failure, I have to go home to Maggie without my guitar.

Jitters is already nodding off to sleep with Laika. I notice she's sharing Mama's pretty scarf with the dog. Laika rests her head on my knee, and I scratch her ears, and then I must fall asleep myself. Sleeping helps the hours pass quickly as the bus heads east, and for some reason, it don't take near as long going back across Tennessee as it did coming. The bus stops just as many places, and I walk Laika around Trailways parking lots while Jitters sleeps on the bus.

Somewhere near Smithville, Laika climbs into our laps, and she's like a big, golden quilt of a dog. I don't even try to imagine Mama's face when she meets her, but at least Uncle Hazard will be happy to have a friend to share his pinecone palace. I could remind Mama of her cat, Miss Amelia, but I don't want her to know that I been reading her diary. I want her to find out in the right way—if there is such a possibility. Jitters wakes up and says, "Read to me. Read me another story from Mama," so I find another diary entry and read real soft to Jitters and Laika.

March 1, 1943
Dear Grasshopper,

I have a secret to tell you. Sometimes I put on my nice-girl face for the world—the one that is quiet, sensible, and hidden. I keep my true feelings locked inside, and no one has found the key. Mother says girls who wear their hearts on their sleeves grow up to become silly women. I don't want to be silly, but I don't want to be careful and quiet either—like Mother insists that I be. Maybe I'm waiting for the day when I can fly too.

Yours truly, Jessie Horace

I go to read another page, but Jitters has already fallen back asleep. I guess this whole trip has really wore her out. As the dark night flies by, I jot down the beginning of a song I promised to write, but my heart aches not to have my guitar to try it out on to see if it's any good or not.

Stepping inside a sweet warm place
On an icy Nashville day
Breathing in all the good fine smells
That seemed to come our way
Hush puppies, dry-rub barbecue, coleslaw too . . .
Moses from Memphis said, "Eat up, it's good for you."

Thank you, Moses
Thank you, Moses
Thank you, Moses from Memphis now!
Thank you, Moses
Thank you, Moses
Thank you, Moses from Memphis now!

The following afternoon, the Trailways bus grinds to a halt in front of the Maggie Store. It takes me a few moments to realize we're actually home. I yawn and sit up to look out the window, and it's true. We're back in the Smoky Mountains, surrounding us on all sides, welcoming us home. Buck, Setzer, Dirty Britches.

Daddy holds Appelonia, and Mama stands next to Grandma Horace, who's got Baby Tom-Bill on her hip. Daddy wipes his eyes, but Mama holds it inside, and for the first time, I see the little girl in her who used to hide her feelings so well. She's not about to fall apart in public for the folks of Maggie Valley to bear witness. Grandma Horace tries to look stern, but I can see for myself the pure relief etched on her face. Pearl, the iguana, is nestled inside Uncle Buddy's shirt, and he stands apart, grim and snarly. If Uncle Buddy were an animal, I reckon he'd be a warthog, always grunting for the next fight. He has brought his Ghost Town truck, and Grandma Horace has her Rambler, which means Emmett must be back from Knoxville, but I don't see him anywhere. Becksie stares at us like we're strangers, her eyes red-rimmed with tears.

Jitters jumps up and down like a jackrabbit, singing, "We're home, Laika! We're home! Wait until you meet everybody!" And I try to feel like she does, but the fact is, I almost feel like a foreigner or something, and I've never felt that way before with my own family. It's as if I left Maggie Valley a little girl and came back home grown up. Even Mama and Daddy look older to me, like the worry of the last few days aged them all at once.

I wave out the bus window, but they just stand there like they can't hardly believe it's us. Louise smiles, holding on to the twins' and Gentle's hands. The twins wrench free and race toward the Trailways, dragging Gentle with them. Cyrus is dressed up like Poseidon again, and Gentle and Caroline have got their fairy wings back on.

The bus driver calls, "Maggie Valley. Next stop, Waynesville." He turns to us. "Good luck with your dog, girls. I'm sure the Smoky Mountains folks will appreciate such a fine rescue dog in their midst to find the lost children."

"Thank you," Jitters says, "and Merry Christmas!"

"Yes, thank you," I tell him. "Merry Christmas."

We get our schoolbags, and I can't help but reach automatically for my guitar case. Jitters whistles for Laika to come on. My head is still crowded with dreams of Nashville, and in a matter of seconds, I'll have to pass through the gauntlet of family and accusation and by-God-how-could-you? We get off the bus together, blinking in the sunny winter day. Uncle Hazard howls at Laika, wagging his tail on the flatbed. The twins and Gentle rush into our arms, hugging like they won't never let go.

Then Cyrus holds up a wooden trident. "Emmett carved it for me while you was gone, so I could truly be like Poseidon."

Carolina hops around on one foot. "Emmett ain't here, but he whittled and carved to keep from going crazy like Mama, Daddy, Grandma Horace, and Uncle Buddy were."

Gentle whispers in my ear, "You came back. Will you read me more of Mama's story tonight? I didn't say a word. I kept my promise."

I kneel down and hug her close to me. I whisper back, "Course I will. There are lots of pages left to read." I stand up. "And we got something else to show you'uns. We brought home a new friend. This is Laika—everybody, meet Laika."

"Named after the first dog in outer space," Jitters says with pride and joy. "We rescued her from a mean old man who swiped Livy Two's guitar. Wait until you hear the whole story how she fought him with her bare hands just like Athena, Goddess of War."

"Quit it, Jitters." I feel my face turning red. "I hardly got a chance to do—"

But Daddy interrupts, "You left your guitar in the land of Nashville?"

Tears flood my eyes, and I can't speak, but I give them a quick nod.

Cyrus asks, "Are you going to leave us again? Is that dog from outer space? Which planet? Why did you leave again? How many minutes were you gone?" Cyrus asks so many questions, a person could lose her mind trying to answer each one.

Caroline and Gentle fall upon Laika, patting on her. "Howdy, Laika. Howdy." Uncle Hazard leaps off the truck to greet her, too, wiggling with joy at this great golden dog. Laika licks his ears, and Uncle Hazard rolls over to show her his belly. I'm afraid to look up and see the grown-ups standing there—a chorus of disapproval.

Jitters asks, "Where is Emmett? Didn't he want to see us?"

Uncle Buddy speaks first. "No, he did not! Can you blame the poor boy? He ain't speaking to neither of you sorry prodigals. He made it back from Knoxville, mad as the dickens. And you"—he points to me—"only a child bad through and through would do her family the way you done. Stealing money from your own. If you were mine, I'd give you a box and five nails—line you up and give you a—"

"You're a fine one to talk about money after how you did Emmett," I blurt out.

Daddy speaks up, sharp and sudden. "Uncle Buddy, these are my children. You hear? They are mine. And they came home from the land of Nashville. So leave off, old man, you leave off. Or I'll give you worse. See if I don't."

Uncle Buddy's face starts working. "Zilpah, you gonna let that feeble-minded son-of-something speak to me that way? You gonna stand there and allow it?"

Grandma Horace says, "For the love of God, hush! His daughters are home."

Daddy says, "That is correct. Hush! The lost children came home."

Uncle Buddy looks so mad he could spit. "The world is against me—as usual. Well, forget you'uns! After all I done for this family? I will take my hat and go. I know where I'm not wanted. Let's go, Pearlie. Let's go see Delia Jupiter. She admires and respects me. Leave this shameful family to its own demise." He gets into the Ghost Town truck with his iguana and takes off, tires squealing and chewing up gravel and dust.

Cyrus asks, "Does Pearl want to go?"

Grandma Horace says, "Maybe Delia Jupiter will take him in and that creature too. I've had it, blood or not. I've had it. I wash my hands of him, Lord forgive me."

Daddy turns to Jitters and me; he could care less where Uncle Buddy gets it in his head to go. He hands Appelonia to Louise and steps forward. "Well, look who came home." He hugs me so tight and says, "Don't you never run off like that again." Then he grabs Jitters too. "You either. Is this your dog?"

I nod, and Jitters says, "We rescued it from a fake blind old man beggar, but he stole Livy Two's guitar, and he almost got Mama's—"

"Jitters!" I whisper a warning, and she shuts up. Thank the Lord the little ones start in asking questions, and Daddy keeps hugging on us like he won't let go. Then Mama hugs us too. She's too worked up seeing us to even bother about Laika. I don't want to cry. I try to be brave like Athena, but it's hard. I'm so glad to be back in their arms. The lady who runs the Maggie Store comes out on the front porch and says, "Well, I see you'uns come back and brought you a friend with you."

"Yes ma'am." I wave to her. "We're back home with Laika."

But the shopkeeper doesn't say another a word. She goes back into the store, which is her way of saying, *I hope you're satisfied with yourself.* It's in what folks *don't* say around here that you know what they're really thinking and feeling. The shame washes over me again, and I want to explain, but what is there to explain?

Mama sees the scarf around Jitters's neck and says, "There's my scarf that went missing. Did you have to go all the way to Nashville to find it?"

Jitters casually steps on my foot and says, "I took it, Mama. I'm sorry, I—"

I interrupt her. "No, she didn't, Mama. I did. I sent it to Mr. George Flowers, the man I auditioned for. But I didn't want him to have it after all. I'm sorry I lied, and I'm sorry I took the ten dollars. I'll pay you back as soon as I can."

All Mama says is, "Weren't you two scared all that long way away? Anything might have happened. Come on, let's get home. We'll sort it out then."

Becksie turns to Jitters, her accusing finger arched. "You should have talked to me first, Jitters. I thought you had more sense than to chase after Livy Two. I have taught you to have more common sense." Her voice is ragged with reproach.

Jitters says, "Rebecca Weems, you don't tell me everything, that's for sure. We all got our secrets. But right now, I have an announcement. My name is not Jitters. My name is Myrtle Anne. I want to be called that from now on. Jitters is a dang baby name."

Everybody stares at Jitters, not knowing what to make of this kid who is no longer acting like Becksie's parrot and handmaiden. Cyrus says, "All right, Myrtle Anne. Nice to meet you!" He shakes her hand and giggles at his own joke.

Gentle says, "Myrtle Anne, do you want to go home and see the whistle pigs? I dressed them up. Mama let me have little bits of yarn. Now they have sweaters. Me and Caroline and Cyrus dressed them up. They are real true pets now."

"No finer pet than a groundhog," Daddy says.

"The mama whistle pig didn't want to wear clothes," Caroline explains.

As everyone gets in the car, Grandma Horace pulls me aside. "Olivia Hyatt Weems, what on earth possessed you to go off on this harebrained escape?"

I whisper, "I thought I could sell my songs and buy our house from Madame Cherry Hat. You gave me Mama's diary, and that was the sign to try, but I failed."

She looks at me hard. "Well, on that fact there is no doubt." Then she yanks me close to her. "Don't you ever pull anything like that again!"

"No ma'am, I won't." It starts pouring the rain as we

pile into the Rambler to head up Fie Top Road toward home; Louise and me hold the babies in the backseat with Uncle Hazard and Laika, while Becksie and Myrtle Anne crowd into the back end with the twins and Gentle. Mama drives, and Grandma Horace and Daddy sit up front. Louise whispers, "Oh, Livy Two. Why'd you do it like that? It's been awful not knowing. Crying and carrying on, sheriff coming over, search parties."

But I only look out the window, kissing on Appelonia's head. I don't want to talk about it or explain myself. I'll have to do that soon enough. I squeeze Louise's hand, and she squeezes mine back. "I'm sorry," I tell her.

"Well, there's somebody who is going to need an even bigger apology than me. Reckon you'd better read it now. Miss Attickson dropped it off earlier." She hands me the letter.

I open the envelope, and a feeling of dread swims over me.

Dear Olivia,

Imagine my surprise when your mother, sick with worry, showed up at the bookmobile demanding to know if I'd seen you or Myrtle Anne? Imagine, again, my surprise when she ASSURED me that YOU told her that I'd asked you to come before school to help me organize books for 1964. I suppose you don't have to imagine my shock and worry at your disappearance. But to pull me into your web of deceit when I tried to be nothing but your trusted friend—all I can say is that I am so very disappointed and heartsick. I have spent nearly two days in a worried daze over you and your sister. I feel somehow to blame too—encouraging you to travel and see the world, but I never meant for you to betray your own family and run off without a word. My own boss heard of your disappearing act and made it clear what I have to do now.

Olivia, it absolutely breaks my heart, but I am very sorry to inform you that your services will no longer be required at the Haywood County Bookmobile. You may come by and pick up your last paycheck. Here is a quote I found recently: "When you betray somebody else, you also betray yourself." Isaac Bashevis Singer is the author of that quote. Maybe someday you will be able to explain why you did what you did, but you leave me no choice to do what I must do. I'm glad you and your sister are home safe and sound.

Sincerely,
Miss Attickson

I feel sick at my stomach. I hadn't even considered the result of including Miss Attickson in the lie. Of course Mama would have gone to her first to find me. I crumple up the letter and shove it into my pocket as we drive past a table under a tarp that says, HONEY—ONE

DOLLAR. BOILED PEANUTS/PORK RINDS—50 CENTS.

Daddy yells, "Stop the car! I see something I want for me and the kids."

Twenty or so jars of honey sit to one side of the table—sacks of pork rinds sit piled up on the other. In between them are bags of boiled peanuts next to another sign that says, BACK SOON. LEAVE A DOLLAR OR 50 CENTS ON THE TABLE. There are a few damp dollars in a cigar box on the picnic table.

Daddy says, "I want some boiled peanuts. That's what I want. Please? Let's get all the kids boiled peanuts and pork rinds to celebrate the lost ones coming home."

Mama sighs and pulls the car over; Louise gets out and puts a dollar in the cigar box for peanuts and pork rinds. She gets back into the car, and Mama eases back on the road to drive the rest of the way home. I watch the windshield wipers chase each other back and forth in the driving rain up the mountain road. Daddy holds his pork rinds and peanuts, but he looks at Grandma Horace. "I got something to say to you. This is my family. These two lost girls are home. There has been a lot of talk. I have said nothing because—I'm bewildered. I am a bewildered man. But I'm saying now that my family is not moving to a land called Enka. My family is staying here in the land of Maggie Valley." He eats the pork rinds, but his eyes never leave Grandma Horace's face. "Is that understood? I am still the father here, and what I say goes."

Nobody says a word. The car is steamy and silent in anticipation of what Grandma Horace will say. Will she throw down the gauntlet too? But it's not Grandma Horace who speaks. It's Mama, her face flushed with deep sadness, who says, "Tom, we have to quit fooling ourselves. Mother is right, as hard as that is to accept. The landlady in Clyde is out of patience. So I'm sorry, but we'll be moving to Enka in 1964, and somehow I am going to find a job—a real job. I've tried every which way to hold this family together here in Maggie, but after nearly losing two children to Nashville and dreams, I can't risk it anymore. I'm sorry, Tom. We're moving to Enka. And that's final. I wish what you did say was law—but it's not."

Tears roll down Daddy's face as he tries to comprehend Mama's words, and I realize that my grand plan to hit it big in Music City USA has brought the Enka plan home to roost, which means we're going. We will be leaving Maggie Valley after everything. "Mama, please?" I say, but then Myrtle Anne whispers to me, "Is this all your fault or all my fault or both our faults?"

Grandma Horace overhears this and says, "We'll be casting no blame today, Myrtle Anne, on anybody. What's done is done, and there are facts to be faced. I'll leave shortly after the New Year and get my house ready, since my tenants will be evacuating." Her voice sounds cracked—as if all the fight has drained out. "And just so all of you know, I take no satisfaction in this wise decision. I know how difficult it is. I am a firm and hard woman, it's true, but I understand more than you think. I am glad to open my doors to my family in Enka. Grandpa Cal, rest his soul, would agree."

Right then, two deer, a buck and a doe, bound out onto the wet road and stop directly in front of the car. Mama slams on the brakes, and we all get thrown forward as the Rambler skids across the pavement. Louise holds tight to Baby Tom-Bill, and I hang on to Appelonia, who laughs like it's a great game. The deer blink at us for a moment before leaping across the road and into the woods. Mama grips the steering wheel, trying to catch her breath and not cry.

Gentle climbs from the very backseat up to the front seat to seek out Grandma Horace's lap like nothing just happened. "Is Enka a pretty place?" Gentle asks.

"Enka is pretty. I have some snowball bushes in my front yard that Grandpa Cal planted, and I'll walk y'all down to Enka Lake, and you can stick your feet in the water. You can join the children's choir, because you, Gentle, sing like God's own angel."

Cyrus sits up. "Hey, how about me? Do I sing like God's own angel too?"

Becksie lashes out, "Good God, hush up with your annoying questions, Cyrus!"

"Why are they annoying?" Cyrus asks, which makes Becksie groan, but Mama says, "I helped my papa plant those snowball bushes."

I want to say: *I know, I read all about it . . . and the girl you were, Mama, would never ever move back to Enka . . . not the girl in the diary . . . she would stay and fight for our home. . . .* But I hold my tongue for now, because I'll be darned if I'm gonna bust out crying, which is what would happen if I tried to speak this minute. My heart is crushed with a lost guitar, a lost job and friend, and now the move to Enka. I wish it were hot summer so I could climb up high into the red maple in our holler and stay there for good.

Daddy says, "I don't agree with this decision to go off to the land of Enka."

Mama says, "No . . . I didn't reckon you would, Tom."

Gentle whispers, "But what about my family of whistle pigs? Can they come too? They'll be scared if I leave them to fend for themselves alone, right, Grandma Horace?"

Nobody answers Gentle—not even Grandma Horace, who knows how crazy Gentle is for those whistle pigs. Caroline says, "Maybe the fairies can take care of them," but this only makes Gentle burst into tears.

Finally, Mama says, "Hush now. We'll figure something out." Another half mile up the road, Delia Jupiter comes strolling out of the woods in the drizzle. She waves and we all wave back as she heads down the road toward Maggie Valley on foot. If Uncle Buddy has gone to see Delia to drown his sorrows and seek her pity and respect, she's not saying. Daddy eats his pork rinds and starts in humming "You Are My Sunshine," and we're quiet the rest of the way home.

CHAPTER FOURTEEN

Glass Birds

I AM GROUNDED until the cows come home or at least until further notice, according to Mama. This is way worse than Waterrock Knob and losing Daddy, because that was impulse, and Nashville was pure calculated planning. Laika may stay but only for the time being, because the family cannot afford to feed another dog. I offer to pay for the dog food, but then I remember that I got fired from the bookmobile. Grandma Horace says, "Well, that animal is not coming with us to Enka; that's all I have to say about the subject. Why not ask the Mennonite fellow if he wants a dog?" But Mathew the Mennonite is away with his family visiting kin in Middle Tennessee, so Laika is here for now. As for the whistle pigs, nobody is discussing them, and Gentle keeps right on caring for them.

Laika adores Uncle Hazard, and the feeling is mutual. The two of them wrestle in the snow and sleep by the woodstove, but I still wonder if that evil Fletcher Partridge is gonna find his way into this holler to claim her back. I feel like sleeping with one eye open just in case. I whisper my fears to Mama, and she says, "That old tramp isn't going to cross a state line for a dog, and even if he did, he'd never find his way to this holler. We got more important things to think about, like how we're going to have Christmas this year with money so low and getting ready to move."

"Do you think I'll get Miss Attickson to give me my job back until we leave?"

"After what you pulled? The job is over. Face facts."

"What about my guitar?"

"Your guitar? That's the absolute last of my worries. The only fact I am facing now is Christmas, and how I'm ten dollars short for presents."

"I'm sorry, Mama." But she isn't in the mood to listen, and frankly, I'm sick of facing facts. I faced the fact of George Flowers. I faced the fact of Fletcher Partridge. And I faced the fact of getting fired, and now Enka. I have faced all the facts I care to face for the moment, and the only thing I want now is my guitar back, but I'm trapped in this house like a prisoner. I am only allowed to go someplace if accompanied by Mama or Daddy or Grandma Horace. Why don't Mama just put bars on the windows and doors while she's at it? Jitters ain't even in trouble because it wasn't her idea. Oh, the injustice! Emmett is not speaking to me either. Fine, who cares? However, I am not the only person in this family who ran off to seek employment and adventure, but try telling that to a short-memory brother who is beginning to bear a resemblance to one great-uncle. Word has it Uncle Buddy is making moonshine deliveries for Delia Jupiter, but that's another subject not open to discussion. *A short memory is not a clear conscience.*

I do manage to get out most of the story of Nashville, except "Myrtle Anne" chimes in with certain chilling details that I purposely leave out—such as the ghost of Spearfinger and the devil-dog man. Now the little ones are having bad dreams, and Mama lets me know it's my fault. But then right out of the blue, she'll hug me so tight I can't breathe, and again, I'll whisper, "I'm sorry."

I do make an effort to be more patient and helpful around the house to make up for all my many faults. I work with Daddy on the banjo. I let him teach me how to play some chords on his claw hammer. As we practice together, he says, "You won't leave again, right, and go off to the land of Nashville? Next time, we leave together."

"There won't be a next time, Daddy."

"Like fun there won't," he roars. "No quitting, Livy Two. You may be grounded in this house like your mother says, but no quitting allowed."

Caroline covers her ears. "Don't yell, Daddy."

"I am not yelling," he yells.

"Yes, you are too, Daddy," Gentle tells him.

Daddy says, "Come here, you two," and they both scramble into his lap and he tickles them. "I'm not yelling. I'm just happy the two lost children came home. It's like they sparked something in my head that I forgot. I don't want to forget anymore. And nobody is quitting! That is the law in the land of Maggie Valley! No quitting!"

Cyrus says, "You're yelling again, Daddy."

One of my many multitudes of punishments is to apologize to the sheriff of Haywood County and write a Christmas card to Mr. Cas Walker over in Knoxville, thanking him for announcing on his radio show that me and Jitters were missing. I write to Mr. Walker and tell him how weren't kidnapped, and I'm sorry for any trouble. I close it with "Merry Christmas." Without complaint, I also help Mama with selling scarves and baby blankets and stack cakes at the Methodist Christmas bazaar, and that gets us a little extra money for the holidays, but that day I also spy Mama cutting job want ads from the local paper, tucking them into her poke beneath balls of yarn. Would she really get a job and move us to Enka all at the same time?

A few of the ladies at the bazaar inquire about my trip and rumors of the upcoming move, but I only reply, "Scarf or baby blanket today?" I am not discussing Nashville or the relocation to Enka with the ladies of Haywood County.

I play with the twins and Gentle and the whistle pigs.

They look real cute dressed up in little sweaters, but my heart ain't in it. Caroline accuses, "You used to be a fun sister," and Cyrus says, "Yeah, what happened to you?" Gentle says, "Never mind. Maybe she'll get nice again. Want to hold Sugar Cookie? She's the sweetest whistle pig of all. Wiggle will bite you if you don't watch it." I try to smile, but sometimes the faces of George Flowers or Fletcher Partridge loom up in my head. I try to pretend every minute of the day that I don't miss my guitar, but I'm scared all my songs are gone with it. It's like I can't hear the music right without my fingers on the strings. I talk to my guitar, and I apologize for losing it in such a foolhardy manner. I know Laika is happy we done what we did, because she looks like a lioness running through snow, but I can't help hankering after what is lost—*Face facts, Livy Two, face facts.*

Louise asks when I'm going to see Miss Attickson to make up, but for now I am too ashamed. I send telepathic thoughts her way—*I am sorry, I am sorry, I am sorry*—but if she hears me at all at the bookmobile, her answer is silence. Then I learn she's off in Memphis for the holidays with that fiancé, Mr. Pickle.

One night after supper, Gentle begs me to read her one of Mama's stories. When we're all in bed and the coast is finally clear, I pick up where I left off and read all the kids some more of Mama's stories. I decide to read a few without stopping in between. I want to cover as much of her story as possible, so I can figure out a way to get her back to the girl she was. If I can do that, maybe I can stop the plans to move away. Maybe I can find a way for us to stay in Maggie Valley if Mama can remember who she was long ago.

March 24, 1943
Dear Grasshopper,

I have no birds to draw for you today, but I have a secret. I'm not supposed to know, but my mama lost a baby she was carrying. She was just a few months along, and I didn't even know, but I heard her crying to Papa about it. Papa said that I shouldn't bring it up to her, but I painted her three birds to make her feel better: a red-headed woodpecker, a Baltimore oriole (that's really for Papa since he likes baseball), and a northern mockingbird. I hope she loves them. They took me a long time to draw.

Yours truly, Jessie Horace

P.S. I wonder what my little brother or sister would have looked like? Sometimes I think I see the baby's little face in my dreams.

April 1, 1943
Dear Grasshopper,

Some folks say that the "ivory-billed woodpecker"

is extinct, and some say it's just an endangered species. There have been reports of sightings. I, Jessie Horace, have seen an ivory-billed woodpecker—TWICE NOW. It's a huge bird, though, growing up to twenty inches tall and living to the age of thirty! APRIL FOOLS! Did I trick you? Hope so.

Papa goes to the doctor all the time now, but he swears he'll be on the mend in no time. He still looks skinny to me. We went over to Sylva to Schulman's Department Store, and he picked out some new clothes. I told him that he looked very dapper. I got some new saddle shoes, and I like them a lot. The three of us stopped and Papa and me had ice cream sundaes, but Papa let me finish his. Mother only ordered black coffee at first, and then the waitress asked if she wanted pecan or chocolate pie, and Mother said, "Well, I'm on a diet so better give me pecan." She ate every bite. For a few minutes, she and Papa held hands under the table. They thought I couldn't see.

May 7, 1943
Dear Grasshopper,

I keep checking the same book of birds out of the library, and it's getting a little worn around the edges since I keep it propped open so I can draw the birds right, but I don't feel like drawing today. I want to build a tree house. Papa can't help me build it, but he could oversee the build-

ing of it. Right away, Mother said (can you guess?) "NO!" But Daddy stood up to her and said, "I want to do this for Jessie." And so we're starting to build a tree house in the front yard. He's telling me how to hammer the wood safe in the branches, so I'll have a level floor, wall, and window. I am going invite Miss Amelia to live in my tree house.

Yours truly, Jessie Horace

P.S. Mama is mad as a hornet about the tree house. She's taken to wearing her green glass eye around, which means ANGRY WOMAN A-LOOSE. She said that a young lady needs no such thing as a tree house, and that I'll send Daddy into an early grave making him fool with it. If he dies and I'm left alone with her, I won't be able to bear it—and that's a terrible thing to say about your own mama. I can't live my life the way she wants me to. I love her but I feel trapped. It's almost Mother's Day . . .

When I'm done, I am near out of breath at the story. "That's all I'm reading for tonight." I have to pull the blankets and pillow over my head when they all plead for more stories. "Hush up now." I sit up in bed. "That's an order. Or Mama will find out and take away the diary." That gets them quiet. Sometimes you just got to lay down the law in this house. Daddy tried to, but Mama said no to him. Now he carries his banjo with him everywhere—ever since Mama flat-out told him no. He picks on it day and night, trying like hellfire to make the songs come back, and I think it's maybe so he can feel like a man again.

The day before Christmas, Mama sees I'm chomping at the bit to run free, so she finally allows Louise, Emmett, and me to hike up a steep trail where Louise says the perfect Christmas tree is a-waiting. Emmett and Louise have to swear they won't let me out of their sight—what does she think I'm going to do? Go back to Nashville? What for?

Near the springhouse I pick up the ax from the stump, and the winter light bounces off the silvery blade. I close my eyes in the frozen holler, letting the December sun fall down all around me until the white gold of it seeps into my skin. I look at Emmett. "Are you speaking to me yet?"

Emmett mutters, "Maybe, maybe not, runaway girl."

"Look, don't do me no favors, Mr. Judge and Jury." I pull a thick sock over the blade of the ax so I won't cut myself or anybody else.

Louise whispers, "Quit it, you two. Let's go cut down the tree. Ready?"

We head up into the woods, Louise the protective barrier between me and Emmett. Fine, two can play this game. My knees still ache from falling on the ice in

Nashville, but who cares? The top of the mountain calls us to come on now . . . faster, faster, faster! *Livy Two, Louise, Emmett . . . don't quit now.* Then we hear it—the scrabble of paws behind us—fly-fly-fly—and I know it's Uncle Hazard and Laika, chasing after us. I hide behind a tall oak, and Louise and Emmett pick other trees. Uncle Hazard zips right past us, his short squat legs racing up the trail. We don't make a sound or even breathe. Laika never even sees us. But all at once, both dogs quit running, backtrack, sniffing, snuffling. We stay still as marble, trying not to laugh, but they spot us anyway and rush up, panting, wagging, as if to ask, *What'd you'uns stop for?*

I glance at Emmett, but he won't meet my eye. Instead, he shouts, "Come on, dogs!" Both dogs race after him, but I'm in no hurry to chop down the tree and get back home to my prison sentence. It feels good to be out of the house and breathing cold, clean air. At least Louise don't hate me. She understood why I had to try and has told me so. When we pass by Delia Jupiter's house, Louise says, "Look," pointing to Uncle Buddy's Ghost Town truck parked outside. "I hope he stays there for good," she whispers, and I nod in agreement. It'll definitely be some kind of business deal, because Uncle Buddy won't do nothing without his palm being greased. Delia Jupiter has probably hired him to make deliveries or clean out her still or something.

I'll never forgive him for stealing Emmett's paychecks last year, claiming he was charging for worldly advice and such. Ha.

"How's your wedding present for Miss Attickson? You done?" I ask Louise as we cut a wide berth away from Delia's house, in case Uncle Buddy is peeking out the window. Ten or so jugs of vinegar sit by her shed. Uncle Buddy told me that vinegar cleans out moonshine stills—and folks that don't clean out their stills wind up dead as a doornail. "You finish it or not?" I ask again when Louise don't answer.

"Don't want to talk about it. You'll have advice and suggestions for me and then some." Louise stops to let some snowflakes melt on her tongue. "No thanks."

"Fine, keep it a big secret then."

"I will."

"Probably uninvited to the wedding anyhow. Wouldn't blame her."

"Quit feeling sorry for yourself. Have you called her yet?"

"What am I supposed to say?"

"How about you're sorry? That'd be a start."

"Maybe divine intervention will happen and they won't get married."

"Did you ever consider that she loves him? She said she wants an old-fashioned mountain wedding with a covered-dish supper. They'll arrive on horseback up at

Cataloochee at the Palmer Chapel and have a feast like in the old days afterward."

"I can't see Mr. Pickle on horseback. He'll fall off, and she'll quit driving the bookmobile to look after his broke-neck self. The whole thing is a tragedy." I look up and realize my sister is already miles up ahead of me, not listening to a single word. "I am speaking to you! Did you hear me at all?" I yell after her.

"Nope!" She races to Emmett, who is waiting with the dogs.

"Where is that Christmas tree? You sure it was this far?" he asks Louise.

"Yes, I know exactly where it is. Come on."

Me and Emmett follow but don't speak. Uncle Hazard and Laika bark at near everything. Then she cries, "There it is! Up yonder." She points straight ahead. "Just waiting."

It's a tall cedar shining like jade and emerald in the frozen sunlight. I take the ax and start to swing at the base. I almost hate to cut the tree down, but I want a Christmas tree in the house too. I don't let myself think about it being our last Christmas in Maggie Valley. I swing the blade, and the wood spits pure bark and cedar fragrance. I feel my hands rubbing raw from chopping, but I keep going. *Chop. Crack. Chop. Crack.*

"My turn." Emmett takes the ax and chops away too. Uncle Hazard and Laika pace around, barking, making sure we're all keeping our minds on the task at hand. *Be careful. Bark. Swing level. Bark. Easy does it.* Then it's Louise's turn, and she chops at the Christmas tree until it falls. The three of us hoist it on our shoulders and carry it down the mountain. Louise carries the front end, and I carry the trunk, and Emmett carries the middle. The needles and branches scratch my face and neck, but it's such a beauty that I can't wait to get it home to the little ones. My brother never says a word to me the whole way down the mountain. The quiet gets wider and deeper between us. I offer up a silent prayer to Livy One in the darkening sky, not to let me and my brother grow up to be the next generation Grandma Horace and Uncle Buddy. I don't intend to send him a fruitcake every Christmas and let that be that.

When we get back home, Mama's gone to the market, leaving Grandma Horace and Daddy in charge. She studies on our tree and says, "I guess I'd better get out my S&H green stamps ornaments." She bought a set of old bubbly lights a while back at the redemption store that's supposed to look just like candlelight. I can't wait to see them shining on the tree. Emmett plays a low tune on the harmonica with the dogs asleep at his feet. Uncle Hazard sleeps stretched out on top of Laika. I wonder what the devil-dog man is doing for Christmas? Moses from Memphis? How about the woe-is-me lady? She must be in Jackson with her husband, loving on her grandbaby. The faker blind man? Is he somewhere playing my guitar? Their faces crowd my thoughts, so I pick up Baby Tom-Bill, breathing in his sweet head, trying to make the faces from the land of Nashville go away. He squirms in my arms, chewing on my fingers, as he's teething. Moses from Memphis is the only one I'd ever care to see again.

Grandma Horace hangs the lights on the branches. Louise takes Baby Tom-Bill from me, and she feeds him and Appelonia an early supper of beans and rice. Jitters strings popcorn and cranberries together on a string with Gentle and the twins. The room glows with Christmas and hope for a moment. One of Louise's pictures hangs on the wall. It's of all of us working in the garden and painting the house around Stella, our scarecrow, and in a corner, Uncle Hazard peeks out of his pinecone palace. She ought to paint Laika into the picture, too, except she won't be our dog for long. Sometimes it feels like the whole adventure to Nashville was a dream, but it wasn't because Jit—because Myrtle Anne is the one who is different.

Myrtle Anne talks to Daddy as she strings the popcorn. "Listen to me, Daddy. You need a manager. All musicians do. That's your problem."

Daddy smiles. "You two lost children came back from the land of Nashville."

She grins back at him. "Yep. I have to write a card to Moses from Memphis."

"Who is Moses from Memphis?" Cyrus asks.

"My new pen pal," Jitters says. "Makes the best dry-rub barbecue in Nashville."

Daddy plays a riff on the banjo. "What will I do in the land of Enka?"

"Same thing you do here, I expect, Tom." Grandma Horace hangs some of Mama's glass bird Christmas ornaments on the tree.

Myrtle Anne says, "Won't it be funny us living thirty miles away from home?"

"That's what they invented telephones and automobiles for, Myrtle Anne," Grandma Horace explains while Gentle plays "Silent Night" on the piano.

Becksie strings the cranberries, her mind far away—on her sweetheart? She hasn't spoken of him since her secret was discovered. In bed later, I overhear her whisper, "Jitters, want to see a picture? Don't tell. He's a Cherokee Indian boy—Henry."

Myrtle Anne yawns. "How many times I got to tell you to call me Myrtle Anne? And if Henry is truly your sweetheart, he should meet us. Y'all should go tie a lover's knot in the woods with some branches and then your love will last forever."

"Since when you did you become such a know-it-all on matters of the heart?"

"Beats me. But this book has great information on love. It's called *8,414 Strange and Fascinating Superstitions.* Look up the subject of 'love.'"

"That's silly, believing all that stuff." But after Myrtle Anne falls asleep, Becksie holds the book up to the window and reads under a shaft of moonlight. I'd like to see a picture of her Cherokee Indian boy, but she'd think I was spying on her if I asked. Instead, I jot down the words to my new song. Gentle wakes with a cry and climbs up into bed with me, shivering from a dream. "Spearfinger's scary. . . . What are you writing?"

"A new song."

"Teach it to me."

"I ain't finished, Gentle."

"You don't sing since Nashville. Please, Livy Two?" So I sing a few stanzas.

Mama's glass birds on a Christmas tree
Sparkle and hang so bright.
Mama's glass birds on a Christmas tree
Shimmer like stars in flight.
Mama's glass birds on a Christmas tree
Dazzle on this holy night.

Gentle falls asleep in my arms, and I look out my window into the starry night to wish Livy One, my sister in the stars, a Merry Christmas. I think about all Mama's quiet Christmases in Enka a long time ago when she was just a little girl, sketching birds. What will it be like to live there? Grandma Horace says she is going to buy beds for the basement that don't flood too often. That's where most of us will sleep. What will happen when it does flood? Will we float around a basement on beds for boats? Will Mama's tree house still be there? Will the kids at Sand Hill Elementary be sweet or hateful? Will we go to the Methodist church every Sunday and get haircuts in Asheville? Will the smell of Enka-Stinka linger day and night in our noses? Will we even notice it after a while? At least Rusty Frye won't be there. Thank the Lord for small favors.

CHAPTER FIFTEEN

New Year Wishes

Dear Grasshopper,

It's Christmas morning, 1943. It didn't snow last night like I wanted it to. Maybe it might snow later. I want to get up and inspect my Christmas presents, but Mother and Papa gave me strict orders last night not to look at a thing. Mother says it's going to be a real small Christmas, but that "Santa Claus" will come. I guess he did, but I'm not allowed to get out of bed. I hope Mother makes cinnamon rolls. I wonder what Christmas will be like when I'm grown up? What kind of grown-up will I be? I hope I don't become some lady who always gets her hair done at the beauty parlor and talks about recipes. Merry Christmas, Grasshopper.

Yours truly, Jessie Horace

P.S. I know I haven't written much, and I'm sorry. Papa's bed is in the living room now. He likes it by the window, because of the sun hitting his face. We eat bowls of cream of wheat together, and I show him my birds. He says I'm an artist with a natural curiosity, which will serve me well in my life. My tree house has a bright red door. I painted it for good luck like I read in a story about a Chinese family. The color is good luck!

On Christmas morning, I read them some of Mama's diary the very first thing while the grown-ups are still sleeping. When we hear Grandma Horace stirring, I hide the diary, and we all gather under the tree around ten identical packages. I suspect they are wool socks, since that's what we get every Christmas, along with candy canes and tangerines. Sure enough, we each get a pair. We put on our wool socks and stick our feet together in the middle so Grandma Horace can take a picture with her old camera that flashes so bright we see stars for an hour at least. Our feet are all different colors—red, yellow, blue, green, gray, black, pink, purple, orange, and brown. Daddy laughs at all the different colors of feet under the Christmas tree, and Mama looks pleased that we like her handiwork. Grandma Horace gets the tangerines and says, "One for each. That's it. Don't be taking more than your share! Then time for church. Oh, here's something for you, Tom." She hands him a present, which he opens and reads aloud, "Daily Proverbs?"

Grandma Horace says, "I thought they'd help you with language and life."

Daddy says, "Well, thank you, Mother Horace," and

he starts paging through it, repeating, "Daily proverbs, daily proverbs."

The front room smells of pine needles and tangerines and hot black coffee. The twins and Gentle are sticky with candy canes, and it feels like Christmas even if Emmett is still holding a grudge. Part of me longs for a guitar under the tree and all sorts of other presents like what I saw in the toy-store window in Waynesville, especially when Caroline asks, "How comes Santa Claus brings us wool socks and tangerines and candy canes, but other kids get dolls and toys and pretty dresses? I wanted new fairy wings."

Mama says, "Well, I do have something else, but just for the little ones." She reaches under a chair and pulls out five packages for the twins, Gentle, and the babies, but Myrtle Anne asks, "How come they all get extra presents?"

Becksie says, "You be grateful, you little brat. It's Christmas! Good gosh!" Myrtle Anne stiffens at the insult and takes her wool socks and tangerine to the other side of the room away from Becksie.

Louise helps the babies open their presents, which are two homemade rag dolls, one for each, that Mama made. Appelonia's got the girl, and Baby Tom-Bill has the boy. Appelonia rocks her baby, and Tom-Bill chews on his. Next, the twins and Gentle tear into the packages. Gentle and Caroline have identical dresses made from flour and feed sacks that Mama's sewn for them. They're real soft with pretty flowers, and Caroline and Gentle both shout, "Fairy dresses," and Gentle cries, "So soft, so soft." Cyrus gets a cape—a fine cape, dyed black from a fertilizer sack—and Daddy says, "All boys need capes when they go exploring to the land of adventure, right, Jessie?" Cyrus puts on his cape right away and says, "I love it! I bet Poseidon had one too! Where's my trident!"

Mama says, "Now, I'd like to hear music from my children on Christmas."

"Me too!" Daddy claps his hands. "I want music from every kid here. Any kind of tune will do. Harmonica, spoons, tambourine, soft shuffle, or clog!"

"All right, come on, Gentle," I say, but then right when we are in the middle of singing "Glass Birds," Becksie bursts into tears and flies out of the room. Mama follows her, calling, "What on earth is wrong with you?"

"Why did it have to happen on Christmas? Why?" Becksie wails in despair. Mama closes the bedroom door behind her, so we can't hear no more, but it turns out later that Becksie has got her monthly period for the first time. *On Christmas Day!* I find Mama in the kitchen cutting up old feed sacks made out of cotton for her to use to soak up the blood that will come every month from now on—talk about a prison sentence. Not only for dresses, I reckon, the material can also be used for something called "sanity napkins." I shudder and sneak out of the kitchen.

I whisper to Louise, "Lord God, I'd give anything not

to be a girl. I swear. I'm willing it not to happen. Keep it away is all I can say."

But Mama overhears this and says, "Don't be silly. My mother had it, I had it, and you'll have it too."

"I don't want to talk about it," I shout. *"Ever!"*

Cyrus asks, "Talk about what? What's a monthly?"

I feel my face get hot as I snap, "Nothing, you tiny-tiny-know-nothing boy! Now be quiet."

Myrtle Anne is far too shocked to even say a word, but she gets over Becksie's earlier insult and makes her a hot water bottle for stomach cramps.

But Becksie recovers from the shock of womanhood quick enough, and after church, she says to me right there in the parking lot of the Methodist church, "I am a woman just in time for Christmas! Mama told me. It's kind of exciting. And you're next, Livy Two! Maybe you'll be a woman, next Christmas."

"Be quiet, all right? Just shut up and keep your old womanhood!"

The little ones have no idea what anybody is talking about. They nag at me to explain, but the second we get home from church, I go out to the barn to milk Birdy Sweetpea. I'm not explaining that stuff to a single soul. Forget it.

Later in the day, Mathew the Mennonite drops by with his daughter, Ruth, bringing us a Christmas present of five chickens. "We thought you might like some for your barn," he says. "Five Andalusian chickens—some of the finest egg layers around."

Ruth and Louise hug each other like it's been years since they seen each other, even though it's just been a month or so. I feel bad that Mathew the Mennonite's wife, Mrs. Alice, thinks we're a bad influence on her girl, but I'm glad Mr. Mathew don't think that way. The little ones get all excited about the chickens, but Mama says, "Thank you very much, Mr. Mathew, but we can't keep them. We'll be moving to Enka once my mother gets the house ready. I expect February or so."

"I am very sorry to hear that," Mathew the Mennonite says.

Mama says, "Well, it can't be helped. Fact of life. Folks move, start over."

Daddy comes out on the porch. "What doesn't kill us will make us longer."

"Stronger, Daddy!" Myrtle Anne corrects him.

"That's right." Daddy says, "I meant that. Hey, chickens! How about that! Thank you, Mr. Mathew. Merry Christmas." He beams with pleasure seeing the chickens. "Hello, you fine chickens! The chickens have come home to—to—to—"

"Roost, Daddy," Becksie calls from the front porch, where she's pressing dried flowers into her flower album. "He got a proverb book for Christmas."

Mathew the Mennonite says, "I see. Merry Christmas, Mr. Weems. I'm sorry you can't keep these chickens."

"Why can't we?" Daddy asks.

Mama says, "We're moving, Tom, remember?"

"Oh yeah, that bad idea. I like these chickens. They're pretty chickens. Can't they stay until we go?" and the little ones all shout, "Hooray! Hooray for chickens!"

Mama says, "No, they can't stay, but Mr. Mathew, we have a present for you. Would you like this big yellow dog? I spoke to the children earlier about finding a home for Laika, and we're all in agreement. If you like, you could have her. I know the children would be very happy knowing she's with you and your family."

Myrtle Anne says, "That's right. And Laika was named after the first dog in outer space, Mr. Mathew, sent there by the Russians."

Ruth kneels down on the ground and pats Laika. "Could we, Father? Please?"

Mathew the Mennonite nods and says, "It's a very fine Christmas present indeed."

"You're welcome, Mr. Mathew," Mama says. "And thank you for being such a good friend to our family and Ruth here too. I know we haven't always been able—" But she stops like she might cry, so she turns and goes into the house.

He looks at me and asks, "And how was the adventure to Nashville, Olivia?"

Myrtle Anne jumps in, uninvited, "It was wonderful, Mr. Mathew. We had a fine time. Scary, but fun, too—Livy Two was *very glad* I came along too, because I'm very interested in superstitions, so I was able to basically be her guide, right? Whoops, I almost forgot I'm baking a pumpkin pie for Christmas. Bye!"

After she dashes into the house, Mathew the Mennonite says, "Olivia, do you know that I found five dollars in my prayer book? I believe it was the day you and your sister disappeared. Would you happen to know anything about it?"

In a low voice, I tell him, "It's the first installment of paying off our debts. We're not a bunch of freeloaders, Mr. Mathew. As soon as I get ungrounded, I'll be finding another job—maybe at the Burger Box or something. You'll be paid in full."

Mathew the Mennonite nods. "Well, I thank you, Olivia. But I am curious. How did you happen to see my truck in Waynesville that day?"

It's true that I am attempting to lie a little less in general, but I can't tell him that we used his truck as a running-away vehicle. So I only say, "Merry Christmas, Mr. Mathew. Sorry we can't keep these lovely Andalusian chickens."

But before he can answer, Uncle Buddy comes roaring up into the holler in the Ghost Town truck, yelling, "Merry Christmas! Get out of the way. Come on, get your eggnog, kids. I'm in a hurry, and I ain't staying where I ain't welcome, but I brought y'all kids eggnog." He hands me a jug of eggnog from the truck window. "Give it to Mama and Daddy now. I hope you're not still tearing off to Lord knows where."

"I am staying put for now." I take the eggnog. "Thank you, Uncle Buddy."

He sees Mathew the Mennonite standing there and says, "And here you go, Mennonite Man, you take one too—compliments of Delia Jupiter. Merry Christmas. And wish that hard sister of mine a Merry Christmas too." He guns the engine and starts to back out of the holler, but Cyrus chases him, yelling, "Where's Pearl? How's she doing?"

"Pearl's fine. Delia's got her. Now move it or I'll run you over, and then who'll be crying?" Uncle Buddy tears off out the holler so he won't get drug into conversation with the adults of the house. I look up at the window to see where Emmett is standing and watching everything, but when he catches me, he shuts the curtain fast. Though he won't admit it, I bet he's glad not to be living with Uncle Buddy at the night watchman cabin at Ghost Town. He still plans to work at Ghost Town after we move to Enka, but strictly as a gunslinger. He says he'll get a ride to and from work like most regular employees of Ghost Town in the Sky. Couldn't be bothered to do that last year though, could he?

On New Year's Eve, we all write our wishes on scraps of paper and burn them in the fire, so the smoke will carry our words up into the air of 1964. I think we all make the same wish about not moving away. I think about it being 1964. We have a new president in the White House now—Lyndon B. Johnson. But everybody misses John F. Kennedy, and Grandma Horace prays for the Kennedy family every day. She don't think much of Lyndon B. Johnson, claiming he's "common as dirt" from Texas. "That man from Texas is no John F. Kennedy, mark my words."

"What'd you wish for, Daddy?" I ask Daddy as he and Emmett play the banjo and harmonica together to ring in the new year.

Daddy says, "I wish to keep remembering. That's my wish."

"What can't be cured must be endured." Grandma Horace puts a wish in the fire.

Emmett says, "You will remember, Daddy." He picks up a stack of flashcards that Louise painted and says, "Try these again."

Daddy begins . . . "Sunflower, fiddle, rain cloud, fork, green stones—I mean peas. Hand, foot, fur—I mean hair." And while Daddy and Emmett do their flashcards, the first song of 1964 comes to me. It's a great relief to know I still got songs in my head, even if my guitar is lost and Mr. Fletcher Partridge is lurking out there somewhere in the darkness. I've got to figure out how to get my hands on a new guitar. That's another wish for 1964.

"NEW YEAR WISHES"

New Year wishes travel on a thin ribbon of
New Year smoke.
They swirl up in the stars in the wrote-down words
from folk.

New Year wishes up a chimney,
Smoky whispers to the world.
New Year wishes, do you hear me?
I'm a Smoky Mountain girl.

Secret longings, resolutions, make it better by and by.
New Year wishes won't you take me far up
with you in the sky.

New Year wishes up a chimney,
Smoky whispers to the world.
New Year wishes, do you hear me?
I'm a Smoky Mountain girl. . . .

CHAPTER SIXTEEN

The Land of Enka

IT'S POURING THE rain the morning Emmett carries Grandma Horace's suitcases out to the car in early 1964. No fooling, she means it. She is going, good-bye, to get the house ready for us. Becksie's got the twins on stools, and she's giving them haircuts. Cyrus has a bowl on his head, but Caroline's just getting a good trim for her long hair. Mama used to give us haircuts, but Becksie's just as good only bossier, so Mama handed over the scissors.

Emmett loads the suitcases into the trunk, and his straw blond hair gets plastered to his skull in the rain. I've given up trying to make him talk to me in the old easy way, and Mama says, "Livy Two, what you did scared him real bad. He drove around East Tennessee for two days looking for you and Myrtle. Are you aware of that?"

"How about him running off to work at Ghost Town last year? I forgave him."

"He'll come around. You'll see. In his own time. He's very sensitive, Emmett is."

Maybe if you call a boy or even a man "sensitive," that gives them permission to act all mean and ornery instead of forgive folks. Only that seems to me a pitiful excuse.

Watching Emmett pack up Grandma Horace, I do see a change in him for the better—maybe not toward me, but it's as if living away up on Buck Mountain with Uncle Buddy marked him in a deep and permanent way. Now he's not in such a fired-up hurry to race off to Hollywood. He seems to prefer being home around the little ones and Daddy. He's even carved out a table and chairs for Gentle's whistle pig family, so they'll feel like they got a home after we move. That's what he told Gentle, and this has eased her a tiny bit, but she loves her whistle pigs, and I dread the day we really have to go and she will have to say good-bye to them.

"You ready to go home, Mother?" Mama calls from inside the house.

"Ready as I'll ever be." Grandma Horace steps out onto the porch in her traveling hat and coat and lace-up brown shoes. "Come say good-bye to your grandmother, children." She waits there as everybody lines up to shake hands good-bye, since Grandma Horace is not a hugging grandmother. The twins wave good-bye from their haircutting stools, trying not to cry. They almost can't remember a time when she wasn't with us. Grandma Horace says, "Enough sniffling. We'll all be back together soon enough. Gentle, tie your shoe."

"I don't know how yet."

"You can make an attempt."

So Gentle squats down and starts trying to tie her shoelace.

"Listen here." Grandma Horace gazes at us through her good hazel eye, but she wears her sapphire glass eye—the one she saves for trips. "You children will mind your mother and father. You will mind them while I'm getting the house ready for your arrival. Is that clear? Remember, you're going to love Enka. I'll take you to Asheville to see the symphony, to the theater, and"—her one good eye falls on Becksie chopping away at the twins' hair—"to get professional haircuts. You'll get some culture and religion if I have to shove it down your throats, understood? And finally, Jessie and Tom, it is my wish that y'all start taking these children to church again on a regular basis. It's one hour a week out of your lives. Surely you can spare an hour for the Lord Jesus Christ. We'll be going regularly in Enka, mark my words."

Daddy walks out on the porch and says, "You leaving today, Mother Horace?"

"I'm going home, Tom. You'll be joining me soon enough. Now if my brother comes sniffing around asking for money or a handout, do not encourage him. Do not! This family is poor as Job's turkey as it is."

Myrtle Anne comes outside with her schoolbag. "I have an announcement. I want to go with you, Grandma

Horace. Today. I'll even go to church with you, and you won't have to beg me. Livy Two got me used to going new places, so I'll try Enka next. I want to get started with my new life right away."

Grandma Horace says, "No. Nobody is coming with me today. I'll have my hands full readying the house. Now Emmett is driving me, and I need Jessie and Olivia to do some cleaning. Lord knows how my renters left things. But I don't need a bunch of kids running loose at my house."

Gentle runs her fingers over Grandma Horace's face. "I love you, Grandma Horace," she says, and hugs her tight around the neck, even though Grandma Horace prefers handshakes.

Cyrus and Caroline shake her hand. "Good-bye, Grandma Horace."

Finally, Mama comes out of the house, ready to go too. Becksie follows holding Baby Tom-Bill, Appelonia tagging along after her. "We'll be fine here, Mama. I'll watch the kids. Jitters can help me, right, Jitters?"

"Myrtle Anne, for the hundredth time!" Jitters glowers from the porch swing.

"All right, Miss Sensitive!" Becksie hides a grin. "'Myrtle Anne' will help me."

Emmett honks the horn. Grandma Horace hoists herself into the front seat, while Mama and me slide into the backseat. I guess I really don't mind going to Enka-

Stinka and doing some cleaning. I want to lay my eyes on the snowball bushes even though I know it's the dead of winter and they won't be in bloom. Will her tree house be there? I want to see for myself what the future holds and just how awful it's bound to be.

"No fair!" Myrtle Anne stomps her foot. "I want to come along too! I beg you!"

I call from the backseat, "No, you can't! Quit making it harder on everybody."

Cyrus calls, "How is Myrtle Anne making it harder on everybody else?"

Myrtle Anne yells, "I'm not making it harder. It's a free country, and I get to say what I want." Then she does the most unforgivable thing of all—the thing that will forever make her *Tattletale Jitters*. "You think you're so smart, Livy Two," she yells, her cat's-eye glasses sparkling. "But why don't you tell the truth for once. Tell Mama how you've been reading all of us her girlhood diary—pages and pages like bedtime stories. And it's the best book I ever read. Mama, you were a real fun girl—even if you're not so much fun now. You were real fun once."

Emmett puts the car in drive, but Mama says in a low voice, "Turn off the car."

I inch away as far as I can in the backseat, but I'm still in smacking distance.

Grandma Horace says, "Never mind, Jessie. Take me home to Enka."

Mama calls, "Hold on. I want to know what you're talking about, Myrtle Anne."

Big blabbermouth holds her hand over her mouth now, knowing she has said way too much. I shake my fist out the window at her, but Grandma Horace says, "There is no call for high drama here. Jessie, I gave Olivia your diary from when you were a child. I found it months ago. You were her age when you wrote it, and the way she loves stories, I thought it would mean something special to her."

"You gave her what?" Mama's voice sounds like she's tiptoeing on glass.

"You didn't want your girlhood things. You wanted to leave them in the past where they belonged. You said so yourself. So I passed on a family heirloom."

"My diary? You gave my daughter my diary? When Papa . . . You had no right."

"I had every right, Jessie Horace Weems. You left it all behind to jump-start your life with Tom Weems, forgetting everything you ever were to move out to the sticks, living a hand-to-mouth existence with a musician husband. Well, you can't leave the past behind as much as you want to. Your children have a right to know who you are."

"With my permission, Mother. I'm thirty-one years old, not a child." Mama whips around and looks at me.

"Did you read it, Livy Two? Answer me. And share it?"

I don't answer. I study my fingers, casting about for a lie. Nothing.

"Did you read my diary and share it? Answer me." Mama's teeth are chattering.

I don't look up. "Yes, I did. I wanted my own sisters and brothers to face the facts of who you are, who you were . . . You wrote a real good story, Mama."

Emmett says, "Law, can I drive now, please?" But nobody answers him.

Mama takes a deep breath. "Where is it?"

"Here." I take it out from under my shirt and hand it to her. "I carry it with me. I kept it with me all the way to Nashville and back. I almost lost it when it was in my guitar case, but that faker blind man dropped it, and I got it back. Me and Jitters had to go chasing down pages in the snow, but we put it back together."

Mama takes it from me, touching the red cover easy and careful-like. The cover is cracked with creases and years, but it's almost as big as a notebook. She speaks to Grandma Horace. "How could you? Without even asking me?"

But Grandma Horace is sitting ramrod straight, not bending a centimeter.

Again, Emmett asks, "What's the big deal, Mama? Livy's right. It was real good."

Finally, Emmett is taking my side, so I say, "Seeing your birds, Mama, and learning about Grandpa Cal Horace and shape-note singing and Miss Amelia and being lonesome and your polite-girl face. It's our history too, Mama."

Grandma Horace says, "See! What did I tell you?"

Mama says, "You always have to be right, don't you, Mother? Always."

"Do you think I enjoy the burden of always being right, Jessie? I'd be more than happy to share the load, believe you me."

Mama puts the diary in her purse. "Emmett, take my mother home. Now." Mama slaps the tears out of her eyes as Emmett starts the car up again. "Drive us to Enka."

Myrtle Anne stands wistful on the porch, but Becksie comes up behind her and puts her arm around her shoulders. Baby Tom-Bill climbs right into Myrtle Anne's arms. Appelonia sits on the steps next to Gentle, who holds one of the whistle pigs, listening to every word. "Bye, Grandma Horace," she says, and the twins cry, "Bye." Then Cyrus calls, "When are we moving into your house, Grandma Horace? Sooner or later?"

Daddy stands there watching when Louise runs out of the house with a painting in her arms. She's got it covered up in plastic so it won't get wet with rain. "It's your going-away present, Grandma Horace. I finished it a few days ago. Hope you like it."

"Thank you, Louisiana." Then Grandma Horace snaps at the sad kids collected on the porch. "Now go on inside. You'll be joining me in the land of Enka, not Outer Mongolia!" But nobody listens. They won't bid her farewell from inside.

Emmett drives off down the gravel driveway, the car dipping and rising over the ruts and gullies in the road. I am tempted to ask Mama if I can read some more of her diary while we drive to Enka, but I know better. The two women in the car, mother and daughter, don't speak the whole thirty miles to Enka. On the Mile Straight, we pass the Candler Furniture Store, Candler Market, Candler Feed & Supply Store, and the Miami Motel & Restaurant, which looks sad, sad, sad. When we drive by the Hot Dog King, I think how good it would be to eat a big old hot dog with ketchup and mustard. Finally, we drive right past American Enka, the plant where Grandpa Cal worked, and not two blocks farther, we pull up to the brick house on Orchard Lane. It looks much smaller than I remember from when I was a little kid. Mama makes Emmett and me stay in the car. She carries Grandma Horace's suitcases up to the door. "I'm supposed to do some cleaning, remember?" I call out the window, but both Mama and Grandma Horace ignore me. Plans have clearly changed since the diary secret was revealed. Emmett and me can't hear what they say, though sharp words are exchanged between the two of them. I say to him, "Hey, look up yonder in the tree there."

"What?"

"Look at the tree branch." I point to what's sticking out—Mama's tree house—then I can't help it. It's hardly raining anymore. I jump out of the car and climb up the chunks of wood steps hammered into the tree. In a flash, I'm sitting in Mama's tree house, smiling down at Emmett. "Come on up," I tell him. "It's great. There's a window and an old stool. You can still see some of the red paint on the door."

Emmett looks toward the house. "Better not."

"Why not? It's Mama's tree house from when she was a little girl."

Emmett whistles. "I can see it fine from here." But he cranes his neck to get a better look. The wood is old and battered but definitely sturdy even after all these years.

Mama runs back to the car in the rain and gets in the front seat, but rolls down her window when I call, "Hey, Mama. Look at me."

She gives me a quick glance and says, "I want you to come down. That thing is as old as the hills, and you could get hurt." She doesn't even look interested. What's wrong with her? What's wrong with all the grown-ups? I'm so tired of the whole bunch of them.

"But it's your tree house, Mama. You loved making

it. You loved it. You were a fun girl, and look what happened to you. Your own daddy showed you how to build it. And you never said a word about it. You always say the past is in the past. But sometimes it's not. Sometimes it's right in front of your face. Come on up! Please?"

"Olivia, you get in this car right now, I am warning you! I've had all I can take today." Her face is pale and scared—as if it hurts her too much to look back too far.

Reluctantly, I climb down and get in the car. I wave to Grandma Horace, and she waves too, but there will be no cleaning today or playing in the tree house. Mama makes Emmett drive out of Enka without looking back. She's a private person, and her privacy's been sorely violated. But how can a good-bye be so quick?

On the way toward home, Mama puts on lipstick and pushes at her hair to give it some shape. Then she says, "Emmett, I need you to do something for me. I want you to drive me to Champion Paper Mill. It's just right down the road. Not so fast, son."

"I know where it is." Emmett heads west down Highway 19.

"What for, Mama?" I ask.

"Never mind, there's just something I have to do, and I have to do it now. Slow down, Emmett—roads are slick as anything today."

"Daddy drove a lot faster than this when he was on the road." He hits a puddle and a wall of water sprays another car.

"Slow down, I'm telling you, or else I'm driving. Understand me?"

"Yes ma'am." Emmett slows down a little. I want to ask her why we're going to Champion this minute, but I don't feel like getting my head bit off anymore today. Mama's eyes are fixed on the road ahead. Emmett turns on the radio to a burst of Little Jimmy Dickens, but Mama reaches over and flicks it off in a flash. "I have to think. I have to concentrate." Then she mutters under her breath, "Old woman. Always right. She'd argue with Christ on the Cross if the mood struck her."

"What are you saying, Mama?" I ask, but she ignores me.

Emmett takes the signs to the Champion Paper Mill like he knows exactly where he's going. I guess he does. It's a pretty famous landmark around here. You can smell it before you can see it. We pull into the parking lot. Smoke pours out of the paper mill and fills the sky with a rotten-egg smell where a logging truck hauls a bunch of fresh-cut trees past us. Without a word, Mama goes inside. We stay still, waiting. "What's she gonna do, you think?" I ask Emmett.

"How should I know?"

"I just asked a simple question."

"Well, quit asking. I don't have all the answers. Shoot, I wish I could get me a job here. Lots of boys my age work steady. Paper mill is steadier than Ghost Town."

"Thought you were going off to Hollywood to seek fame and fortune?"

"Can't leave Daddy right now. Or Mama. Not yet." He sounds matter-of-fact.

"I should have sold my songs back in Nashville. I should have tried harder."

Emmett groans with disgust. "I can't believe you're still even thinking like that. Didn't you learn a thing watching Daddy dream big and not get jack for it?"

"So I should quit? Live a life where I never try? Moses from Memphis told me—"

But Emmett interrupts, "I don't want to hear about your dang old Moses from Memphis. You never should have gone in the first place, and you know it."

I don't know what to say. I watch the raindrops streaming down the window. Finally, after more than thirty minutes, the car door opens and Mama slides back inside, flushed with excitement. "I've done it. I'm facing facts. I've got all these children and not near enough time in the world to knit scarves and baby blankets to support y'all. If all goes well, they'll offer me a job. Now, not a word to Grandma Horace."

"Heck, why didn't you let me go inside and apply too?" Emmett starts up the car.

Mama says, "No, Emmett, not yet. You can work on Saturdays, selling pulpwood the way men do around here, but that is all I'm allowing. I want you back in school after the last year of not going at all. I mean it. You need an education."

"Do you want to work at Champion? Is it your heart's desire, Mama?" I ask.

"When you get grown up, Livy Two, life can quit having a thing to do with 'want.' It won't be easy, but I think we can make it work if I can figure out how to do it."

"Does this mean we're moving to Canton instead of Enka?"

"Of course we're moving to Enka, eventually. But after what Mother pulled, giving away my private girlhood thoughts without asking, telling me how to raise my kids, offering unsolicited advice at a regular clip—I'm flat wore out is all. Your grandma may think she is right about some things, but she's not right about everything. She is not. If they give me this job, we'll be able to pay the landlady back rent, and we won't be beholden to a soul, including blood. Now don't ask me any more questions—we will move to Enka very soon, but I want to try this first."

"But who'll watch the babies if you work full-time?" I ask her, but Mama don't answer. "Mama?"

"Quit! No more questions, I told you. I'm thinking!" Mama bites a fingernail, her mind calculating on how in the world to pull this off. I stare at the mill smokestacks, twisted, white tornado shapes. On the way home, I see a sign that says: JESUS CHRIST IS THE LORD OF HAYWOOD COUNTY. If he is, I sure wish he'd make my daddy all well again, so Mama wouldn't have to work at the paper mill. I don't even know what the right decision is anymore—Enka? Maggie Valley?

"Mama, just one more thing?" I ask, but Emmett answers, "Now what?"

I pay him no mind. "Could I at least finish reading your diary to the little ones, Mama? I've already faced facts the way you said, and I know I've lost my guitar forever, but do I have to lose your story too?"

"Livy Two." Mama shoots me that warning look.

But I don't care. "And while we're on the subject of facing facts, Mama, I have another question. Why couldn't you even look up to see your tree house that Grandpa Cal showed you how to build? Do you want to forget every single thing about the past?"

With an exasperated sigh, Mama hands me her diary. "Go on. Read it all if it'll make you happy. Keep reading it to everybody the way you're doing. Maybe you'uns will learn something from it, though Lord knows, I don't know what. The past won't change a thing."

CHAPTER SEVENTEEN

Goose Boy Betrayal

THOUGH I HAVE every intention of apologizing to Miss Attickson, I keep putting it off. I don't know how to even begin. Now it seems like I've said sorry to everyone except the most important one of all. I start a dozen letters to her, but they sound awful. I try to leave a message for her at the main library office, but I hang up the second I hear, "Haywood Public Library Services. May I help you, please?"

Toward the end of school one day in late January, Mr. Pickle hands back our papers that we wrote on the Seven Wonders of the World. On mine, he wrote, "Nice job." I take the paper and look at his wedding ring finger, which is empty. In a few months it won't be. How can Miss Attickson even love him the least bit? It's a mystery to me, but I'm relieved that Mr. Pickle (with his clogged sinuses and ginger lozenges) has stayed out of my business, not questioning my motives or feelings of remorse and not holding a grudge that I dragged his fiancée into my world of deceit. As far as I'm concerned, I'm just another seventh-grade student to him—nothing special at all.

The final bell of the day rings, and I see the bookmobile pull into the parking lot. My heart starts to pound. Today is the day. I've ignored it the last few times, but I can't wait any longer. Louise and me head outside to the school bus, but she gives me a nudge. "Go on. Do it."

"I am. You don't have to tell me."

"Then just do it."

"I will, Louise. Stop pestering me."

She sighs and goes on ahead to the bus, where Becksie and Myrtle Anne and the twins are already waiting. I walk over toward the bookmobile, but I don't go inside. Maybe too much time has passed to beg her pardon? I study the ground where the snow's all melted and gone slushy like dirty ice cream run over with tire tracks.

Becksie, Louise, Myrtle Anne, Caroline, and Cyrus watch from the window of the bus. I turn my back to them so I don't have to see their faces. My hands feel sweaty, and I might throw up. This is the hardest apology of my life. What if she hates me forever?

Myrtle Anne calls, "You want me to go in there with you, Livy Two?"

"No, I do not, thank you very much."

"Are you sure?"

"Yes, I'm sure. I can do it myself."

Becksie yells, "Stop being so dramatic—you're just trying to get attention."

"Wait a second." Myrtle Anne gets off the bus and races over to me. Then she says, "Lean down."

"What?"

"Just do it."

I try to be patient and lean down—she puts her acorn necklace around my neck. "For good luck, Livy Two. I want it back, but I bet Miss Attickson don't hate you too much." She runs back to get on the bus. Rusty Frye leans out of the back window and says, "Hey Loretta Lynn, you gonna beg for your job back? Gonna lick the bookmobile lady's boots? Please, oh please, can I get my old job back? I'm real sorry I run off to Nashville seeking fame and fortune!" Cackling comes from inside the bus. . . . I kick a few rocks and wish a violent death on Rusty Frye, where the vultures pick his bones clean.

The bus driver, Pokey McPherson, honks the horn. "Knock it off back there, Frye, or you're walking. Hey, you coming or not, Weems?"

"Not today," I tell him.

"Suit yourself." Pokey honks for some other kids to get on the bus. I can't wait another minute to do what needs doing. I push open the door to the bookmobile, but what greets my eyes is both a shock and surprise. Miss Attickson doesn't notice me at first because she's busy ordering around her new employee, Randal, the goose boy. She says, "Randal, please shelve the health books. Then check in the returns and record the fines."

Randal limps over to a shelf with some books, and they both see me at the same time. Clancy, the goose, helps Randal by toting some of the books on his feathery back. Both Clancy and Randal look absolutely at home in the bookmobile, so I know this is not their first day—not by a long shot. Why didn't somebody tell me that Miss Attickson had hired the goose boy in place of me? Tears sting my eyes, but I blink them away quick. I won't bust out crying for this trio. Clancy honks at me. *Honk. Honk.*

Randal says, "Be quiet, Clancy. Hey, Livy Two."

Miss Attickson keeps quiet—waiting for me to make the first move. My leg starts shaking, and I can't hardly hold it still no matter how hard I grind my heel into the floor. From somewhere nearby, a dog starts barking and then howling. I can't concentrate, so I blurt out, "I come to see you."

"Yes, I can see that. Did you want your final paycheck? It's here somewhere."

"No, I didn't come about that. I mean, it's not why I'm here." My voice trembles.

Randal says, "Miss Attickson, would you mind if I went outside for some fresh air? Me and Clancy could use a breath of fresh air."

Miss Attickson says, "Go on, Randal."

And even though I hate and despise that goose boy for stealing my job, I am grateful that he makes himself scarce. The door clicks shut behind them, and Miss Attickson gets right to the point. "I thought I would see you before now. You came home from your disappearing act quite a while ago."

"Yes ma'am." I pick out a corner of her desk to stare at, and I notice it has a little torn piece of tape on it. It looks like it's been there a good long while.

"Care to explain?"

"Ma'am?"

"Why didn't you come to see me before now?"

I focus on the ripped tape, not moving my eyes. If I can keep all my attention on that corner, then I won't cry. "Well, after I got your letter, I reckon I was too ashamed. I never meant—I never meant to scare you like I did."

"What did you think would happen, Olivia, leaving the way you did with your little sister? Vanishing into thin air?"

"I thought that I had the whole thing figured out. I would go to Nashville, sell my songs, and come home and buy our house to get Madame Cherry Hat off our backs."

"Who?"

"The landlady."

"I see."

"And then it got all mixed up—I mean, I guess you heard."

"Bits and pieces."

"And I was going to come see you to explain, but your letter scared me. I don't blame you—I betrayed you, no doubt. But I thought I'd be a success—and everybody would understand. Even you. But I failed in Nashville, so I had to come back with bad news. And—well—I'm sorry. I guess that's it. I am very sorry for what I did. We're supposed to be moving to Enka real soon, so I want to say sorry, in case I . . ."

Miss Attickson sighs and begins organizing papers. She blows her nose, so I know she's feeling bad too. I stand there, waiting. Nothing. So I say real soft, "See you later, Miss Attickson."

"Wait. Olivia. Look, I'm sorry that I had to fire you. That was one of the hardest things I've ever had to do, but I had no choice. I felt betrayed by your actions. I thought we had an honest friendship where we could tell each other things. Was I wrong?"

I stop at the door, waiting. "Well, I couldn't tell you about Nashville. I'm sorry."

"At any rate, Randal is a good worker," she continues. "Loves books like you do."

"That's good." But I don't know what else to say. Our

sentences hit the air and fall flat. Our old easy way of talking is gone. Finally, I come right out and ask it. "You reckon I can still come to your wedding?"

Miss Attickson gasps. "What kind of question is that? If you didn't come to my wedding, then I'd be really upset with you. I want all of you Weems children there. I'd like you to read something or sing. I would be very sad if you didn't come, Olivia."

"All right. Just checking." I feel hot and unsteady. I can't keep staring at the tape stuck to the corner of her desk.

"I heard your grandmother moved back to Enka already."

"Yes ma'am. She did. She's waiting for us to join her, but Daddy don't want to go, and Mama, well . . . Anyhow, it's all up in the air. But Grandma Horace calls every night to check on our progress. And to remind us of how much we'd better be missing her, I think. She gave me my mama's diary from the 1940s—full of her girlhood stories. Mama drew birds. She was a member of the Audubon Society back when she was little."

"Was she? That's a real gift. Did your mother mind you reading it?"

"At first—that was a fight—but she's come around. A little."

"Have you read *The Diary of Anne Frank*?"

"No ma'am."

"I'm going to order it for you. I just checked it out to a child over near Fine's Creek. I need some more copies. But it's by a Jewish girl who would have been about your mother's age. She wrote her diary during World War II, hiding in Holland in a place called the Secret Annex from the Germans."

"Did she get to come out when it was over?"

"No, the war was still going on when the family was discovered and sent to concentration camps."

"I want to read it," I tell her, but I don't look up at her.

"And here is your last paycheck. I could have sent it, but I hoped you'd come."

There's something so final about the words "last paycheck." I don't even want to see it, so I say, "Miss Attickson, about that? Would you please give it to Mathew the Mennonite when you see him? I'll sign it so he can cash it, but I want to keep paying him for all his work on the smokehouse. I'd rather do it this way. He'll know."

"I can do that."

"I'm learning to face facts. I don't know if you know this, but I lost my guitar in Nashville, and then I came home and found out I'd lost my job too." My voice tears a little, but I have to say it. "Miss Attickson, I didn't run off in order to make things hard for you—I was trying to do right by my family. It just turned out wrong." I breathe in the smell of all the books to stay calm—it's one of the finest smells in the whole world.

"Olivia?"

"Ma'am?"

"Even though I was furious with you, you're a brave girl—full of heart. I hope you have many more grand adventures in your life—when you're older. And I hope you'll always come back and tell me about them. Will you do that?"

I give a quick nod and turn and leave the bookmobile, for I can't stay another moment. I pull open the door and leap down the steps past Randal and Clancy, and the line of kids he's been holding at bay to give Miss Attickson and me privacy. I start running toward home, and I race by Mathew the Mennonite driving past me in his truck. Laika is sitting up front like she's queen of the world. I call to him, "Hey, Mr. Mathew, Miss Attickson has got something for you!" I keep running so that anyone who sees me would never suspect I been crying. I vow that these are the last stinking tears I will cry over Nashville, a stolen guitar, and a near lost friendship.

That night at supper, Mama says, "Well, I got some big news to tell you children. The Champion Paper Mill called. I got a job. As secretary. Starting tomorrow." She means this for us all to hear, but she looks directly at Becksie. "So I have a plan in mind."

Becksie puts down her fork without a word. "What? Why are you looking at me?"

"Becksie, Daddy can't watch Gentle, Appelonia, and Baby Tom-Bill on his own. He just can't. Emmett's going back to high school. You're the oldest girl. I hate to say it, but the oldest has to make sacrifices."

"What?" Becksie picks up her fork and starts stabbing at her beans.

"I want you to leave school for just a few months until we get back on our feet."

There is gasp from the little ones, and Myrtle Anne says, "You want Becksie to leave school? How will she do her homework?"

Cyrus asks, "Won't she get in big trouble?"

Gentle says, "I don't need to be watched. I know my way around just fine. And I can help Daddy."

But Mama shakes her head. "You'uns kids can bring Becksie her homework to her each day, so she won't get behind. She's not the first child to leave school to help out. And it's only temporary."

Becksie's face is white. "You expect me to stay home to watch the babies instead of going to school?"

"Just for now is what I'm telling you," Mama says. "I'll talk to the school. It's allowed at age fifteen under special circumstances. And it's only until we move to Enka or Daddy can go back to work, right, Tom? Whichever comes first."

Daddy nods like he's been told this over and over, but Louise says, "Why can't I stay home, Mama? I hate school, and Becksie's Maggie Queen."

But Mama says, "No, she is the oldest girl. She stays. And now we'll have money and benefits. We'll be able to get out of debt. Do you know what a relief that will be?"

But we don't know, not really, and Becksie just sets there trying not to cry. Then Myrtle Anne drops the firebomb. "Becksie, since you can't come to school right now, could I be the Maggie Queen in your place? Just a stand-in so the kids won't forget you?"

That does it. Our big sister shoves her plate away from her and runs away from the table. We give Myrtle Anne black looks, but all she says is, "What? She can't do it right now. I'm just stating the facts. Besides, this is only temporary, right, Mama? Right?"

Mama says, "Myrtle Anne, eat your supper. Every one of you, eat up."

Daddy says, "That's right. I guess we'd better eat."

And so we do, but Mama goes off to check on Becksie, who yells, "I'm fine, Mama! Please leave me alone!" from behind the closed bedroom door. Daddy looks down at his food, but he don't eat; it's like he wants to say something but can't figure what exactly. Then he says, "It never rains but it . . . it . . ."

"Pours, Daddy, pours," Myrtle Anne supplies the answer.

"I was going to say that." Daddy reaches for a biscuit and slathers it with honey.

Cyrus asks, "Then how come you didn't?"

After I get the little ones ready for bed, I read them more of Mama's diary. Louise and Myrtle Anne gather round, too, but Becksie's buried under the covers, a sad lump in the bed. And Emmett has the new *Legion of Super-Heroes* comic book, so he's more interested in Saturn Girl and the planet Titan than Enka 1944.

Before I start reading the diary, I hear Daddy in the front room playing the banjo. Then the phone rings, and Mama answers it. It's Grandma Horace calling up like clockwork to check on the state of things, and Mama talks real formal and stiff to her, like Grandma Horace is some stranger checking up on us. "We're doing just fine. And how are you? Are you taking care of yourself? I'm not sure yet. No. Yes. No. Not yet. No. I appreciate your concern. I have to go now. Good-bye." I notice that Mama doesn't tell Grandma Horace the news that she told us at supper.

January 5, 1944
Dear Grasshopper,

A cedar waxwing is a bird that is crazy for fruit. There is a word for it too. "Frugivorous!" Isn't that a fine word? This bird loves fruit so much it can even get drunk and die from eating too much fermented fruit. I told Mother about the cedar waxwing, and she said that if Uncle Buddy were a bird, that's what he would be.

I've written to the Audubon Society about starting a magazine for kids on birds in the mountains. I'd call it "Jessie's Smoky Mountain Music Notes" because each birdcall is like a perfect little music note—and when they're all singing together, it's like little melodies. What do you think of that? I like the name a lot. I could write all sorts of stories on birds in the Smokies. They include red-winged blackbirds, yellow warblers, chimney swifts . . . and golden eagles fly in the fall. I sure wish there was a magazine because most kids think birds are all the same but they're not.

Today I went with Mother across the street to our neighbor's house, because the lady who lives there is as old as the hills with skin like oatmeal that's been sitting there too long. Her name is Mrs. Buford. Mother says it's our Christian duty to help folks. The dishes were piled up high in Mrs. Buford's sink, and the old lady was listening to one of her stories on the radio. Mother offered to do the dishes and the old lady said, "All right." Then she looked at me and said, "Come listen to my stories with me." It was about a doctor with a nurse named Judy, but the news came on about Hitler, and Mrs. Buford turned it off and spit at the radio.

Then I heard Mother scream, and ran to the kitchen. She pointed at the edge of the sink, where I saw the biggest spi-

der of my life. At least the size of a silver dollar—and next to it was an egg sac about the size of a fifty-cent piece. Mother kept saying, "He, he, he!" And I think she was trying to say, "HELP!" But she couldn't get the word out. Then she said, "Wolf Spider." I felt the shivers go through me. Even the name "wolf spider" sounded deadly.

I didn't know how to kill it, so I scooped it up in a napkin and ran outside and dropped it in the marigolds. Next I came back inside and got the egg sac and ran it back to the marigolds too. Mother sat down at the table and had a drink of water and caught her breath. Then she said, "Let's go home." And we did. I told Papa all about it, and then I read him some of Huckleberry Finn, and he went to sleep.

Yours truly, Jessie Horace

P.S. I dreamed of millions of wolf spider babies hatching in the marigolds.

Cyrus yells, "Wow! Wolf spiders. That's the best one yet."

Caroline shudders and says, "I don't like wolf spiders. No, thank you."

Gentle says, "Read another, another!"

"Not tonight, tomorrow." I tuck them under the covers as Myrtle Anne calls from her bed, "Hey, did you say sorry to Miss Attickson, Livy Two? Did she forgive you?"

"Yeah."

"Told you she would. Didn't I tell you? I told you so. Next time, you shouldn't be so scared. Next time, you should just march up to the person and tell them you're sorry. Now give me back my acorn necklace, thank you. And have you thought of how you're going to get another guitar? You've hardly written any songs since Nashville."

"I think I know that, Myrtle Anne! I've been thinking about a new guitar."

"Do you think you're the first musician to lose an instrument? Not likely."

Becksie pokes her head up. "I am trying to sleep. I've got a long day tomorrow, since I won't be going to school like a normal girl. I'll be stuck here like some slave. It's not fair. Livy Two and Louise, you'd better not forget my homework or I'll wear you out, got it? I'm not about to get behind even if I'm stuck here with green noses and dirty diapers."

Louise says, "I won't forget, Becksie. And we can trade off anytime you want."

But Becksie just turns over in her bed, ignoring us all.

CHAPTER EIGHTEEN

Hey, Loretta!

THE CHAMPION PAPER Mill asked Mama to be a secretary, since she graduated from school with good grades and she knows the boss from high school. Mama can't hardly believe it. Neither can the rest of us, but it turns out that she was in a high-school play *Romeo and Juliet* with her boss in Enka. He wasn't her boss then. He was some skinny kid named Charlie who ran the light board. Mama played Juliet. Daddy was in the play, too, only he was in the chorus on banjo. It makes me think of Rusty Frye or Billy O'Connor. Could they ever be my boss? I'd like to die before I ever let the likes of them order me around.

Daddy has lots of questions. "Why are you doing it again? When?" He asks the same questions over and over again, until finally, out of patience, Mama snaps, "I'm doing this for us, Tom. I'm taking this job at Champion for the children—I'll work for a year, and then you'll be back on your feet, and we'll be all right. Becksie will go back to school—I'm not going to sacrifice her education, but I need these months to get ahead until you're well, and you will be. Look how far you've come. This is going to be hard, but I have to be the breadwinner until you're ready to start auditioning again. It's the right thing to do."

"But I want to work now, Jessie Weems."

"The doctor says you still need more time."

"More time for what?"

"To recover your wits, I guess."

"I repent that."

"Resent, Tom. The word is 'resent.' "

"That's what I said, by God, that's what I said."

It is *not* what he said, but Daddy's face is gloomy, which means he is in no mood to be corrected by Mama or by a kid.

Mama will be gone five days a week, seven A.M. to four P.M. It means we'll have a real salary coming in and trips to the dentist and doctor. But nobody really knows what to feel about her working full-time. Except for Becksie. She makes her feelings heard loud and clear, slamming things around. After four, Becksie will be off the clock to do homework. It's not the best plan. Except we all know that Daddy can't watch the kids on his own. If Grandma Horace were here, she would never have stood for this—but Mama's made us swear not to tell her. She says that we're to handle our problems and our family in our own way, without Enka casting down judgments from on high. The move seems to get pushed further away, and I don't know what to think.

Right before she starts work, I ask Mama, "What about the dumping and the pollution in the Pigeon River? Folks say Champion is one of the causes. Did you know that? I seen chunks of black and brown and foamy white floating down the river, and cars always need new paint jobs on account of how the pollution just tears up car paint. That's what Miss Attickson told me. Grandpa Cal did die of cancer, which is on the rise, and—"

Mama says, "Good Lord, not you and Miss Attickson too. All I know is that I got a family to feed, and I intend to do it. I'm a secretary. I'm not standing at the river's edge pouring a bucket of chemicals into the water."

"Yeah, but you work there, and so—"

"Set the table," Mama roars, her hands trembling. And I do. I set the table.

After her first day at the mill, Gentle asks Mama, "Was it fun?" And so Mama pulls Gentle onto her lap and says, "Fun? Well, let's see, I answered the phone. I learned about paperwork and how the payroll works. I learned that my boss likes his coffee with milk and sugar. I answered the phone some more. I learned about filing, which means what papers go where and so forth. And you don't smell the paper-mill smell after a while. It becomes something else."

Gentle's lower lip trembles. "But I missed you all day. It's too long."

"Hey, what does it become, that stinky smell, Mama?" Cyrus wants to know.

Caroline stands on the back of Mama's chair on a lower rung. "Do you like your boss? Is he nice to you? Is he a yeller? I hope he's not a yeller."

"No, he's very professional and no-nonsense, so I like that. But it sure feels funny being in an office all day." As she's talking, Gentle hiccups a sob and won't let Mama go. "Now, no tears." Mama kisses her head. "We'll get used to it, I promise. Okay?"

Daddy holds both Appelonia and Baby Tom-Bill on his knee. "Well," he says, "we had a good day, right?" He looks at Becksie like he's asking a question. Becksie sighs like she don't even have the energy to get mad. "Well, I washed clothes and chased after the babies. Then I swept the floor and put the beans on—I am mighty sick of beans, let me tell you. Pots and pots of beans. When I grow up if I *never* have to look at another bean again, it will be just fine with me. So yes, I guess Daddy is right, it was mostly a good day. We made a cake to celebrate your first day as a working woman, Mama." She shows us a lopsided chocolate cake.

Gentle dries her tears. "I frosted it. Becksie let me. It got tilted in the woodstove."

The worker bus takes Mama to the Champion Paper Mill in Canton every morning before we even wake up. Emmett goes to high school during the week in Waynesville, which he says is all right—"Not my favorite place in the world, though"—but he works on Saturdays, cutting trees that have no rot or decay to gather for pulpwood, and that brings in five dollars a week or so. He has to make sure the trees are the right size, or the paper mill won't buy them from him. He loads it all up in the backseat of the Rambler. It's only a winter job, because he's determined to be a full-time gunslinger at Ghost Town this summer—no night-watchman duties. Good thing workers get to ride the chairlift up to work for free. Maybe I could get me a job there, too, at the Mad Hatter or Custard's Last Stand.

We all help out a lot more at home now that Grandma Horace is gone, and I swear, it's beyond tiring. I don't see how Becksie keeps up with Baby Tom-Bill, Appelonia, Gentle, and Daddy all day. But she's doing it with her "game-face on," according to Louise, though to me she's more like a pressure cooker just a-waiting to blow. She makes Daddy clean the kitchen, and she's taught him how to scrub the counters and the floor. He does a good job. It's too cold to be outside much yet, so Daddy plays the banjo for the babies and follows Becksie's orders. And Becksie does her homework after school. She goes out to the smokehouse in her coat with a blanket and studies every single subject, and when she's done, she gives Louise a folder of her homework to take to school. Yet I notice that as the days pass, Becksie is not actually speaking to Mama, and it's curious to me—Mama not speaking to Grandma Horace and Becksie not speaking to Mama.

Emmett and me take turns getting breakfast; Mama does supper; Louise and Myrtle Anne make lunches. I still milk Birdy Sweetpea, but Emmett chops the wood now. The twins clean the front room and feed the chickens. Gentle dusts the furniture and straightens the books and tends to her whistle pigs that love her. We all take turns with Daddy watching the babies, who can make a mess quick as anything, pulling books off the shelves, tipping over the bag of cornmeal. Baby Tom-Bill has a bad habit of taking off his diaper. Both Appelonia and Baby Tom-Bill follow Uncle Hazard around, who ducks under a chair when he sees them headed his way. Appelonia climbs on top of everything like she's practicing to be a future high-wire artist. Sometimes it feels like our family is one big music composition, with all the notes playing their different tunes, but if one note is out of place, the whole piece sounds wrong. Like an F-sharp and G on the piano, which are Becksie and Mama right now, and, to be honest, Mama and Daddy too. He can't wrap his head around why she's working at Champion when he feels it should be him with the real job. When she gets home from work, he follows her around. "I need a job at Champion too. Or someplace."

"Your job is to get better. The doctor said you'll be able to work again someday if you work on getting better now, which means flashcards, practicing the banjo, exercise."

"Someday! What the heck does someday mean? My memory's not so bad."

Mama says, "I'm too tired to argue, Tom. You are working by being home."

"I need to find my music again. I got to. No fooling, Jessie."

"And I've sent the check off to Clyde. We're catching up, Tom."

The phone rings, and Myrtle Anne answers it. "It's Grandma Horace."

Mama says, "Tell her I'm putting the babies to bed."

"Again?" Myrtle Anne asks, but she does it.

In between my chores, Daddy makes me listen to him play the banjo, and asks, "When do you think I'll be ready to audition in the land of Knoxville, where that grocer man has a radio show? What's his name again?"

"Cas Walker, Daddy. He throws chickens off roofs to

customers. Remember? The ones who catch them get to keep them."

"Yes, he lives in the land of Knoxville, where I played banjo for lettuce."

"A lettuce commercial is what you did."

"That's what I said. It used to be so easy. Easy as breathing. I want it back. Now."

"You got to keep trying." I clean Baby Tom Bill's face, which is covered with honey.

"I am trying. What do you think I'm doing? Casting flies?" he yells at me.

"Catching flies," Becksie corrects him.

Daddy stands up and walks out of the house, not quite slamming the door. I wish I could think of ways to help. I'm too young to drive, and Emmett's in school. How could we find a place for him to make music closer to home? It ain't realistic for him to go off to Knoxville when he's not ready to audition just yet. There, I said it—he's not ready.

One Saturday morning in early February, Louise and me head down Fie Top, swapping turns pulling the wagon to load up on essentials, plus a salt lick for Birdy Sweetpea. At the bottom of Fie Top Road at Highway 19, Rusty Frye rides by on his bike with a bunch of buddies. Even though I've seen them all at school, and they make jokes about me running off to Music City USA, they haven't bothered with me much—until now. Rusty Frye skids to a stop. *"Hey, it's Loretta. Sing us a song, Loretta! Or wait, are you Patsy or Dottie or Kitty or just Miss Nashville?"*

We keep walking, heads down. Louise says, "Ignore the possum breaths."

"Better make up your mind, Loretta! *Nashville wants to know*, right, boys?" Rusty hollers, clapping his hands. "Grand Ole Opry, whoooo!"

Louise stops, turns, and says, "You'uns can just shut up now! Go on, beat it!"

Rusty and his group of friends laugh and fall over each other like they're killing theirselves with the hilarity of the situation. Only Billy O'Connor hangs back, not joining in the fun, but not meeting my eye either. I reckon he can't help being spineless. Finally, he says, "Leave them alone," which irritates me, so I tell him, "We can fight our own battles, thank you." He blushes scarlet, but too bad. *You are the company you keep!*

"Hey, Loretta," Rusty yells, "are you a honky-tonk gal now?" More laughter erupts from his posse. They circle us with their bikes, closer.

"Fine, laugh it up, boys," Louise tells them, "but one day, my sister will be on the Grand Ole Opry, and where will you be? Pumping gas? Moonshining? Your pitiful lives are mapped out, but not hers and not mine."

Rusty gets ugly all at once. "You just think you're better than us, Louisiana Weems. All you Weemses think you're better than everybody. Got nothing and you are nothing, Tater and Turnip Girls!"

Billy O'Connor tugs on Rusty. "Come on, let's go. Let them alone."

"Leave off, Billy. Always defending them. Hey, Loretta, I bet they laughed at you in Nashville, didn't they?" Rusty gets in my face. "I bet they're still laughing."

And then I can't stand it. I leap on Rusty Frye and start whaling on him. *Pow, pow, pow!* From far away, I hear Louise call, "Livy Two! Quit!" But I am fast into the fight, and my hatred for this mean boy flames up like fire. "I don't think I'm better than you, Rusty—I know it!" One punch for George Flowers, another for Fletcher Partridge, another just for him! Blood spurts out of his nose. Good! How about another? *Pow!*

"Ow, get off, you girl! Get off!" He covers his face to duck my blows, but I'm way tougher than the likes of him—I am Athena in battle—Athena only fights when the situation is dire. *Punch!* "I am better than you, Rusty Frye, and don't you forget it."

Louise tries to pull me off him, but blood is in my own mouth. Damn him for making fun of me, and I don't care if God strikes me dead for thinking like that. Next thing I know, Emmett shows up out of nowhere in

Grandma Horace's Rambler, the back end loaded with pulpwood for his Saturday delivery to Canton. He pulls over and leaps out of the car, yanking me off Rusty Frye. "You knock it off, Livy Two! You're gonna hurt that boy!" He pins my arms back, but I wrench away to try to throw more punches. "He was by God asking for it. Let me go!"

"Behave yourself." Emmett holds me tight and looks at Rusty. "And you. You leave my sisters alone. I don't know what happened, but I'm betting she was provoked."

Rusty Frye stands up, wiping his bloody nose. "Boy-howdy, your sister is crazy. Crazy as a loon. Lock Loretta up at the loony bin! Nashville don't need no crazy singers."

"What did you say to me?" I holler.

"I said you're crazy as a loon! You can take that to the bank too!"

A few cars slow down to stare at the fuss, and Emmett yells at them, "What are you looking at, South Carolina? Bunch of tourists! Party is over."

Then I hear the sound of a familiar truck. I try to stand tall and strong like Athena, but Miss Attickson don't even spare us a glance.

"Go on and get out of here," Emmett tells the boys, and they don't argue, but Rusty can't help himself. Pedaling off, he shouts, "See you later, Crazy Loretta!"

The three of us stand there in silence as cars come down the mountain from Cherokee. Finally, Louise asks, "You all right?"

"Yeah, I'm okay." I kick at some gravel. "I guess it's always going to be this big joke to everybody that I went to Nashville to try to make it in the big time."

"Do it right next time, why don't you?" Emmett says. "Don't run off like a thief in the night, worrying folks. You hear me? Just say, 'I'm going to Nashville, like it or lump it.' Then folks won't have no call to be scared or make fun of you."

"Look who's talking?" Tears spark my eyes. "You run off to Ghost Town last year without looking back. So I'd quit talking so big if I were you."

"Yeah, but I didn't just vanish. I said where I was going right from the start."

"I thought I was doing right, Emmett."

"All right, but Livy Two, you couldn't have been more wrong."

Louise says, "I think she knows that by now, Emmett. Come on."

"That's right, I do," I inform my brother. "And I don't need you to tell me that over and over again. I knew it in George Flowers's office. I'm not a complete fool."

"Well, good! I'm glad to hear it." Emmett and Louise head inside the store, but I sit down on the steps to wait, hugging my knees. I'm still warm from the fight. Is it a terrible thing to say that it felt great to beat the holy living crap out of Rusty Frye? I close my eyes, rubbing my skinned elbows that ache from the fight. When I open my eyes again, they land on the beat-up building across the street that's been there forever. The sign in the broken window still says, FOR RENT. The words stick in my head. For Rent. I write down the phone number in my song notebook that I keep in my back pocket.

CHAPTER NINETEEN

For Rent

EMMETT AND LOUISE don't tell on me for beating up Rusty Frye when we get home, and I am grateful. On the way back, I make a decision. Since Mama won't tell us or Grandma Horace when exactly we're moving to Enka, I'm going to pretend we're staying right here in Maggie Valley; otherwise, life will just hang in limbo. No thanks. I go into the closet with the telephone, so I can have some privacy and call the number on the FOR RENT sign. It rings seven times, and finally a man answers. "Hello?"

"Yes sir, I'm calling about the building for rent in Maggie Valley."

"And for what business purpose do propose to use my property? How much are you willing to pay up front?" He sounds bossy, formal, and familiar all at the same time.

"That's what I want to talk about. I know how to get it to make money for you, so I could pay you more on the back end." Does that sound professional? In the least?

"Is this a child?"

I know the man's voice, but I can't place it. The line is crackly, not to mention it's a party line, too, because somebody gets on the other line, and says, "That you, Gert? Hungry for pancakes?" The man says, "This is not Gert. I am on the line, madame."

"Oh dear, my mistake. Bye." *Click*. I don't hear anything, and I'm afraid he's hung up on me.

"Sir, are you there? Could we set up a business meeting?"

"I'm not interested. I don't mix children and business. Good-bye."

"Story of my life," is what I'd like to say, but all I say is, "Please listen to me."

"Give me one reason why I should not end this call right now?"

"I'm calling on behalf of my father, Tom Weems, a professional banjo player. We want to make your building into a musical venue place."

"A musical venue place?"

"Yes, where folks gather to play music."

"I'm aware of the definition. What would you call such a place?"

I don't know what I'm going to say until that very moment. It pops right into my head from Mama's diary. "Jessie's Smoky Mountain Music Notes."

"A little long for my taste."

"Maybe, but it's named for my mother. I play the guitar, which was recently stolen, but I am going to get another either through the Sears catalogue or a pawnshop."

"Resourceful."

"And my brother plays the harmonica, and my little sister, Gentle, plays the piano, and boyhowdy, can she sing. She's got a voice that—"

"Sounds like you have a crowd living there."

"That's not the half either. My sister Jitters—her name is Myrtle Anne—she is our manager and will handle all the business and make sure you get your cut. My other sister Becksie will handle the popcorn and lemonade. She's also good at talking to folks. And we'll invite other professional musicians to play too. In my opinion, there's no sense in the Grand Ole Opry hogging all the music, right? We can create our own music place right here in Maggie Valley in your building, if you'll rent it to me."

"Why would I do that?"

"Because, nothing personal, but it's just standing there. And it's been empty for as long as I can remember. And unless you have any better offers, I think you ought to take a chance. We could fill the place with music and tourists from Ghost Town. My daddy needs a place to play his banjo for folks, and I need to play my guitar."

"That building's run down. All sorts of problems."

"And I got all sorts of ideas for fixing it up. My sister Louise is an artist, and she can do portraits. She could do a mural on the outside of the building and make a sign. My brother sells pulpwood and works at Ghost Town in the Sky in the summers, but he's real strong and could do any repairs."

"You've given me a lot to digest, but my instinct tells me to say no."

"No?"

"That's right. No."

"Wait. Please don't say no just yet. My mama has started working at the crack of dawn at Champion, and I'd like to find a way to ease her burden, if this becomes a profitable business. She makes the prettiest mountain scarves and baby blankets."

"Like I said, I don't think so. Good-bye."

"Wait! Please, mister."

"Young lady, don't you even want to know who you're dealing with?"

"I already do know. It's you, Mr. Pickle. Isn't it?"

"That's right, it's me. And given our relationship and your reputation to go tearing off without a word to a living soul, I do not believe this is a good idea."

I pretend he didn't make that last unnecessary comment and ask with great politeness, "What was the building used for when it was open, Mr. Pickle?"

"It was a feed-and-supply store—belonged to a cousin.

It went out of business, and lately my family's been asking to see if I can turn a profit with it. But I'd—"

"Have you had any calls? At all?"

"I am ending this conversation. Make sure you do your homework. Good-bye."

The line clicks. I hang up the phone, steaming. He's wrong—dead wrong—so I sit there in the closet, sending wishes and prayers to Livy One up in the Seven Sisters. *Please let this work. Please let crabby Ichabod Crane change his mind.* Mr. Pickle don't know it yet, but this is not over. I'll make it happen, and nobody, not Mama, not Mr. George Flowers, nor the new president of the United States himself is going to stop me. We're going to open us a place and call it Jessie's Smoky Mountain Music Notes.

A pounding comes on the door, and it's the twins and Gentle wanting another Mama story. "Why do you have the phone in the closet?" Cyrus asks.

"You ever heard of privacy?" I open the door to Cyrus in his Poseidon cape.

Cyrus considers and says, "Nope. Can you come and play Poseidon and Amphitrite with me and Caroline? Gentle's dressed up like Iris, goddess of the rainbows. She's been telling stories of the Greek gods to the whistle pigs through the floor. And don't forget Mama's story too. We want to know what happens next."

"All right. Come on, Poseidon, Amphitrite, and Iris." I grab Mama's diary and take the little ones outside to the garden, which is just warming up now in March. Caroline and Gentle wear long white nightshirts, but they've made crowns of clover and daisy chains for necklaces. Cyrus runs around with his trident, holding it up high to check the wind. The wet earth smells like spring, and I gather the kids close to me on an old blanket. Daddy follows us out to the garden and says, "Hey, I want to listen. I want to hear Jessie's story." He sits down with us on the grass, and the little ones climb into his lap and fool with his hair. He don't mind, and I begin to read.

April 29, 1944
Dear Grasshopper . . .

Papa felt well enough to come out to the garden, and he showed me a plant called love weed. The love weed looks like a big plate of orange noodles, and I think it's real pretty. But Papa says once love weed takes hold, it's hard for other flowers to get a chance because love weed can get too strangling. It's near time for the touch-me-nots to start popping. They're the prettiest flowers. You touch them with your finger, and they burst with little seeds that go flying in the air. But Papa says his favorites are the pretty-by-nights, because they bloom around four o'clock each day. I love looking at the flowers from my tree house. I want to sleep in my tree house one night, but Mama won't let me.

I almost forgot. Uncle Buddy sent a postcard from Needles, California, and says it's hotter than the devil's oven out there and folks got shiny metal sculptures in their front yards instead of bushes. He said he's going to be a "desert rat" in a tin trailer for the time being. Uncle Buddy's only been to visit us one time in my whole life, because he's got the wanderlust, according to Mother, and won't ever settle down anywhere.

I sometimes wonder if Mother holds a grudge against him because she has to wear a glass eye. By accident, Uncle Buddy shot out her real eye with a slingshot. I think her different-colored glass eyes are pretty. She has a collection and lets me polish them. When I was little, she used to put one on the table if she had to leave the room, and she'd say, "Just remember, I am watching you, no matter where I am in the house, I am watching you, Jessie." I believed it too!

Yours truly, Jessie Horace

May 15, 1944
Dear Grasshopper,

The red-tailed hawk enjoys feasts of rabbits, tree squirrels, and even prairie chickens. They like to sit up high and look out for their prey. The tail is more rusty-colored than red, and this hawk is a master at soaring and flying through the skies. I wish I could be like a red-tailed hawk, floating in the air, barely moving my wings at all.

And Grasshopper, I am so sorry that I lost you. I beg your forgiveness. I lost you for a whole month. I can't believe

I got you back. I am crying as I write these words. I never knew how bad it was to be missing something. The longer you were gone, the more I missed you, but Mother said it was my own fault for being so absentminded. She said it's one of my worst faults.

It all started when I left you at the beauty salon in Asheville, where Mother likes to get her hair done, and she made me get mine done too. I hate it. The lady cut my bangs too short and made the back and sides poof out. I looked like a yellow-bellied sapsucker, which is all right for a bird but not a girl . . . and so I left in tears and forgot all about you, and I couldn't remember where I'd put you.

Papa thought my hair looked pretty, but he has to say that, being related to me. Mother said she'd get me another diary for my next birthday, but I couldn't wait that long or replace you. You are not replaceable, dear Grasshopper. Not in the least. Then joy of joys—the lady from the beauty salon called up and said she had found a child's diary. I will be much more careful, and when my children misplace things, one day, I will try not to be so hard on them.

Yours truly, Jessie Horace

P.S. Papa is not getting better. I would have told you sooner, but I thought you were lost. I don't know how much I'll be able to write for a while, because Mother is going to need me more than ever. Miss Amelia has taken over the tree house like it's her castle. I still sneak her saucers of cream at night.

When I finish reading, Caroline says, "Grandma Horace was bossy then too."

Gentle says, "Well, some people are just born bossy. That's what Grandma Horace says. Some folks are born bossy, and some are born good-natured."

I tickle Gentle. "I guess so. I guess she's right. As usual!"

Daddy plays a few notes on the banjo. "My wife wrote that story?"

"That's right. A long time ago," I tell him. "Daddy, you know what?"

"What?" He stands up and stretches his legs and picks up his banjo.

"If we found a way to have a music place in Maggie, would you come play the banjo? I bet we could fill it with tourists from Ghost Town and mountain sightseers."

Daddy says, "How can we find one?"

"We will . . . I promise. Nashville don't get to hog all the music."

He looks at me like he wants to believe me, but all he says is, "I reckon I'd better practice." He takes his banjo and whistles for Uncle Hazard to go with him. They head up to the woods together, and pretty soon, we hear the sweet melodious twang of Daddy's banjo. He plays better in the woods than in front of us watching his every move, correcting him, telling him how to do it right. The better he gets, the less he likes to be told how to do things or reminded of the right words.

The twins jump on top of me and I tickle them too, and Gentle starts laughing. We get muddy rolling around on the ground, but it's so good to feel spring coming. As we come up for air, I tell them all about my idea for Jessie's Smoky Mountain Music Notes and how I'm going to need their help real bad to make it work. "We're going to have to get that mule-headed Mr. Pickle to change his mind."

Cyrus asks, "How will you get him to change his mind?"

Caroline says, "Could you trick him?"

Gentle asks, "Put him under a fairy spell?"

"I don't know yet, but maybe. It's the most perfect building, I swear, and here's why." As I start explaining, the eavesdropping music manager yells from the bedroom window, "What are you'uns talking about? Are decisions getting decided without my approval? Hold it right there. I am the music manager. I have the family's best interests at heart. Not another word without me." Myrtle Anne flies out of the house and down to where we're playing in the garden. I got no choice but to tell her every last detail too, and she is thrilled by the prospect of putting her managing talents to work.

CHAPTER TWENTY

Please, Mr. Pickle

A FEW WEEKS later, the family's officially declared music manager, Myrtle Anne, grabs me in the hall during recess to say, "We got a business meeting with Mr. Pickle. Come on. I finally got him to say yes to a meeting."

We march straight up to his desk where he's working, and the first thing Myrtle Anne does is whip out her notebook. "Hello, Mr. Pickle. How are you today? You said for us to come see you during recess for a meeting. Here we are."

"So I did. But at the moment, I'm grading papers. How about tomorrow?"

Myrtle Anne says, "This won't take long, Mr. Pickle. I think my client explained the whole thing to you. We'd give you all the ticket sales until we paid you back in full."

"You're asking me to *front* all the money? And what client do you mean?"

"Her, of course!" She points to me. "My sister. Olivia Hyatt Weems."

Mr. Pickle puts his pen down and stares at Myrtle Anne, who is only getting started. "I went to Nashville with her, Mr. Pickle. It turned out to be a business trip for both of us. I think Maggie Valley needs a music place, and since our move to Enka has been put on hold, I think your place would work just fine. What do you got against children and music?"

"Not a thing. But how do you children propose to pay for repairs to get the building into shape? That won't come cheap, hiring workers, and how will you even get an audience? I don't have the energy or inclination. I'm sorry."

"Have you discussed this with your fiancée? She might want to know," I say.

"I have not. This does not concern her in the least."

"Well, how do you know that?" Myrtle Anne asks. "Don't you think your future wife would want to know about business propositions? In fact, Mr. Pickle, I was talking to my sister, Becksie, about that very idea last night. She's stuck home watching the babies since Mama went to back to work, so she has time to think, and she's also got a head for figures. And she thinks you ought to make it an extra-credit project for students. You know—math or something. Because we'll be sawing, cutting, measuring—and all the kids who help get extra credit. Anyhow, that's just a suggestion from the Maggie Queen to her subjects." She laughs at her joke. "Get it? Subjects? Math? Extra credit?"

"I get it." Mr. Pickle blows his nose.

I jump in and add, "And everyone knows the Weems family pays their own way and don't accept charity from nobody. This way the kids who do the work for Jessie's Smoky Mountain Music Notes will get rewarded. It won't be some do-gooder charity project. Fair enough?"

"You girls offer a fine argument. But I don't have time to run a music place. I am a full-time teacher with sights on being principal."

Myrtle Anne says, "Well, then, this seems like the perfect chance for you to spice up your job résumé—leading a bunch of kids working to bring music to Maggie Valley. That's what Becksie thinks, and I think so too."

The bell rings, and Mr. Pickle is out the door like a shot to collect the class. Myrtle Anne says, "We're wearing him down, slowly but surely."

The next time Grandma Horace calls, I answer the phone and she's already talking. "Is that you, Olivia? Is your mother home? I want to know what's going on. Do I order these beds or not? She won't return my calls. I'm very upset."

"She's not here at the moment. Hey, Grandma Horace, guess what?"

"Hay is for horses, not grandmothers. Where is she?"

"Grandma Horace, guess what?" I twist the black phone cord around my finger.

"I don't guess. Either say it or don't. I am losing my patience."

"I got real good news. We're in the process of possibly renting a building from my teacher, Mr. Pickle, to open a music place right in Maggie Valley. We can run it whether we live in Maggie or Enka. We'll be commuters if we have to be."

"What? A disaster in the making, if you want my candid opinion."

I did not ask for her candid opinion, but all I say is, "And guess what we're calling it if it works out? Jessie's Smoky Mountain Music Notes. After all the birds in Mama's diary that she drew when she was a little girl."

"Sounds like a terrible plan to me. What does your mama think?"

"We're not telling her. It's a surprise. Becksie and Myrtle Anne came up with the business plan. My job is to focus on the music and get Daddy ready to play. Louise is going to paint the mural and maybe do mountain portraits of tourists, and Emmett, he—"

"I have heard enough. You let me know when it all comes to fruition or absolutely nothing. Be sure to tell your mama I called. Does she get my messages? I heard a rumor she's working full-time at Champion, with all you children left to run wild. I am very concerned. We had a plan. We had a very good plan."

"Grandma Horace, you can't believe everything you

hear. I promise that we're not running wild," I tell her. "I'll have her call you."

"I didn't know she'd be so mad about the diary."

"Just think, it'll be Daddy's official return to music too."

"Oh, Lord. Good-bye." And the phone clicks dead.

We start the next phase of Wearing Mr. Pickle Down. I pull Cyrus, Caroline, and Gentle down the mountain in the wagon one Saturday when I know he is testing eighth-graders for high school. Becksie is taking the tests, too, even though she's been home-schooling herself. She is not about to be left out of high school. If anything, this whole setback has made her more determined than ever to get herself educated. She's putting together a whole book of wildflowers with scientific names and explanations for a science project.

After the test takers are all gone, the twins and Gentle stand in Mr. Pickle's classroom door and bust out singing "Little Darling Pal of Mine," just like I directed them to do as a kind of audition. They sing right on key, and the twins give Gentle her solo, which even makes the janitor stop to listen. When they're done, the janitor is wiping his eyes, but all Mr. Pickle says, "Way to hit those notes. Good-bye."

"Wait!" I tell him. "Here are the blueprints for the building. Louise made them up. And a sketch of the mural for the outside. You're going to love it. Just one look."

"Miss Weems, this is bordering on harassment," Mr. Pickle says. "I told you I'm not going into business with you. I don't know how to make that any clearer." With that, he sends us packing. I don't say a word as I guide Gentle into the wagon first.

"Now what?" Cyrus climbs into the wagon. "Didn't we sing so good?"

"You sang fine." I start to pull the wagon down Highway 19. "He don't have a lick of sense is all."

"But why didn't he like us?" Cyrus wants to know.

"How should I know? Maybe he's tone deaf. No more questions for ten minutes."

"How long is ten minutes? How many seconds?" Cyrus looks pained.

Gentle says, "Livy Two will think of something. Right?"

Caroline says, "I'll write a secret note to the fairies and ask them for a favor."

I don't answer a one of them—they're just little kids who think it's all a game. I pull them back up the mountain in the wagon, but they're so heavy now I make them walk part of the way. I try not to feel too awful discouraged, but that Mr. Pickle sure is hardheaded. I wouldn't fool with him if his building wasn't so perfect and Daddy didn't need this so bad. And if it's truly successful, Mama could help run it—leave Champion and sell her scarves and baby blankets again. I just have to figure out a way to be more convincing instead of "bordering on harassment," whatever that means.

The next thing we do is start a letter-writing campaign. Louise comes up with that idea. We all write—pleading, begging letters. The little ones write in childish scrawl. Gentle dictates her letter: *"Dear Mr. Pickle, Please give us a chance to sing our songs for you."* Caroline writes: *"Dear Mr. Pickle, The fairies will bring you good luck if you rent us your building. I know it."* Cyrus writes: *"Mr. Pickle, Why won't you rent us your building? How come?"*

Me and Louise write haiku, since Mr. Pickle's been teaching us haiku in English class, and we want to show that something is rubbing off. One goes:

Your tired old building
Fiddles, guitars, banjos sing
Music in mountains!

Next, the twins draw pictures of musical instruments and kids singing onstage and a clapping audience, and Louise makes a poster in the comic-book style of the *Legion of Super-Heroes*—Saturn Girl, Superboy, Lightning Lad—all ordering Mr. Pickle to say yes. Emmett drops by to see Mr. Pickle and to deliver the letters and pictures, but if our teacher reads them, he's not saying.

Every day at school, I look for some kind of sign, but he is not bending an inch. Daddy keeps asking, "When do we open our music place, Livy Two? When, honey?"

"I'm working on it, Daddy. I promise." But by April, I'm so tired of begging. Why should the Grand Ole Opry of Nashville get to have all the fun, and why should a perfectly good building sit right here in Maggie Valley collecting dust and cobwebs? I don't know where to turn next, and I feel like a giant failure—like I was in Nashville. Just when I sit down one evening to figure out a new business plan, I hear a knock on the door.

Mama calls, "Livy Two. Somebody wants to see you. You too, Myrtle Anne."

I come to the door, and who is standing there but Mr. Pickle and Miss Attickson, who's holding a thick bunch of papers—our letters and drawings to Mr. Pickle.

Miss Attickson says, "Mrs. Weems, I wonder if I might speak to Olivia and Myrtle Anne? My fiancé would like to discuss something with them in private."

"In private? They do something wrong?" Mama looks alarmed.

"Nothing like that," Miss Attickson assures her. "It's regarding—"

Myrtle Anne interrupts, "It's a business meeting. We'll tell you all about it later, Mama. We promise."

Daddy appears from the kitchen. "Can I come too?" I nod, and the five of us head to the smokehouse, where

I light the lantern and the room fills with yellow light as we sit around the table Mathew the Mennonite built us.

Miss Attickson says, "Children, I read your letters. Mr. Pickle shared them over breakfast at the Pancake House, and frankly, I have never been so surprised in all my life. Isn't that right, Mr. Pickle?"

Mr. Pickle nods his head. "Yes, that's correct." He looks like he'd rather not remember breakfast.

"I had no idea. And now my fiancé would like to say something to you. We've had many heart-to-heart talks, and so what he is about to say comes from both of us."

Mr. Pickle clears his throat and blows his nose. With a pained expression on his face, he says, "I would very much like to open this business with you Weems children, on a trial basis. I don't know where exactly we'll get the money, but I think the idea of an extra-credit project and students working together is all right."

Daddy asks, "What's he talking about?"

Myrtle Anne says, "Mr. Pickle is talking about Jessie's Smoky Mountain Music Notes, Daddy. We're going to have a place for you to play your banjo again for folks. We'll be renting his building. I'm glad you seen the light, Mr. Pickle. Mighty glad."

"That's right, Daddy," I tell him. "You won't have to drive all the way over to Cas Walker. Or any other place. You'll be able to play right here. All of us will."

Daddy swallows hard and nods and says. "Well, Mr.

Pickle? That's your name? And you're the library lady. I thank you. My children thank you."

Mr. Pickle says, "You're very welcome, Mr. Weems."

Myrtle Anne says, "Well, can we shake on it?"

Mr. Pickle extends his hand and we both shake it. "Thank you, Mr. Pickle," I tell him. But he says, "Remember, it's a trial basis through the summer, with the possibility of going up to Halloween if all goes smoothly. I'll be watching every move and penny."

When we got back outside, I whisper to Miss Attickson, "How in the world did you get him to change his mind?"

She puts her arm around my shoulders and says, "Don't you know me by now?"

"Thank you, Miss Attickson. I swear you won't be sorry."

"I don't expect I will be." Miss Attickson smiles and says, "Come on, Leonard. These children need their sleep." Mr. Pickle starts the car, and they drive off out of the holler together. The plum sky is filled with crystal stars, and I whisper a thank-you to Livy One, my sister, who must have heard us wishing and praying with all our hearts for Mr. Pickle to come to his senses and see the light.

CHAPTER TWENTY-ONE

Uncle Buddy Flies Away

THE HARDEST THING is keeping the whole thing a secret from Mama. But each time she starts to pester one of us with a question, we only say, "You'll spoil your surprise," so she lets it go until she can't stand it and asks another question. Finally, Daddy says, "It's a secret, Jessie. It's a secret between me and our children, so no more questions." When he puts it that way, Mama backs off, but not before saying, "Have you studied the facts of whatever this scheme is you got cooking? I mean, have your fun, but I do hope it's a worthwhile project."

I have no doubt in my mind that it's worthwhile. Right from the very beginning, Jessie's Smoky Mountain Music Notes feels like a barn raising in slow motion, working every day after school and Saturdays, with Mr. Pickle playing taskmaster. All the students in the class are going to get extra credit and be able to say they had a hand in starting a new business—all except Rusty Frye, who won't lift a finger, but who wants that rodent around anyway? Billy O'Connor offers benches from his church, since the church is getting new ones. I ask him, "How come you're not out there bowing and scraping to the call of that fool as usual?" We look out the window to where Rusty is popping wheelies in the parking lot.

Billy says, "Maybe because I'd rather be in here working with you?" I got no answer for that, but my cheeks get hot. I walk away from him without a word. I sure hope nobody heard him. A Cherokee Indian boy comes in the door swinging a bucket of paint. He nods at Becksie, and I see them swap shy looks until finally, Becksie says, "Quit staring at him, Livy Two. This is my friend Henry. He lives over in Cherokee. He's an actor in the play *Unto These Hills* about the Trail of Tears, and he's come to help out. It's not a big deal."

Henry says, "Nice to meet you," as Becksie introduces him all around. Then she shows him what wall to paint. So her secret sweetheart is real.

A month before we're set to open, we're all working inside the building. Emmett is sanding the benches from Billy O'Connor's church, and Becksie is cleaning out a popcorn machine that we bought for five dollars from the pawnshop in Waynesville. Mr. Pickle comes inside from collecting the mail and waves an official-looking document. "Attention, workers, please? It's from the fire marshal. He's inspected the place and said it's not up to code.

Bad news. Not good, not good. I knew this thing was a terrible idea. You can all go home."

"What does that mean? Not up to code?" I ask.

Emmett says, "It means we can't open this place. Unless we bring it up to code. How much would that cost, Mr. Pickle?"

"A few thousand dollars. At least. The wiring is old, which could short-circuit, start a fire. A tragedy waiting to happen. And we need a new roof. Who knew? Who knew? I did. I knew better."

"A few thousand dollars?" It might as well be a million. I put down the rag I'm scrubbing the windows with. I feel the news like a punch in the gut.

Mr. Pickle looks stricken and says, "I'm sorry, children. I truly am sorry, but I didn't realize—Miss Atickson and I thought it could be a gathering place for music and folks, but I told you from the start that I am not a businessman. I didn't take things like the fire marshal into consideration." His face is covered with little red splotches, and actually I feel sorry for him.

Daddy's painting a wall, and says, "That's okay, Mr. Pickle. We'll do it anyhow. Let them try and stop us. We'll figure out a way. We have to do this for my wife, Jessie. She wrote a book when she was a little girl—a diary book—with Smoky Mountain birds! So we can't cancel this plan. We won't."

"Daddy," Emmett tries to explain it to him, "the fire marshal could officially shut us down on opening night."

Daddy looks surprised. "How could they do such a thing?"

"We're not quitting, Emmett," I tell him. "We're not. We've come too far. We are not quitting. Don't worry, Daddy."

"Fine." Emmett starts sanding the bench again. "We're not quitting, but somebody better come up with some bright idea fast, or all this work will be for nothing. It looks hopeless to me. We're gonna need a miracle of some sort."

"Then, by God, we'll get one!" Daddy thunders, and picks up his banjo and starts playing. He's only got one song—"Mountain Dew"—ready to play, and I can tell he's nervous. But folks will know that song and sing along if Daddy don't get too scared in front of them—if there even are folks, with that bossy fire marshal tossing his weight around with mean letters.

Louise and me write a polite letter back to the fire marshal of Haywood County, asking him to please give us a little more time to fix the wiring and roof and not shut down work yet, even with kids on the premises. We type it up real professional. The fire marshal does not answer us. I guess he's just another busy man with better things to do. I'm about sick to death of all the busy men in the world. Finally, we decide to go see him for ourselves one day when school lets out early. Emmett drives me, Myrtle Anne, and Louise over to Waynesville, but the fire marshal's secretary says, "The fire marshal is a very important man with important matters to attend to every day. We got your letter, and he doesn't have time to fool with you and your school project. We'll discuss the matter *only* when you bring the building up to code. Wouldn't that be a terrible thing to have a fire on your opening night and have folks go up in smoke or get scorched with third-degree burns? You want the roof caving in on your heads? It's the law!" She slams the door in our faces, and we head back to the car, where Emmett is waiting on us.

"No luck?" He's listening to Loretta on the radio singing her sad song "Success."

"No luck." Myrtle Anne's cat's-eye glasses get steamed up with unshed tears. It's been hard on her, handling all the business details on her puny shoulders.

Louise says, "It's like that secretary couldn't wait to say no. I didn't even have a chance to show her the blueprints and mural sketches."

Emmett shakes his head. "Come on, at least we can do something else while we're in Waynesville." He doesn't say what, but pretty soon we wind up in front of the pawnshop on Main Street. He turns back to Louise and Myrtle Anne. "You'uns wait in the car. Come on, Livy Two."

Myrtle Anne says, "What for? Why can't we come too?"

Louise says, "Hush, Myrtle Anne. Let them go."

"Why should I?"

But Emmett just motions me to come on, and we head into the pawnshop that is packed with everything. We go by the household appliances, bikes, wagons, tools, and chain saws to the row of instruments hanging on the back wall. Five guitars hang above my head. He looks at me and says, "Pick yourself one."

"What?"

"You heard me, pick yourself one. Pick yourself a guitar."

"We can't afford it yet, Emmett. Forget it." I start to walk away.

"Yes, we can, Livy Two. I'm buying it. I want you to get yourself a guitar. You can't very well prepare for an opening night without practicing a lick. You ought to be playing day and night to get ready. Folks won't pay to hear some amateur kid. Or they'll pay once and never come back again. Is that what you want?"

"No, course not."

"Well, then, pick one."

I study the guitars hanging on the wall. One is sapphire, almost the color of the guitar Daddy got for me from the Sears & Roebuck catalogue, swiped by the evil faker blind man. But I see another that's bigger, one I could grow into—it's a Fender acoustic guitar—price tag, twenty-five dollars. I always heard the sound of a Martin guitar is the best, but there are none to be seen in this pawnshop. I look at Emmett. "Why are you doing this?"

"You know why." He looks at the wood floor.

"Emmett, things ain't been right since Nashville. Now all of a sudden you aim to buy me a guitar. I don't get you."

"I'm trying to make it right, Livy Two."

"But what I did was wrong."

"Yeah, but I was wrong too. I want to do this, and I don't want to argue about it. All right? Aren't you gonna say anything?"

I swallow hard. "Fine. I want the Fender acoustic then, but down the road I'll get me a Martin."

Emmett reaches up and lifts the Fender off the wall and puts it in my arms.

I try a chord. It's out of tune, so I tune it, and the C chord sounds beautiful. Deep and strong. I can play again. I can write again and hear how the songs sound. Daddy got me my first guitar; Emmett is getting me my second. I look at him. "You sure you sold enough pulpwood to pay for this?"

"What do you think I am? Get you in here and get your hopes up?"

"Thank you, Emmett." We go to the cashier to pay for my new guitar. I can't hardly believe it. I play it while the cashier rings up the order.

"One lucky kid," says the clerk, "for your big brother to sell his collection of *Legion of Super-Heroes* comic books to me." He hands Emmett the receipt.

"Emmett, I thought it was pulpwood!"

"Drop it. I wanted to do it. Now leave it."

"All right, but I won't forget it." I follow him outside with my new Fender acoustic.

"Good."

As we reach the car, Myrtle Anne leans out the window, pointing to my guitar, and yells, "About time! What kind is it?"

"Fender acoustic."

"Alleluia! Is it any good? You could have asked my opinion, you know."

In the end, it's Uncle Buddy who gives us the miracle we need. He does something so terrible, so generous, and so unexpected that nobody can believe it. He has himself a heart attack on a moonshine run somewhere over in East Tennessee. Somebody finds him dead on a street called Fruit Jar Alley, and Grandma Horace calls us up on the telephone to deliver the pitiful news. Mama gathers us together to pray for the restless soul of Uncle Buddy. *Uncle*

Buddy is dead. How can that be? He seemed far too mean to up and die.

The day after his death, Grandma Horace drives Grandpa Cal Horace's 1927 Model A Ford up into our holler. I'm practicing on my Fender acoustic, but I quit when I see her. Will she be crying and carrying on for her brother? We hold our breath as she climbs out of her car, weary, but not crying. She gives us a hard look before she says, "Don't stand there staring. Somebody get my grip. Didn't expect to be back here so soon."

Myrtle Anne asks, "Are you sad, Grandma Horace? Do you want a hug?"

"I do not need or desire a hug. Where is your mother?"

Gentle says, "But I want a hug," heading straight in the direction of Grandma Horace's voice.

"Very well." Grandma Horace allows herself to be hugged by Gentle.

Cyrus says, "Mama took off work from her job today so she could be here when you came. I like your car, Grandma Horace. Where'd you get it?"

Caroline says, "Be quiet. You weren't supposed to say that, Cyrus. Grandma Horace, were you ever my age?"

"Your age? Of course I was. Now what's this job talk?" Grandma Horace asks.

"Was everybody in the whole world my age once?" Caroline asks, but right then Mama comes outside onto the front porch. "Mother, you're here."

"Jessie. Yes. Here I am." They stand there a moment until finally, Grandma Horace, ramrod straight, says, "What's this news I hear about a job?"

Mama tucks a loose lock of hair behind her ear. "I meant to tell you. I've been working at Champion, but I wanted to get used to it. You remember Charlie Walsh? He's a boss there. My boss. Anyway—I'm glad you're here. Delia Jupiter's having fits over Uncle Buddy. I had to sit with her."

Grandma Horace says flatly, "You have a job? At Champion?"

"Yes, Mother. Now, could we go inside? They'll be bringing Uncle Buddy over soon." Mama looks upset, but she's holding her ground.

"Are you sad at all, Grandma Horace?" Cyrus peers up at her, tugging on her hand. She stops and peers right back down at him with her good eye.

"What? Sad? Good Lord, no. If anything, I'm mad. Your great-uncle Buddy just couldn't be reasoned with. Now, no tears. We'll bury the dead, but we'll have no nonsense with high drama and carrying on like a pack of shouting Baptists. Now, somebody fetch Grandma a glass of sweet tea. I'm parched."

Louise says, "I'll get it for you."

Becksie says, "No, I will. I want to tell Grandma Horace all about the new schedule and me staying home from school to watch the babies."

Grandma Horace expels a big sigh. "So this is what happens when I turn my back?" She looks at me. "And you? A new guitar?"

"Yes ma'am." I play a few chords of "Mama's Biscuits," a song I wrote when I was a kid, but she's not listening. She turns around. "Now none of you kids fool with your Grandpa Cal's car. I won't tell you twice. It's an antique. And as for you, Jessie, I'd like an explanation about this so-called job of yours." She follows Mama inside, with Becksie tagging along behind filling Grandma Horace in on all she's been missing.

The miracle of Uncle Buddy isn't his heart attack in Fruit Jar Alley. It's that he was still officially the night watchman at Ghost Town, and it turns out that he had a life insurance policy, of which he left every penny to Emmett. The news comes like a bolt out of the blue. Nobody even knew Uncle Buddy had a policy or suspected that an ornery old man would be thoughtful enough to leave it to Emmett. It's near three thousand dollars, which is all the money we need to finish paying the back rent and get Mr. Pickle's building up to code so the fire marshal will open up Jessie's Smoky Mountain Music Notes. There might even be some left over for the bank, but maybe I'm counting my chickens too fast.

Uncle Buddy bequeaths one last gift too. In his handwritten will, which is all of one sentence, he wrote:

In the event of my untimely passing,
my iguana, Pearl, will go to Jessie Weems's kid,
Cyrus Weems, my grandnephew,
to take care of since he likes critters.
That is all.

Uncle Buddy don't leave nothing for the girls or Grandma Horace or Mama. Not even a note. I guess it's no secret that Uncle Buddy always did prefer the boys, and Daddy's not blood to Uncle Buddy, so he don't get a thing either.

Our great-uncle's body gets brung over from East Tennessee and laid out in our front room, because Grandma Horace don't want him in her living room in Enka. So he's getting a true mountain funeral. Nobody has the money to pay for a fancy one, and Emmett don't want the money he inherited to line some undertaker's pockets. Although he left no explanation as to why, Uncle Buddy requested a burial way over in Soddy Daisy, Tennessee, but Grandma Horace says he'll just have to put up with Maggie Valley as a final resting spot. "Make no mistake about it, folks have to be kinder in life to get their last requests met in death," is her only explanation.

Mama and Grandma Horace take turns setting with the body, but us kids linger at the door, trying to hear scraps of conversation from the grown-ups. Some folks from Ghost Town come down the mountain to pay their respects, including Clare Whelan, the blacksmith, and her husband, another blacksmith. They come along with some of the gunslingers, musicians, and even the sheriff of Ghost Town. One says, "Hear he didn't break a single jar when he collapsed."

Another stirs sugar into his coffee and says, "That's Buddy for you."

Emmett says Uncle Buddy played poker with every one of them. Even crying Delia Jupiter comes, and brings Cyrus the iguana in her cage. Cyrus takes Pearl to our bedroom, where he's fixed up the corner for her. Pearl stares at us with black, blinking iguana eyes and slithers out her tongue in a greeting. Uncle Hazard growls at Pearl like she's a dinosaur come back to life, but he does it back-stepping all the way.

In the front room, folks sing songs like "Amazing Grace" and "I'll Fly Away." Grandma Horace leads everybody in a prayer for Uncle Buddy. I try to feel sad—or something akin to sorrow, but all I feel is relief. He won't be around to say hateful things about "a box and five nails" or get his nose out of joint because somebody looked at him wrong. Before they get him ready to go to the graveyard, I walk into the front room with Louise and Emmett on either side of me. We stand next to where he's laid out in a black suit, his hands folded across his chest. I can't hardly breathe. I ain't never seen a dead person before. His face looks waxy and pale, his lips almost blue. Mama comes up behind us and hugs us to her close. "You children all right? I'm proud of you for being brave. He was a hard man, but he couldn't help himself, bless his heart. Grandma Horace will have the Methodist preacher say a prayer for the repose of Uncle Buddy's soul."

Because the little kids are scared about the strangers in the house and Uncle Buddy being dead in the front room, I take them for a long walk up into the woods. Even Emmett, Becksie, Louise, and Myrtle Anne come along. We leave Appelonia and Baby Tom-Bill at home, but I bring Mama's diary with me, because I have another page they need to hear. We wind up back in the garden, and I start to read another excerpt. Daddy joins us and listens too. He pulls Gentle onto his lap, and she leans back against him.

July 27, 1944
Dear Grasshopper,

A bobolink is said to sing the prettiest of all the birds, with his little voice just pouring out of his throat. He used to be called a "rice bird" because huge flocks of them would gobble up rice. I read that the boy bobolink looks like he's wearing a tuxedo backward. I have only seen a picture of my papa in a tuxedo on his wedding day.

A few days ago, Papa died. The funeral was yesterday. I am pretending that it happened to someone else, so I can write down the facts, since Mother says I need to face facts. But last night, after Papa's funeral, I dreamed a spider bit me on the hand when I was shutting the curtain. Right off, my two fingers, pinky and fourth finger, got real numb. In my dream, I thought maybe I was imagining the numbness, but then it began to spread. I called Mother, but she didn't hear me, and I called Papa, and he came to me, and I tried to talk to him . . . but by this time, my fingers were swollen up to the size of large black carrots, and my hand wrinkled up with poison. I didn't know my own hand. Papa didn't say a word but kept patting my hand. Then we were back at Papa's gravesite, and Mother said, "You'd better take care of that black carrot hand." Finally, I woke up. I was afraid to go back to sleep.

The house is full of macaroni and cheese and Jell-O salad with too many marshmallows. Somebody put sugar in the cornbread, and who eats sugary cornbread? We sang "sacred harp" singing at the funeral, since Papa requested it. Afterward, folks said, "I'm sorry for your loss," but what do they have to be sorry for? It wasn't their fault. I had to put on my nice-girl face, though, and say thank you. Then I went and hid in my tree house. I looked down at the snowball bushes and sunflowers I planted with Papa.

Yours truly, Jessie Horace

P.S. Mother hasn't cried yet.

Nobody says a word when I finish, but the tears we can't cry for Uncle Buddy come pouring out for Grandpa Cal, a gentle man we never even knew, who loved our mama, loved our grandmother, planted snowball bushes, sunflowers, and helped our mama build a tree house. We love him just the same as if we'd known him all our lives.

A little while later, Mama and Grandma Horace come out to the garden to find us. Mama's holding Baby Tom-Bill, and Grandma Horace has Appelonia by the hand. I look up at Mama and ask her one more time, "When all this is over, are we going to move to Enka?"

Daddy says, "I don't want to move to the land of Enka."

Cyrus asks, "Yeah, but is that going to be our new home anyhow?"

Mama starts to say something, but Grandma Horace says, "What is the plan, Jessie? Out with it. Are you going to leave us all in the dark?"

"I've made up my mind." Mama sets Baby Tom-Bill down on the blanket to play. "I've been going back and forth, and Mother, this is very hard for me to say, but we're not moving to Enka. We're staying here in Maggie Valley. I know you'll be disappointed, but my job at Champion is sustaining us. We're catching up. On our own."

Grandma Horace says, "Sustaining you? What about your daughter? The job is not sustaining Rebecca if she's sacrificing her education. And how is she expected to watch those babies and a blind child and a daddy on the mend? How, pray tell?"

"I watch myself!" Gentle says, a note of anger in her voice.

Mama says, "It's just for a little longer. Until Tom is back on his feet. He's so much better now. And I've promised Becksie it's not forever. Not by a long shot."

Daddy nods. "I'm close. I know it. I'm getting better, Mother Horace. I—"

Becksie says, "You promise me, Daddy?" gazing hard at him.

He nods, and we wait to see what Grandma Horace will do next. She takes a deep breath and says, "So that's it? You're truly not coming? After all I've done, getting the house ready? Waiting on you to come and live with me? I have a basement full of beds from a store in Marshall. They delivered them. Set them up for me."

"The children can visit you any time," Mama says. "They'll need those beds."

"Stop. Just stop." Grandma Horace holds up a trembling hand and blinks hard with her one good eye, her blue glass eye lonesome, looking at nothing. More singing comes from inside the house as folks serenade Uncle Buddy away to a peaceful good-bye. After a few moments, Mama and Grandma Horace leave us to walk out to the edge of the field to watch the sun set over the mountains. They stand apart, careful not to touch.

CHAPTER TWENTY-TWO

Cataloochee Wedding

September 22, 1944
Dear Grasshopper,

Did you know that lovebirds come all the way from Africa and some of the species are called peach-faced, masked love, and Fischer's lovebirds . . . ? They're really parrots, but they love to cuddle up together and groom each other too. I would love to have a whole flock of lovebirds one day.

Mother says something has to be done about my hair. I like my hair. I like the way it frizzes and rises in the air around me. I like my hair just the way it is, but Mother wants me to wear it in tight little Jane Eyre topknots.

I have a secret—one more of many, I guess. The secret is I would like to cut my hair as short as a boy's and then have no more fuss about it. Why can't I? I can't help it if my hair has a mind of its own. Mother might be surprised. I might just do it one day.

Yours truly, Jessie Horace

P.S. I have dreams about Papa, but he is always standing in a crowd of folks. I miss him more than I can say.

I read that passage aloud the night before Miss Attickson's wedding, which takes place a month after they put Uncle Buddy in the ground. I'm just glad he's not next to Livy One on Black Mountain. They say sometimes the dead come back and visit, but Uncle Buddy has not come here to our holler. Rest in peace, Uncle Buddy—sorry you didn't get Soddy Daisy like you wanted, but Maggie Valley's a nice place.

The time has come for Miss Attickson to get hitched to Mr. Pickle, and I'm relieved I don't hate him like I used to. We'll open Jessie's Smoky Mountain Music Notes when they get back from their honeymoon the first weekend in the summertime. Emmett's money paid the workers to bring the building up to code and fix the roof, so the fire marshal had no choice but to give the building a clean bill of health.

Louise whispers, "I can't hardly believe the wedding day is tomorrow. I bet she'll be beautiful. You think she'll like my painting?"

Becksie says, eavesdropping, "Of course, she will. She'll be a radiant June bride."

Mama hears us and says, "Go to sleep! We've got us a long day tomorrow. I want you rested."

"But we're waiting to hear the daddy whistle pig, Mama," Gentle explains.

The whistle pig daddy has moved in under the porch to join his family. We lie awake in bed waiting for him to start rooting and grunting. When he gets going, it sounds like he's moving furniture or something.

Gentle says, "I wish I could take my whistle pigs to the wedding."

Caroline sits up in bed. "You can't bring a family of whistle pigs to the wedding. I'm not bringing my chickens. Chickens and whistle pigs don't belong at weddings."

"Well, I know that!" Gentle replies. "Don't you think I know that?"

Cyrus sits up. "How come whistle pigs and chickens can't come to weddings? Who made that rule up? Is it against the law?"

"Never mind about the chickens and whistle pigs. You'uns kids need your sleep," Mama calls from the front porch, where she's sitting with Daddy. He's practicing his banjo tune for the wedding. He wants to play "Wildwood Flower," and it's starting to sound pretty.

I'm relieved Miss Attickson don't hate me like I thought she might forever. I reckon it'll never be the same like it was—us working together and driving books around to kids through the mountains—but I know she'll be a part of my life. Always. Heck, she can't wait for Jessie's Smoky

Mountain Music Notes to open. Come tomorrow, we'll be going to a traditional Baptist wedding and covered-dish supper. I sure hope Mr. Pickle don't fall off the horse when he comes riding over the mountain. Some more rooting and grunting takes place under the house.

Louise says, "I think I hear the daddy whistle pig."

"Me too," I whisper back.

Gentle sits up in bed. "That's him, all right."

We lie in bed and listen. As my eyes get heavy, I think of the first time I saw Miss Attickson. She was reading books to a crowd of kids in the bookmobile. I hope she don't change one bit when she becomes Mrs. Pickle. I roll over in bed and think of Grandma Horace, who will not be coming to the wedding. She says Grandpa Cal's car would never make it to the top of Cataloochee. Maybe that's partly true, but the real truth is she's still so mad at Mama she could spit.

The wedding day dawns bright and beautiful with an early summer breeze floating through the bedroom window. Myrtle Anne paces the room, reading a superstition poem about brides: "'Married in white, you have chosen aright; married in red, you'd be better dead; married in yellow, ashamed of the fellow; married in blue, your lover is true; married in green, ashamed to be seen; married in black, you'll ride in a hack; married in pearl, you'll live in a whirl; married in pink, your spirits will sink; married in brown, you'll live out of town.' That is from page one ninety-eight from *8,414 Strange and Fascinating Superstitions*, in case any of you'uns are interested."

I throw a pillow at her. "I can't believe you ain't returned that library book yet! Are you crazy?"

"I can't help it. I'll pay for it somehow. Just one more! 'Happy is the bride the sun shines on.' Well, looks like Miss Attickson is going to be happy. It's gonna be a real sunny day. Let's go to the wedding!" She starts humming "Here Comes the Bride." Then she stops and says, "Hey, I wonder which one of us will get married first?"

We all look at Becksie, who's brushing out her long dark hair, trying to catch her reflection in the window. "What?" she snaps. "Don't be looking at me. It won't be me. I feel like I already raised a bunch of kids, and I'm not even fifteen yet."

Up on Cataloochee, we have to cut through a path of stinging weeds, beggar lice, and pokeberries to get to the Palmer Chapel. The chapel itself is filled with all sorts of wildflowers—dog hobble, Dutchman's britches, fairy wands, and flaming azaleas. Gentle uses her cane to get where she is going, but she's completely at home in the mountains, lightly resting her hand on Caroline's arm. Gentle and Caroline have already pressed mountain laurel flowers to their earlobes, so they will look like fancy ladies with petal-white earrings at the wedding.

I smooth out Mama's old dress that she took in for me. We're all in hand-me-downs of one sort or another—all except for Becksie. Mama bought Becksie a new "imperfect" dress from Schulman's Department Store in Sylva, because of the sacrifices she's had to make by leaving school this year. Good thing the wedding is on a Saturday and Mama didn't have to take off work. Becksie's still not happy about being home with Daddy and the kids, but she got one of the highest marks on the eighth-grade test for high school and, fingers crossed, she'll be able to start in the fall if Daddy can start working again and Mama quits being a secretary. Mama says, "One day at a time, children. We can't solve all the world's problems in a day, but Daddy truly might be better by fall."

Cyrus asks, "How long would it take to solve the world's problems, do you think?" but nobody answers him.

We stand outside the church, waiting for Miss Attickson and Mr. Pickle to ride across Cataloochee on horseback so they can get married at the Palmer Chapel. Before long, I spy Miss Attickson with Mr. Pickle following her. She's in a white wedding gown that hangs down off the horse a bit. Mr. Pickle wears a black suit and looks more like Ichabod Crane than ever, but he can't help it, and they're both beaming. Myrtle Anne and Becksie jump up and down with excitement. A swirl of tiny purple butterflies follow the bride and groom, and Caroline cries, "Fairies!" and Gentle says, "I feel them. Everywhere."

I stand near Randal and his goose, Clancy, who've also been invited. He nods at me, and I nod back at him. I can smell the covered-dish supper that will be waiting after the vows are exchanged—fried chicken, baked ham, potato salad, green beans with bacon, creamed corn, corn on the cob, biscuits, homemade pickles, chicken 'n' dumplings, sweet potato pie, barbecue, cheese grits, and Lord knows what all else. I could faint from hunger with all those smells rising in the air.

Mr. Pickle climbs down and helps Miss Attickson off of her horse. They head into the Palmer Chapel, and we follow along behind them. I'm real glad they found a preacher who don't mind guitars and banjos in a church, because Miss Attickson wanted real mountain music to celebrate her wedding day. I notice Miss Attickson's Memphis relatives crying in the corner, and I guess they're sad to be losing their girl. I'd like to tell them that they could come visit anytime, and I'd also appreciate talking to them about Moses from Memphis after the ceremony. Wonder if they've heard of him?

Daddy picks his banjo, slow and steady, Emmett plays the harmonica, and I have my Fender acoustic guitar. I feel like I been playing it forever. I hate to say it, but I think I like it better than my old guitar. Me and Emmett play "Wildwood Flower," and Daddy mostly follows along. He's still real shy playing in front of folks, and I hope he gets over it quick. I look at Louise's beautiful painting of Miss Attickson standing in a field of wild sunflowers, and I know she will love this gift from her new husband most of all. Mr. Pickle already paid Louise, and she put the money into a savings account in the Bank of Waynesville and called the account Jessie's Smoky Mountain Music Notes.

Mama holds Baby Tom-Bill, who has on a sailor suit. Appelonia sits on Louise's shoulders up high where she likes it best of all. Us Weemses gather into the pews and start in singing "Anchored in Love," another old Carter song. As Miss Attickson and Mr. Pickle come up the aisle, Mama smiles at Daddy, and he smiles too, but goes back to his banjo—he's nervous, I can tell, about playing. Will folks say he plays different since the accident? Will they judge him? I expect we all know the answer to that.

Myrtle Anne whispers to me, "I sure wish I could have got a new dress for the wedding. Don't you? I think we all should have got new clothes this day."

I elbow her to hush up.

"Ow, I'm just saying, Livy Two."

But I don't pay her any mind. It's a fact of life that Myrtle Anne can't help herself about such things. Besides, why would we waste our money on a bunch of frilly dresses when we're on the verge of opening Jessie's Smoky Mountain Music Notes? The preacher greets Miss Atickson and Mr. Pickle, and the ceremony begins in this little mountain church up on Cataloochee. A red bird alights on the windowsill like he's setting there ready to watch the whole thing.

CHAPTER TWENTY-THREE

Jessie's Smoky Mountain Music Notes

Halloween, 1944
Dear Grasshopper,

I can't believe this is the last page. Well, I've done something very dramatic in honor of my last entry. You won't believe it, but I cut my hair as short as a boy's. It's like a little cap and no more tangles. Hooray! Mother is not speaking to me, but folks say it's very becoming. It was time for a change. After all, I'll be fifteen very soon. It's way too short for me to ever need a beauty parlor in Asheville, and this makes me more happy than I can possibly say. We're going to do "Romeo and Juliet" at school, and the director wants the new boy to play his banjo in the play. His name is Tom, and he plays a coffee-can banjo. He made it himself. He'll be part of the chorus. I'm playing Juliet. You'd think it was a Broadway production the way Mother is carrying on, but I'm very excited about the part. The director says I can wear a wig or just have short hair. It's my decision. Do you know how many times I've heard that sentence in my whole life?

"It's your decision, Jessie." Not many, let me tell you! Even though Halloween is for kids, we're going trick-or-treating as William Shakespeare's characters!

Yours truly, Jessie Horace

P.S. Don't tell a soul, but I visit Papa's grave a lot and put flowers on it—mostly sunflowers and cuttings from our snowball bushes. I want to make sure he's not lonely and that he knows I haven't forgotten him. Tom followed me one day on his bicycle, and he played Papa a song on his coffee-can banjo. The Audubon Society wants to give me a scholarship to go to a fancy boarding school in Chapel Hill, and Mama wants me to go, but I can't. I can't leave her alone. I'm real mixed up these days. I don't want to go off to Chapel Hill, which makes Mama so mad—we've had such fights. But maybe I should go. Why does everything have to get decided all at once? Why does Mama yell at me, but put on her nice-woman face to all the neighbors? Nothing I do is ever good enough, but one day I will surprise her. Maybe I'll surprise everybody—even myself.

Mama's diary ends right there. It drives us crazy. We want to ask her, but how? We're still so busy keeping Jessie's Smoky Mountain Music Notes a secret from her. After Mr. and Mrs. Pickle's wedding, the local newspaper, the *Smoky Mountain News*, runs a little announcement about out business, and we even have to hide the paper from her, and so does her boss at Champion, Mr. Charlie Walsh, when I call him up on the phone and beg him to keep it a secret. But I read it over and over again.

JESSIE'S SMOKY MOUNTAIN MUSIC NOTES TO OPEN, JULY 1964

The Weems family of Maggie Valley and local schoolteacher Mr. Pickle are opening "Jessie's Smoky Mountain Music Notes" for all musicians to come and showcase their talents. The Weems family will be performing, along with their daddy, who suffered a head injury last year, but has recovered to join his children onstage to play the banjo. Folks will remember Tom Weems from Settlers' Days, 1962, and his duet with Ellie Ketteringly, who will be joining the family to play her fiddle along with professional musicians from Ghost Town. For further information, contact the Weems business manager, Myrtle Anne Weems, either at the Maggie School or at "Jessie's Smoky Mountain Music Notes" located on Soco Road, Highway 19, in the heart of Maggie Valley.

Although I know Mr. George Flowers won't give a rip, I can't help myself. I cut out the article and send it to the devil-dog man. Then he and that stiff, high-haired secretary of his can see that Nashville isn't the only home to good music.

So Pearl, the iguana, won't get too lonely missing Uncle Buddy, Cyrus totes her in her cage down to Jessie's Smoky Mountain Music Notes in the red wagon. Pearl seems happy with Cyrus, as much as an iguana can appear happy, and Uncle Hazard keeps a respectful distance. Caroline and Gentle practice singing and playing the piano in their fairy wings, and Becksie and Myrtle Anne rehearse a clogging routine for after the tickets are sold but before intermission when they'll be selling popcorn and lemonade.

Louise's mural is more beautiful than I ever could have imagined—she's painted every single bird from Mama's girlhood diary on the side of the building. I can't wait for Mama to see it. She's so tired from working such long days at Champion that she falls into bed early every night and is gone before we wake up. She still has stacks of scarves, baby blankets, and sweaters left to sell, but because she's been far too busy to think about her old career, I've decided to have a corner to sell her knitting on opening night.

After much discussion, Myrtle has decided that Jessie's Smoky Mountain Music Notes will be open on weekends in July, while we're getting started, and then we'll start adding more nights if it goes all right. We have to play it by ear. I can't believe my sister has such a head for business and details, but she does, and she and Mr. Pickle have gone over every dime, so it's all accounted for.

~ ~ ~

On opening night, Emmett drives the Rambler with all of us packed inside. We make Mama ride blindfolded so she won't know where we're going. Mathew the Mennonite's truck is parked in the parking lot. There are other cars I don't recognize. I suddenly recollect playing in Asheville almost two years earlier, and how scared I was, but I'm not scared now. I'm nervous, but not scared. I can't wait to get up there and sing for folks.

"You ready, Mama?" Emmett asks as he helps her out of the car. We climb out and stand with her. Louise takes off her blindfold. Mama looks up at the mural on the outside of the building painted with flying birds of every breed and color. She gasps and takes a step backwards like she's not sure what she's seeing. "What is this place?" Then she spots the sign, JESSIE'S SMOKY MOUNTAIN MUSIC NOTES under a twinkling row of Grandma Horace's Christmas lights that she bought with S&H Green Stamps.

Daddy says, "I been learning all the bird names myself. That there's a bobolink, a red-tailed hawk, finches, a condor, parrots, yellow warbler, mockingbird. More than I can even name. Look at all those beautiful birds. Our girl, Louisiana, is responsible."

"I'm looking, I'm looking," Mama says, hardly able to believe it. "How did you'uns do this? How in the world?"

"It was easy. Well, not that easy. Mr. Pickle rented us his building, Mama," Myrtle Anne explains. "Mrs. Pickle had to twist his arm a little, but he came around."

Cars and trucks continue pulling into the parking lot, and Mama says, "Who are all these folks? How do they know about it?"

"Guess they like music," Emmett says. "Come on, we'd better get inside."

Daddy carries Appelonia, and Mama holds Baby Tom-Bill on her hip and wipes the tears out of her eyes. The twins and Gentle head inside the building together. I get butterflies in my stomach. It's really happening. The sound of an old-fashioned car pulls in the parking lot behind us, and we turn to see Grandma Horace driving up.

"Excuse me! Hello there!" she calls from the car. "I do believe one of you grandchildren could come hold open the car door for your Grandma Horace. I have taught y'all a thing or two about being ladies and gentlemen." But it's Daddy who goes over and opens the car door, and she says, "Thank you, Tom, and thank you for your call, Rebecca. I would have come anyway, seeing as how it was announced in the *Smoky Mountain News*."

"Did you drive all the way from the land of Enka?" Daddy asks Grandma Horace.

"I most certainly did." She takes his arm. "Hello, Jessie."

"Hello, Mother. Did you know about this? Were you in on the secret?"

"I heard rumors but didn't believe them for a minute. I see I have been proven wrong. That doesn't happen often, as you well know, Jessie. At any rate, I'm here for your big night. And your night, too, Tom. The ladies at church cut out the clipping in the newspaper for me." Grandma Horace is dressed up for the occasion in a fancy church hat.

Becksie says, "I'd better get in there and start the popcorn. The clipping's at home in the Everything Box, Mama. We just didn't want you to see it."

Mama keeps shaking her head like she can't hardly believe it. "This is like a dream, this night. What am I seeing?"

Grandma Horace glances at the side of the building to study the mural of Mama's birds and the tender care that Louise has taken with each one. "Well, I know what I am seeing, and I intend to get a good seat up front. Come on."

Mama and Daddy walk arm in arm into Jessie's Smoky Mountain Music Notes for a night of mountain music with Grandma Horace leading the way. Myrtle Anne grabs me by the hand and says, "Hurry up! I'm supposed to be tearing tickets and greeting the masses."

A few minutes later, Mr. Pickle climbs up on the stage to announce the evening and play the mandolin. Mrs.

Pickle joins him, singing along while he plays "Listen to the Mockingbird" on mandolin. Ellie Ketteringly, the best mountain fiddle player around, is on next and makes her fiddle do all the bird calls of a mockingbird. Gentle, Caroline, and Cyrus come out and sing "Little Darling, Pal of Mine," and Gentle steals the show with her solo, hitting the rafters of that old feed store. Folks give her a standing ovation.

Then it's Daddy's turn. It's his first time to play in public, other than Miss Attickson's wedding, and somehow that was different.

Myrtle Anne introduces him and says, "Ladies and gentlemen, please welcome our daddy, Mr. Tom Weems, back to the stage after a long absence."

Daddy comes out on the stage with his coffee-can banjo. "My son, Emmett, made me this coffee-can banjo. He heard that I had one back when I was a kid, and so he thought I should have another one. Anyhow, so here it is, and I come here tonight—to—play—for you." Daddy's sweating as he looks out at the crowd, and all of a sudden I'm scared for him. Maybe it's too much? He strums a chord, but his fingers fumble on the strings, and he says, "Think I'll start over." But the same thing happens again, and he can't seem to find the right notes.

"Sorry, folks. Let me try that again."

Becksie waves to me from behind the popcorn machine. "Do something."

Nobody's making a sound, but I feel the audience getting anxious, so I take the twins and Gentle back out to Daddy and set them on a bench. I warn, "You'uns sit still for Daddy or else!" Next, I whisper into his ear, "Play to them. Play to all of us. Play to Mama. Please, Daddy. You're ready, I swear you are."

The lonesome sound of Emmett's harmonica pierces the air, and Daddy studies the twins and pats Gentle's hair. She grabs his hand, then lets go, and Daddy's fingers find the right chords. He starts to play his banjo, and the sweet chords sound just right. Folks start in clapping. *"Welcome home, Tom Weems."* I join in real soft on my Fender, and me and Emmett and Daddy play together. We play one song—"Mountain Dew"—but near everybody knows all the verses, so the audience sings along. One by one, folks get up and start clogging at the foot of the stage. Little kids, big kids, married couples, teenagers, old grannies—not ours, but Grandma Horace is tapping her foot in her sensible black shoe. People can't help themselves but dance to Daddy's music. Mama's face is radiant, and for the first time in a long time, I see joy in her eyes.

CHAPTER TWENTY-FOUR

Chasing Rainbows

IN LATE SEPTEMBER after a rainy morning, the sun spears through the clouds, and we have our usual picnic on top of the hill behind our house. Daddy and Mama sit on a quilt under a shady tree with all of us gathered around. We've gone back to Daddy's old way of church—giving thanks to every living thing around us. Mama makes a real good picnic with tomatoes, squash, and apple butter on cornbread. She and Daddy share a glass of blueberry wine; they're a picture together, with the wind blowing and the leaves just starting to change, with hints of raspberry gold in green. I read an Emily Dickinson poem about the Sabbath and how folks keep it in different ways. Our way is more like Emily Dickinson's compared to Grandma Horace's of dresses, stockings, suits, and preachers. When I'm done reading, Becksie says, "Grandma Horace wouldn't like that poem."

But Daddy says, "Why not? It's a fine poem, and here we are living in the land of Maggie Valley, and I'm playing music again." He smiles, holding Baby Tom-Bill, the spitting image of Daddy, and I realize for the first time that maybe running away to Nashville back at Christmas was a disaster, but in another way, it jolted Daddy—sent a spark through him. It's like he's waking up more and more all the time. Can something that was so awful wrong have shiny bright bits of right to it?

Daddy looks around. "Is there a radio playing? I hear a Bob Wills tune."

Louise looks up from sketching. "No radio, Daddy."

Cyrus asks, "Oh no, Daddy, are you having auditory hallucinates again?"

Gentle says, "Auditory hallucinations, Cyrus."

"Well, I never get them, whatever they're called," Cyrus complains. "And I want them. How can I have them too? What's the secret?"

Daddy shakes his head. "No secret, but I hear a Bob Wills tune playing. That's okay. I like Bob Wills."

Mama asks, "You all right, Tom?" as she wipes Apelonia's face.

"Yes, I am. Are you, Jessie?" Daddy kisses Baby Tom-Bill on the head.

"I'm fine. I'm so glad to be working at Jessie's Smoky Mountain Music Notes instead of facing the paper mill at the crack of dawn tomorrow. I still can't believe it's working out, but it is."

I'm glad too. We all are. The first night led to even

more business the second night and more the third. Then Mr. Pickle and Myrtle Anne made a decision to keep it open every night of the week until Halloween and then open up again in the spring. Mama and Daddy are running it themselves now, and Mama's even selling her scarves and baby blankets to tourists who have the money to spend ten dollars on a jar of honey or twenty-five or thirty dollars on a homemade baby blanket or scarf or sweater. Thank the Lord for tourists. It'll get lean again, come winter, but if we can watch our money and be careful, we can eke out a living at Jessie's Smoky Mountain Music Notes.

"My sunburn hurts," Cyrus whines. "I got sunburned fishing with Emmett yesterday, right, Emmett? How come sunburn got invented, Mama? Why?"

And while Mama thinks up an explanation, I write a new song on my Fender acoustic. I won't have much time to work on it, as it's getting late and we all have to gather at Jessie's Smoky Mountain Music Notes tonight for a Sunday night show. Myrtle Anne says, "I checked the reservations—fifteen folks coming tonight."

Becksie says, "I need to get there early to start the popcorn. I already did my homework for school. I'm so glad to be back in school."

"Not me," Emmett says. "It's awful. A terrible place. I prefer Hollywood. One of these days. You watch me. I'll be on *Gunsmoke* or *Bonanza* or both of them. I swear it."

"Send us a postcard when you get there," Louise tells him.

"You'd better believe I will!" Emmett picks up a stick and starts to whittle. "If you're lucky."

Cyrus looks at the sky and cries, "Hey, look at those clouds. They're like Poseidon clouds . . . and there's a rainbow. Hey, Iris, Goddess of the Rainbow. There's one up in the sky right now."

We all look toward the sky, and Daddy says, "It's a beauty, all right."

And it is a beauty. It's one of those fine fat rainbows of red, orange, yellow, green, blue, and violet—rising like an arch across the sky over the mountains.

Becksie says, "Hey, guess what? Spanish for rainbow is 'arco iris' . . . just like the goddess. Good thing I'm taking Spanish now to teach you'uns a thing or two."

Gentle says, "I want to go get it. Let's go get the arco iris."

"Come on Iris, Goddess of the Rainbow! Poseidon commands you!" Cyrus grabs Gentle's hand, and Caroline grabs the other, yelling, "I'm Amphitrite. And Uncle Hazard can be Triton, my fishtailed son. Come on, Uncle Hazard. Good boy."

Gentle says, "That's right. I am the Goddess of Rainbows, so let's go find it!" And with that, the twins and Gentle and Uncle Hazard, barking his fool head off, race up and down and up another hill to go catch it. Appelonia toddles after them, and baby Tom-Bill chomps on a blade of grass, watching while I work on a new song.

"JESSIE'S SMOKY MOUNTAIN MUSIC NOTES"

Jessie's Smoky Mountain Music Notes hit
all the different keys,
Mourning doves, red-winged blackbirds,
yellow warblers, chickadees.
Jessie's Smoky Mountain Music Notes soar
high up in the trees.

Jessie's starry light on each of her kids shines so bright.
Her gentle hands moving fast like swallowtails in flight.
Her love, it fills our house so big and wide and deep.
Jessie's girlhood stories forever we will keep. . . .

I love you more than anything, Mama.
Thank you, Mama, for always loving me. . . .

Acknowledgments

WHEN I FIRST began to write *Gentle's Holler*, the first of three Smoky Mountain books, I wrote it snappy, sappy, and sent it out lightning speed, hoping for a book deal yesterday. Naturally, the rejections flooded my mailbox. It was my son, Flannery, who said, "Mom, the daddy is a nice banjo player, but something should really happen, don't you think?" And my friend Amy Goldman Koss said, "You absolutely can write this book, but those kids have been sitting in the garden for eighteen pages. What about plot?" But it was Richard Jackson who offered the most memorable comment in his rejection letter: "Nothing your characters did surprised me." And the fact is—he was right. So I took Amy's, Flannery's, and Richard's words to heart, and I decided not to worry about selling the book anymore and making it happen "fast." I began to really write the story and honor the Weems family, and somehow, I came to write three books of this big Smoky Mountain family of Maggie Valley, and I hope one day that more will follow.

I would like to thank my editor, Catherine Frank, who truly helped me find my way through the muddle and listened to me at every stage. Her notes were so specific and helpful that I was able to find the heart of each book. I would also like to thank Regina Hayes of Viking Children's Books for believing in the Weems family from the beginning, when Melanie Cecka first brought an early draft to her. My amazing agent Marianne Merola's insight and humor have been a great gift through all three Smoky Mountain novels. I would like to thank my copyeditor, Nora Reichard; my proofreader, John Vasile, for Nashville geography help; and Kendra Levin of Viking for her patience and help in the finishing touches. Thanks very much to Nancy Brennan for her brilliant book design.

Ellen Slezak, Keely Madden Kovalik, and Denise Hamilton all read the manuscript at various stages, and I would like to thank them for their wonderful comments and notes. I am indebted to Thelma Rifkind and her love of birds, which led me to the Audobon Society and my own new appreciation of birds. Toni Buzzeo found *Gentle's Holler* early on and has championed the Weems family in Maine with students and librarians. I am very grateful for the support of my writer and reader friends: Diana Wagman, Donna Rifkind, Diane Arieff, Amy Goldman Koss, Lienna Silver, Heather Dundas, Carol Hughes, Elizabeth Dulemba, Cecil Castellucci, Candie Moonshower, Gretchen Laskas, Cynthia Leitich Smith, Alexis O'Neill, Tom Christie, Catherine Landis, Barbara

O'Connor, Cynthia Lord, Sandra Tsing Loh, and all the writers on Diane Davis's YA Writers Group list-serve and Katie McAllister's YA Novelists' list-serve. Susan Patron, Annie Ayres, Lori Special, Laurie Reese, Mary Voors, Ellen Ruffin, Ellen James, and Clare O'Callaghan are some of my most favorite librarians in the world! I have made so many connections and friends in all my online communities, and I am very appreciative of their support. I am immensely thankful to Vicki and Steve Palmquist and Kari Baumbach at Winding Oak, who have updated my Web site and are now setting up my author visits across the country.

I would like to thank the librarians at the downtown Nashville Public Library who helped me find old newspaper headlines from 1963, and I would like to thank Tomi Lunsford and Warren Denney, who took me on a tour of Nashville and helped me figure out the geography. Lori Gunnell also gave me a quiet few days in the "other" mountains of Yosemite to work on *Jessie's Mountain*, and I am thankful for her friendship. I would very much like to thank the family of Jill Hunt, and her parents, Becky and George Fain, who helped me when I was researching TBI—Traumatic Brain Injury.

Megan Flatt is a great kid who wrote my first fan letter and pointed to a great place where I could start the second novel—Daddy's homecoming. I am very happy to know a little girl named Lilly Grossman, of La Jolla, who loves fairies and dancing and stories. I am very grateful to the University of Tennessee and the Festival of Children's Reading. I finished *Louisiana's Song* on a summer night in Knoxville during that festival, and I began writing *Jessie's Mountain* on another summer night in Maggie Valley in Ernestine Upchurch's cabin with my daughter Norah. Shirley Fairchild was an enormous help in describing Halloween, death, weddings, and other mountain rituals of her childhood. In Catherine Marshall's book, *Christy*, there is a character, Fairlight Spencer, and in a way, Shirley Fairchild is my "Fairlight Spencer." I have so much more to learn from her, and I feel so lucky to know her and her husband, Raymond Fairchild, a great banjo player in the Opryhouse of Maggie Valley, North Carolina.

I would like to thank all the hundreds of schools I have visited and all the students, teachers, and librarians who have welcomed me and my Smoky Mountain stories and music into their libraries and classrooms. It's a great gift to be able to do what you love, and I love writing books for kids, and I hope that some of the young writers I meet grow up to write their own stories one day.

When I was a young mother with little babies, I found *Oral History* and *Fair and Tender Ladies*, and Lee Smith's words gave me so much comfort in those early days of motherhood in a brand-new city with very few friends. I would also like to thank Robert Bradley, "the Apache Kid"—also known as the boy from Ghost Town.

Finally, I would like to thank my mother, who gave me a library card every time we moved (ten states!) and let me check out all the books I wanted. I would like to thank my father, who said, "You can do anything you want to do if you put your mind to it." I am grateful to my sister, Keely, and my brothers, Duffy and Casey, who allowed me to dress them up (not always willingly) and make them characters in stories when we were growing up. I would like to thank my husband, Kiffen, whose infinite patience and love sustains me every single day. My daughter, Lucy, drew Jessie's birds, and I'm so very glad that she did. And last of all, I thank my children—Flannery, Lucy, and Norah—whose bright, shining faces are illuminated in the Weems children.

Property of:
Hall Middle School Library
200 Doherty Drive
Larkspur, CA 94939